M000187974

VEIL OF MIST

LELA TRILOGY BOOK TWO

TESSONJA ODETTE

Copyright © 2018 by Tessonja Odette

All rights reserved.

No part of this book may be reproduced in any form or by any electronic or mechanical means, including information storage and retrieval systems, without written permission from the author, except for the use of brief quotations in a book review.

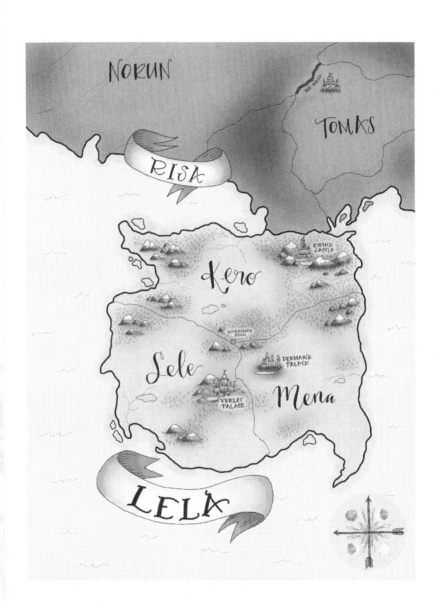

1

NEW BEGINNING

Cora

One kiss. It was a moment of fire, of sweetness, of uncharted new worlds. It felt like a warmth radiating through my chest, a lightness in my head, and a shortness of breath.

As we parted, my lips tingled with the memory of his. With every subtle movement he made away from me, I felt colder. However, not so cold that I would say I felt unpleasant. Far from it. The warmth still encircled my chest, but there was now a yearning to close the distance between us, to never part. To always have our lips touch like that.

"I'll take that as a yes," Teryn said. He reached a hand to my cheek, which my flesh eagerly accepted.

"Yes, I'll marry you." The words felt strange in my mouth, as if I spoke in a new language, but my body responded with giddy excitement. I felt like my smile would stretch my face into oblivion. "But only in a year."

The statement brought a sober quality to the air around us, but I knew it was for the best. I couldn't lose all my wits in a single kiss.

"In a year," Teryn echoed. "That will give us plenty of time to spend together. I meant what I said. I want to know everything about you."

The thought of someone eager to know me to such an intimate degree would normally send my stomach churning, but not this time. Not with Teryn. I blushed. "I think I can accommodate."

"Plus, now that we're engaged, we can be seen visiting together."

"No more sneaking into my room at night?"

Teryn laughed. "No. We'll have plenty of time together during the day. Maybe you can accompany me home to Dermaine for Larylis' coronation? You can see my kingdom."

"I'd like that."

"Then after that, we can return to Ridine. Together."

I thought about returning home to Ridine Castle, where we'd last been as prisoners, and shuddered. "I would love it if you were there with me. It would mean a lot."

"Then I'll be there." He smiled, and for a few moments we held each other's eyes, lost in silence. His eyelids seemed to grow heavy, and he blinked, ending our spellbinding stare. "I should let you get some rest. We have all day tomorrow to talk more. And the day after that. And the day after...well, you know."

As much as I didn't want him to go, it was late, and I needed some rest in a proper bed for once. "Tomorrow, then."

Teryn squeezed my hand, then stood, making his way to the hidden door. I followed him, watching as he pulled the tapestry aside. He paused. With a single stride, he was in my arms again, lips crushing mine and bringing about another round of that fiery warmth. I was about to pull him closer when he gently pulled away. He opened his mouth, but no words came out. Instead, he gave me a sly grin and made his way into the servants' hall.

I stared at the tapestry, hoping for the sound of returning footsteps. None came. I was filled with the most satisfying disappointment I'd ever felt. Who knew longing could feel so wonderful and terrible at once? I was beginning to understand why love was said to be for fools.

Now I had become one.

I turned from the hidden door and threw myself on the plush bed. My mind spun with the events of the day. I'd been freed from Verlot's dungeon and dressed like royalty. I'd been offered a marriage to Teryn's brother, Larylis. I'd been heartbroken and distraught. And now I was engaged to a man I'd unwittingly become smitten with.

After befriending a unicorn and fighting a magic war, I hadn't thought anything could still surprise me. I was wrong.

I climbed under the covers and sank into the luxury surrounding me. As I closed my eyes, thoughts of Teryn were interrupted by thoughts of returning home, being princess, living indoors, and rebuilding trust with my brother. The sinking in my gut threatened to sweep away my joy. *Not tonight.* I returned to thoughts of Teryn and the tingling of my lips, still hungry for another kiss.

Mareleau

My eyes fluttered sleepily as we walked through the dimly lit hall of Verlot Palace. Larylis squeezed my hand, and I shook my head to clear my mind. Sounds of harp, shuffling feet, and muffled laughter followed in our wake. I felt as if I'd never been down these halls before. Every step I took seemed significant, like each one was sealing my fate.

In a way, it was.

I was now a married woman, hand-in-hand with the man I loved, the man I'd fought for. The man I'd lied for.

As we made our way along the procession to the wedding chamber, each step we took brought us closer to consecrating our marriage—and closer to the conversation I was dreading to have.

At the end of the hall, we came to a set of doors I'd never cared to enter before. Two guards pulled them open and stepped aside. A candlelit room was illuminated within. My heart quickened.

Larylis and I exchanged a brief glance, then turned to face our retinue. The harpist ceased his playing. The crowd quieted.

Breah, one of my chambermaids, came to me and began loosening the laces of my gown, removing pins, jewels, and sashes, then let down my hair until it cascaded past my shoulders in waves of gold. A young man went to Larylis and removed his cloak and tunic until he was left in a plain undershirt and trousers.

I pursed my lips as our audience watched our

undressing as if it were the most normal process in the world. Of all the ceremonial flair I would have wanted on my wedding day, this would have never made my list. I never understood the ritual procession to the wedding chamber. Why did an audience need to witness such a thing? *At least our kingdom has advanced beyond the need to fully witness the consummation.* I shuddered at the thought.

I scanned the crowd, finding my mother as the only familiar face aside from Breah. It was no surprise Father was missing from the procession, just as he had been from my wedding feast. He'd afforded me no luxury during the signing of my marriage contract, no Gods-priest to conduct our ceremony. Nothing but a contract and a quill. His actions made his message loud and clear: *I do not approve of your marriage.*

When Larylis and I were stripped down to our under-clothes, the harpist recommenced, and the group cheered. I kept my chin high and my chest pressed forward, despite my state of undress. I would not blush beneath their gaze.

Mother clasped her hand to her heart and addressed the crowd behind her. "It is now time for the bride and groom to become true husband and wife. Wish them many blessings, so they may bring forth an heir." Another cheer followed. I swallowed a lump in my throat.

Breah curtsied before me, bowing her blonde head. "Is there anything you desire to be brought to you before we bid you goodnight?"

"Wine." The word came out in a rush.

Mother's mouth opened, then snapped shut. She raised an eyebrow as she looked down at my abdomen.

"For my husband," I amended, placing a hand on his arm. "My husband would like wine. I do not."

Breah nodded and entered the crowd. A moment later she produced a goblet and bottle of wine and handed them to Larylis.

Mother narrowed her eyes at me, and I met her gaze with a look of innocence. Before she could say anything, I addressed our retinue, "Thank you all for celebrating our wedding night. You have made this moment very special."

I looked to Larylis. He remained silent until he realized I was prompting him to speak. "Yes, thank you. My...wife and I are...overjoyed that you could be part of this." His voice was devoid of all emotion. He looked at me as I furrowed my brow, but I couldn't meet his eyes. "Now get out of here so I can make this woman my wife." Laughter had returned to his voice, no matter how stilted it was.

The crowd erupted in raucous cheering and departed down the hall. Mother lingered a moment longer before following them. We entered our room and closed the door.

The silence that hung in the absence of the party felt like a shroud. My breaths became shallow, and my limbs trembled as Larylis and I took in our chamber, looking everywhere but at each other. The room was elegant and spacious, and the bed enormous, piled high with plush pillows and velvety blankets, all in shades of deep red. Tapestries displaying romantic scenes of courtship and lovemaking spanned the walls.

"It's beautiful." My voice sounded like a child's. I turned my head and smiled at my husband.

"It is," Larylis agreed without looking at me. He set the

wine and goblet on a table next to the bed, then moved to stand at the window on the other side of the room.

I went to the table and poured the wine, draining the goblet in two gulps, then filled another. The burn of the fiery liquid was pleasant, creating a buzzing in my mind and a calming in my stomach. I took another sip, letting my muscles relax.

Larylis turned toward me, eying the cup. "What about the baby?" The pain in his voice was raw.

I averted my gaze and drained another goblet. I swayed to the side as I set it back on the table. *It's time for that conversation.*

I sat at the edge of the bed and put my hands in my lap. "I'm so sorry, Larylis. It was the only way."

"Was it?"

I looked over my shoulder at him still standing by the window. "Yes! You heard how insensible my father was! It was a last resort. I waited until I was sure nothing else would work. I told you I would do anything to avoid marrying Teryn. Did you not think I meant it?"

Larylis strode toward the bed. "But you lied! You lied about us. You made *me* lie. My own brother thinks..."

I stood and went to him, placing a hand on his shoulder. "He wasn't mad. If he was, he wouldn't have helped us the way he did."

Larylis shrugged away from my touch. "That doesn't matter. Teryn thinks I betrayed him. He thinks I bedded his betrothed."

"It isn't far from the truth. We both agreed it was what we wanted."

"I agreed to love you. To kiss you. To have passionate,

stolen moments. But we agreed not to go too far. We agreed not to..."

"I know. And we didn't."

"Are you even conflicted about what you've done? Our families think we not only had a treasonous affair, but that we also made a baby from it. Neither of those claims are true, and they almost got us killed."

"But they didn't."

Larylis turned away from me. "How do you not see the problem here? Our marriage is built on a lie."

Tears pricked my eyes, and my throat felt dry. My voice came out weak and quavering. "This is what we wanted. *You* are what I've always wanted. I'm sorry I lied, and I'm sorry I hurt you, but I had to do something. *Someone* had to do something."

Larylis turned back around. His face was crestfallen. "You're right. I did nothing."

"That's not what I meant." But it was true. He'd done nothing to stand up for me or our love.

Larylis released a deep sigh. "What you did was wrong. I don't know if things will ever feel right between me and Teryn because of it, but I know why you did it. I just wish you hadn't had to."

"We can wish all we want, but what's done is done. We're married. We're together. I know you love me, and I love you."

Larylis reached out and put his hands on both sides of my face. "You're right, I do love you. This may not be the wedding of my dreams, and you may not be the sweet girl of my childhood, but you are *mine*. I promised to know and love the real you, and that's what I'm going to do. Forever."

My smile stretched over my face. In that moment, as Larylis looked into my eyes, deep into my flaws, past my lies, and beyond my cunning, I felt truly seen for the first time. My father may have seen me as a soiled traitor, and my mother may have thought me an irresponsible harlot, but Larylis knew the truth. Beneath it all was a girl in love becoming a woman.

Our lips melted together, lighting a fire of passion between us, a fire that burned in the most delicious way. I was both excited and terrified as we fell together onto the bed.

Larylis pulled his face a few inches away from mine and brushed my tangled hair away from my cheek. "Mareleau, Princess of Sele, daughter of King Verdian and Queen Helena, do you take me, Prince Larylis, Crown Prince of Mena, son of King Arlous and Queen Bethaeny to be your husband in life and love?"

I brushed my lips gently against his. "I do."

2

MORNING

Cora

"Good morning, princess."

The sing-song voice startled me from sleep. I raised my head from the plump pillow, and Lurel's face, framed with wisps of dark-blonde hair, came into view.

She held a waif-like hand toward me. "I'm here to get you dressed and fitted, Your Highness."

I clasped her hand and let her pull me to sitting, but my heart sank when I could no longer feel the warmth of the blankets. "If I could bring one thing home with me from Verlot, it would be this bed."

Lurel giggled. "I'm sure you have lovely furnishings in your castle."

I stifled a laugh, knowing how wrong she was. It dawned on me how much work would need to be done upon returning to Ridine.

Lurel beckoned me to the vanity and sat me before

the mirror. "I wish I could go with you to Ridine. I've never been to Kero." She began to brush my long, dark-brown hair. Despite all the work she'd done on it the day before, it had returned to a mass of wild tangles. She furrowed her brow at the brush as if it were somehow responsible, and her frown deepened as she redoubled her efforts.

I cocked my head, sensing conflict in her. Even though my empathic powers were strong, she took no effort to read. She wore her feelings so openly, I had to tighten control over my power so as not to feel them myself. "What's wrong, Lurel? You seem upset about something."

She met my eyes in the mirror and sighed. "It's just that...I heard the saddest news this morning."

"What's that?"

"Princess Mareleau is married to Prince *Larylis,* not Prince Teryn."

I suppressed a grin, remembering last night's kiss. Twice. "Why is that a sad thing?"

"I just don't understand it. She was promised to Prince Teryn. Something awful must have happened. I've heard the most terrible rumors."

"I wouldn't give too much weight to rumors."

She giggled. "Mother says the same thing. I just hate to think Princess Mareleau married the wrong man."

What will she think when she hears about my engagement to Teryn? I pressed my lips together. "I'm sure you'll see the truth for yourself. If she seems happy, then there's nothing to worry about."

Lurel nodded. "You're right. Now, come. It's time to have you fitted."

"For what?" I asked, following Lurel to the center of the room. She left me there and opened the door.

In walked two women carrying boxes of colorful fabrics. They curtsied as they approached me. "Your Highness."

"You're being fitted for a new wardrobe." Lurel clasped her hands proudly together. "Ordered by King Verdian himself."

I raised an eyebrow. "Why would he do that?"

"Rumors say Sele and Kero are allies now," she explained. "King Verdian is helping you and your brother reclaim your titles."

That rumor, at least, seemed to be true. The seamstresses fluttered around me, taking measurements and holding different shades of fabric in velvet, lace, silk, and brocade. Was this a display of King Verdian's wealth? To show I was in debt to his goodwill? Whatever the case, I could do nothing but accept the attention.

A sound of disgust came from behind me. I turned to see Lurel pulling my dusty, grime-covered cloak from the wardrobe. My heart fluttered at the sight, delivering a rush of memories—Roije offering me the cloak the night I'd found Valorre, sleeping beneath its warmth during my travels, meeting Teryn, cutting the hem to wrap his wound at the Battle at Centerpointe Rock.

"She'll need a new cloak," Lurel told the women.

"That's not necessary. It will be good for my journey home," I said.

"We can make you a much better one, Your Highness. One without...whatever this is." She pointed to a stain that was unmistakably blood.

My throat constricted at the thought of discarding it,

but I couldn't think of a convincing argument. "At least let me keep it until my new one has been made. I'll leave it behind when I depart."

Lurel widened her eyes both at me and the cloak before she returned it to the wardrobe. "As you wish, princess."

When the women were finished with their work, they repacked their things. "We will return with your new garments with haste," one said.

"It's no rush. Take your time."

The women exchanged a look. "King Verdian says *with haste*." And with that they scuttled out of my room.

Lurel pulled a dress from the wardrobe and brought it to me. "Until your clothing has been made, you'll have to wear another one of Princess Mareleau's dresses. This one is from when she was eleven, so it should fit you even better than the last."

I examined the gown in gold and cream taffeta with ivory lace at the hem and sleeves. "You're saying I have the body of an eleven-year-old?"

Lurel hid her laughter behind a hand. "An eleven-year-old *Mareleau*. This one is quite modest compared to the last, but it should suit you for the day." She pulled the gown over my head and secured the buttons and tightened the laces. She was right about it being more modest. It was simple and high-cut at the chest, but the length was perfect. She placed a pair of brown slippers before me.

When I looked in the mirror, I was satisfied with what I saw. Modest or no, at least I looked like a princess.

"Now you're ready," Lurel said.

"For what?"

"For the meeting, of course."

"Meeting? I was never told of a meeting."

Lurel seemed unperturbed. "King Verdian announced it this morning. Everyone will be there."

"Who's everyone?"

"The king, the queen, Princess Mareleau, Queen Bethaeny, and the twin princes. Oh, and your brother, King Dimetreus."

My heart felt warm when she mentioned the twin princes, but it did a flip at my brother's name. I hadn't seen him since we'd left Centerpointe Rock. "My brother will be there?"

"He's waiting outside your door to accompany you."

A grin stretched over my face, and I all but ran to the door with Lurel hurrying at my heels. Flinging the door wide, I found Dimetreus and was struck by his change in appearance. Last I'd seen him, he'd been worn and aged with hollow cheeks and thinning hair. Even though he'd been in a dungeon for the best part of the last few weeks, color had returned to his flesh, and his eyes shone with their bright green hue. His hair still bore more gray than it should have for his age, but it had been nicely combed. The beard sprouting from his chin reminded me of our father.

My eyes filled with tears as I ran into his arms. "Dimi, I'm so glad to see you are well."

Dimetreus patted me gently on the back. "So am I." His voice held a hoarse quality, as if he'd lost some of it to Morkai's torture and control. Yet, his tone was far gentler than it had been during that time.

We parted, and he offered me his arm. I brushed the tears from my cheeks and placed my hand in the crook of his elbow. As we walked, I felt like I was floating on air. I was engaged to the man I desired. My brother was well and at my side. I thought there was no way my morning could get any better.

I was right. It was about to get worse.

THE MEETING

Teryn

I stood outside King Verdian's study, trying to keep my composure despite my foot's insistence on tapping a tune on the marble floor.

Movement caught my eye, and I turned, smiling as Larylis and Mareleau strolled toward me, arm-in-arm. As much as the sight warmed my heart, they were not whom I was hoping to see.

Larylis cocked his head as they approached me. "Do you know what this meeting is about?"

I shrugged. "King Verdian, Queen Helena, and our mother are inside."

Larylis pointed his thumb at the closed door. "What are you doing out here then? Are you trying to force us in first?"

I laughed. "I'm waiting for Cora. We can wait together. They can't remove our heads all at once."

Larylis' shoulders relaxed while Mareleau remained unreadable as always.

"How was your...um...wedding night?" I asked, trying unsuccessfully to keep a straight face.

Larylis landed a playful punch on my arm, and Mareleau scowled, color rising in her cheeks.

"That good?"

"Is this what brothers are like?" Mareleau said under her breath.

I was about to execute a witty response when all thought was stripped from my mind. Cora rounded a corner, walking with Dimetreus. My breath caught in my throat as I tried to keep myself from grinning like an idiot. Memories of our first—and second—kiss flooded my mind. My legs begged me to run to her, but I forced them still, admiring her from afar as she drew near. It was almost comical how tiny she looked next to her towering brother. He loomed even larger than before, now that he was no longer stooped beneath the control of a sorcerer. Being in good health proved him to be wide-chested and well-muscled, looking nothing like the man I'd watched cower beneath Morkai's demands.

Dimetreus offered us a bow as they approached, and Cora gave us a tight-lipped smile. She too, it seemed, was trying to keep her composure. Dimetreus released her hand from his elbow and kissed it. "How about you let Teryn walk you in?"

She blushed and came to me, barely meeting my eyes as she took my arm. It was strange how much one day had made all the difference in the world between us. The woman who had once held me at her mercy by knife-point was now blushing at my side. The air surrounding us felt like it was sizzling. We locked eyes, and I knew she could feel it too. I wanted nothing more than to bend down and kiss her like I had last night. *Later. We have all the time we need.*

"Shall we?" Larylis raised his brows and looked at the double doors. Mareleau bit her lip.

"I suppose," I said.

Larylis tapped on one of the doors, and they swung open. Guards greeted us and nodded for us to enter. The heavy silence made it seem dark in the study despite the daylight streaming in through the windows, illuminating shelves of books, lavish chairs, and an immense, mahogany desk. King Verdian sat behind the desk and motioned for us to sit as well. Queen Helena and my mother, Queen Bethaeny, sat to the right of Verdian.

"It is time to make plans moving forward," Verdian said in his gruff voice. "The death of King Arlous makes it imperative that Crown Prince Larylis," he annunciated each of the last three words with clear disdain, "be crowned as king as soon as possible."

Mother nodded. "Coming from war, we must secure our kingdom."

"I understand," Larylis said, sitting high in his chair, Mareleau's hand clasped tightly in his. "We can prepare to leave at once for Dermaine."

"And, of course, Princess Mareleau will be crowned as queen." Verdian's words were laced with venom.

"Agreed," Mareleau said, reflecting her father's tone.

"You will depart for Dermaine tomorrow morning." Verdian turned his gaze from Mareleau to Dimetreus. "Of equal importance, King Dimetreus must return to Ridine and bring strength back to his kingdom. He will sign the Tri-Kingdom Peace Pact of Lela, securing our long-standing alliance. As allies, Sele and Mena will provide him members of council and military, as well as household staff. We are going to great lengths to return peace to our land."

King Dimetreus bowed his head. "You have my deepest gratitude." Perhaps it was my imagination, but I thought I heard a hint of mockery in his voice.

Verdian continued, "Princess Coralaine must secure her position as well and return to Ridine. My brother, Lord Kevan, will serve as your Head of Council. Tomorrow he will accompany you and your retinue on your journey to Ridine. You will be given horses, a traveling coach, and several guards from my Royal Force, as well as two more men from my household to serve on your council. One of these men will be my other brother, Lord Ulrich. However, before joining you, Lord Ulrich will accompany Queen Bethaeny, the two princes, and Princess Mareleau to Dermaine. The day following the coronation, he will escort Mareleau, additional guards from Dermaine, and three more men for your council to Ridine."

Mareleau flung herself forward in her seat. "What? What do you mean I'm going to Ridine? My new home is Dermaine!"

Verdian stood and fixed his daughter with an icy stare. "You will go where you are needed. Princess Coralaine is returning to a role she hasn't held since she was a child. Since Kero has no queen, the princess will also need to serve as Lady of Ridine. She knows nothing about running a royal household and needs to learn her duties both as princess and future queen. Considering your upcoming coronation, you will have plenty to share with her."

"That's absurd," Mareleau said.

"That's not necessary..." Cora began, her voice decreasing in volume until it disappeared beneath Verdian's gaze.

"You children think you know best," he walked to the front of his desk, "when you know nothing at all. Arlous and I had decades of experience, and yet..."

And yet he still died, was left unsaid.

Verdian's fierce expression faltered for only one moment. "Being king and queen isn't a game. It's a duty. It isn't about love and romance. It's about protection, obligation, and strategy."

Mareleau swallowed hard. "Will Larylis be coming with me to Ridine?"

"Of course not. His place is at Dermaine."

"When will I return to him?"

"When Lord Kevan and Lord Ulrich give word that you've done your job."

"But I'm pregnant! I can't travel."

"No one knows you are pregnant yet, remember? Every person in this room is sworn to secrecy. Until it is proper for you to announce your condition, you will act like any other woman."

My heart raced as I sat forward and cleared my throat. "King Verdian. I'd like to go to Ridine as well. Since Cora and I are engaged—"

"No. You've thought it so wise to abdicate your duties

to your untrained, unprepared brother. Now he'll need *you* to guide him."

My mouth felt dry. "For how long? Cora and I have only a year—"

Verdian slammed his fist on the desk. "Did King Arlous teach you it's acceptable to argue with a king? You will do your duty. You will see to it until it is done. I don't care about weddings, engagements, and babies. I care about the strength of our land."

Cora and I exchanged a glance. The disappointment in her expression mirrored my own.

Queen Helena went to her husband's side and placed a hand on his shoulder. "My love, they are young. They don't know any better. They will learn, just like we did."

Verdian growled a curse under his breath.

Helena shined her glowing smile at him. "You have yet to mention what *we* will be doing. Will we be present for our daughter's coronation?"

Verdian looked at her with disgust. "I don't have time to watch Mareleau play dress-up."

Helena pursed her lips and put her hands on her hips. She looked as if she were about to argue but seemed to think better of it. Her eyes lighted on her daughter for a moment before she returned to her seat.

My mother was the next to speak, her apprehension palpable. "What about the arrangement you'd made with Arlous? When Mareleau and Teryn were promised, it was agreed that you would make Mareleau your heir. Upon inheriting their thrones, our children would rule Sele and Mena together as one kingdom. Does this agreement still stand with Larylis in Teryn's stead?"

Verdian put his arms on his desk, eyes unfocused.

Then he raised his head and looked at Mareleau. "If I die before naming a proper heir, yes, my rule will go to my daughter. And our kingdoms can go to the wolves."

Larylis

"It isn't fair." Mareleau stomped to the bed and fell upon it. "He's clearly punishing me. He's punishing *us*."

I closed the doors to the wedding chamber and stood in the middle of the room, eyes heavy, mind empty. It wasn't that I was surprised; I'd known there would be a price to pay for our marriage and for Mareleau's lie. It was a price I'd already accepted. I just hadn't realized we'd have to pay it so soon.

Quiet sobs brought my attention back to the bed where Mareleau laid with her hands over her eyes. Her tears woke my heart from its brief reprieve, and I went to the bed and pulled her into my arms. For all her ferocity, she was surprisingly fragile. I was beginning to learn how much she hid behind her bold, beautiful mask. Would I ever truly know her at all?

"We just found each other. I don't want to leave your side ever again." She raised her head, and I saw a hint of fierceness return to her eyes. "I am to be Queen of Mena. What right does my father have over a queen?"

I kissed her forehead. "I don't know, but he is your father. Right now, he's the most powerful ruler in Lela. Mena and Kero are broken. We need an alliance with Verdian."

"So, you're on *his* side?"

I tried not to laugh, recalling when she'd called *me* the dramatic one. "Of course not, but the best thing we can do right now is keep our heads down. Prove our worth. Prove our marriage is strong and our kingdoms are stronger. Then figure out what is expected of you at Ridine. When the time is right, we'll make a plan and get you home."

Mareleau groaned. "It's so cruel. How could my father send his pregnant daughter to the other side of Lela?"

My hand froze in the midst of rubbing her back. "You know you aren't pregnant."

Mareleau rolled her eyes. "But *they* don't know that. If I were, I'd deserve the utmost care." She turned her chin up, looking much more like her usual self. "Thank goodness, though. I don't know what I would do if I had to birth a brat at Ridine. It's probably infested with rats."

"Let's...not talk about that."

"About what? Rats?"

"No. About...the pregnancy."

She frowned. "Lare, you promised you'd try to forgive me."

"I am trying, but I still feel raw about it." I hesitated, wondering if I should say what was really on my heart. "I don't like hearing you speak so carelessly about it. I want a child with you someday. It's important to me."

"I'm sure we will. Someday." She turned her face toward mine, a sly smile playing on her lips. "In the meantime, we only have a few more days together to practice."

My heart quickened as I leaned my lips toward hers.

Knock, knock, knock.

"Who would visit us at our wedding chamber?" Mare-leau scowled at the door.

The visitor knocked again.

I groaned and dragged my feet to confront our intruder. It was Teryn. My mouth went dry, and desire drained from my body at once. "Brother."

Teryn smiled. "I hope I wasn't disturbing anything."

"Not at all." I shifted from foot to foot. It had been easy to joke with him earlier that morning, but that was before my mood had turned sour. Now, seeing Teryn standing outside my wedding chamber, I could think of nothing but the debt I would forever owe him. "What brings you here?"

Teryn looked past me into the room. "I actually wanted to speak with Mareleau."

I turned and saw Mareleau pause in the middle of smoothing her dress to cock her head. "Me? What do you need from *me*?"

I wasn't sure if I felt guilty or delighted about the edge in her voice. *Could I still be harboring jealousy about my brother's former interest in my wife?* At least I knew how Mareleau felt about *him*. I suppressed a smile and opened my arm to welcome him into the room.

He approached Mareleau. "I have a favor to ask."

"Another one?"

Teryn smiled. "Yes. First, thank you for helping me with the directions in the servants' hall last night. They worked perfectly."

"And I thank you for what you did for me and Larylis." It was clear in her tone that she considered them even now. How wrong she was. We could never make up for what Teryn had done for us.

"Would you help me with something else? I want to do something for Cora, but I'm clueless when it comes to these things. It's our last night together for who knows how long, and I want to make it special."

Mareleau's jaw moved back and forth while she considered his request. "I'll see what I can do."

4

PAWN

Cora

I paced along the far wall in my room. *I've gone from prisoner, to princess, to pawn, all in the span of a day.* It wasn't anything I hadn't seen coming. I'd known that even though the rulers of Mena and Sele were allowing me and Dimetreus to reclaim our kingdom, they wouldn't do so easily. Verdian didn't trust us. But I never would have predicted the level of control he'd shown over our lives today.

Teryn and I have just been engaged, and already we have to part. My shoulders fell, remembering our kiss, remembering the plans we'd made to go to Dermaine and Ridine together. Why was Verdian so intent on keeping all of us separate? He seemed to have a particular disdain for his own daughter. And she was somehow already pregnant! There was obviously much I didn't understand.

I heard the doors of my room spring open, and I turned to find Lurel skipping toward me, smiling wide, and carrying a large box in her arms. "I have the best news, Your Highness!"

The tears streaming down her cheeks made me question the validity of her statement. I wasn't sure whether to comfort her or bounce on the balls of my feet. "Oh, and what news is that?"

"I am to be your chambermaid! I get to accompany you to Ridine!"

"And you're happy about that?"

"Of course I am. I've never been outside of Sele."

"Then why are you crying?"

She set the box at her feet and wiped her eyes and cheeks. "I'm just so excited, Your Highness. I thought I would have to say goodbye to you after how fond of you I've grown. I wasn't keen on returning to Mareleau's service, although I really shouldn't say that—"

I laid a hand on the girl's shoulder. "I understand. I'm happy to hear you'll be joining me. But won't you miss your family?"

"My father will be there. Although I'm sure Mother will remain home—"

I held up a hand. "Who is your father?"

"Lord Kevan, of course."

"Lord Kevan is your father? Wait...you and Mareleau are cousins?"

Lurel nodded, frowning. "Probably why she hates me so. Although, I shouldn't say that either. She has always treated me well. She just prefers when I'm quiet." Her smile grew wide again. "But you've never reprimanded my speech before, have you, Your Highness?"

I laughed, although beneath it was a slight apprehension. Was Lord Kevan a man to be trusted? If he was anything like Verdian, I doubted he had strictly pure motives.

Lurel gasped, bringing my attention back to her. "What am I doing talking about myself? I brought you something." She bent over the box and removed the lid. "The seamstresses finished some of your garments."

She pulled the first item out of the box—a cloak of deep-blue wool with rich, brown leather running along the front seams and bottom hem. "It's your new riding cloak. Do you love it?"

I took it from her and draped it over my shoulders, securing the silver clasp. With a gasp of surprise, I realized the clasp was in the shape of a mountain—Kero's sigil. It had been years since I'd seen the symbol of my kingdom. "Yes, it's perfect."

Lurel went to the wardrobe. "Can we throw this one out then?"

I took the tattered cloak from her hands. As sentimental as it made me feel, there was no sense in keeping it. "I suppose." I folded it in my arms and began to hand it to Lurel when I felt something hard beneath my palm. "Wait." I reached into the cloak for the source. When I pulled it free, a large, purple crystal was in my hand.

"What is that?" Lurel's eyes grew wide.

I froze, and the old cloak slipped to the floor. "Oh, it's nothing." I stooped to retrieve the cloak, and in the same move, shoved the crystal into an inner pocket of my new garment. How could I have forgotten Morkai's crystal all this time?

Lurel titled her head, looking for what I'd held in my hands a moment before.

"Here. Do what you will with it." I pushed the cloak

into her arms. "What else is in the box?" I was less curious and more hoping to distract her from asking about the crystal.

The diversion worked. She dove back into the box and withdrew a gown of royal blue silk. "This is amazing. You have to wear it for dinner."

"Tonight?" I looked out the window at the sun beginning its descent toward the Verlot Mountains. Dinner would begin before the next bell. I looked back at the gown. "It's too elegant for a simple dinner."

Lurel blushed and giggled behind her hands. "I think Prince Teryn would like it."

I felt heat flush my cheeks. "I take it you heard about our engagement."

She nodded. "I also heard he'll be leaving tomorrow. You might as well put this dress to good use. Besides, do you really want to keep wearing Mareleau's hand-me-downs?"

I couldn't help but smile at Lurel's innocent sass. I looked from the silk gown to the modest taffeta dress I was wearing. "You're right. I'll wear it."

I STOOD BEFORE THE MIRROR, AND THIS TIME I COULD CALL myself anything but modest. The silk fabric shone like a deep-blue sapphire, the neckline plunged, and the tight bodice of blue and gold brocade forced my bosom into two visible mounds. The sleeves opened at the elbow and trailed halfway to the hem of my skirt. The skirt itself bloomed away from my hips, sweeping down to my feet like a shimmering waterfall. My hair had been pulled up and away from my face, secured with pins and pearls. Brown, curling tendrils framed my face and spilled to the nape of my neck. I'd thought I'd looked ravishing the first time I'd been dressed at Verlot, but now I knew what a dress made specially for me looked like.

I felt my chest tighten and stepped away from the mirror. "I can't wear this. It's too much. I should be going to a ball or something, not dinner."

"Princess, you must wear it. You look amazing! All eyes will be on you."

"That's what I'm afraid of. I don't need anyone looking at me." I sat at the vanity and raised a hand toward my hair to remove the pins.

Lurel stopped me before I could succeed. "Your Highness, please don't make me tell you. I'm already terrible at keeping secrets."

"Tell me what? Lurel, if there's something—"

I was interrupted by a knock and turned as the doors opened to reveal Mareleau.

Lurel sighed. "Just in time."

I looked from one girl to the other. "What's going on?"

Mareleau strolled into the room, hands on her hips. She was dressed in a lavish gown of shimmering gold damask with an overflowing bosom that put mine to shame. I no longer felt overdressed. "Your presence has been requested," she said with an air of indifference as she approached me. The way she swayed her hips when she walked reminded me of Luna and Ciela, and I was struck with a sudden aching for the Forest People.

"Who requests my presence?"

Lurel rolled her eyes. "She's very difficult to surprise. I nearly had to tell her."

Mareleau popped her hip to the side. "Just play along, all right?"

I raised an eyebrow but stood from my chair.

"One more thing." Lurel scurried to the box and pulled out the remaining item. It was a lightweight cloak in a cream color with gold stitching lining the hems. She draped it over my shoulders. "You might need this."

"Why?" Before Lurel could answer, Mareleau linked her arm through mine and pulled me from the room.

As we walked arm-in-arm down the halls of Verlot, taking leisurely steps, my heart began to quicken. Who was she taking me to? My stomach churned, imagining me in my gown in front of King Verdian.

The silence grew heavy between us. I was beginning to think we'd walk the whole way without saying a word, until Mareleau finally spoke. "I never properly introduced myself," she said in a disinterested tone, staring straight ahead. "I'm Princess Mareleau of Sele, daughter of King Verdian and Queen Helena."

No kidding. I imitated her formal introduction. "I'm Princess Coralaine of Kero, daughter of King Jeru and Queen Tiliane."

"Yes, the woman who almost married my husband."

I turned toward her and scowled. "I wouldn't say I even came close to marrying your husband. However, you very nearly married my betrothed."

Mareleau smirked but didn't meet my eye. "I hope you aren't too disappointed. We can't all get our first choice."

I stopped and pulled away, putting my hands on my hips as I looked up at her. "Larylis wasn't my first choice, Teryn was. I was only considering my duty to my kingdom."

Mareleau walked on, forcing me to trail in her wake. "Good. That's what I needed to hear."

My mouth fell open. "You could have asked. We aren't enemies, you know. It's clear we're both pawns in this. We should be able to be honest with each other."

Mareleau shrugged but gave no response.

"Look, I didn't ask you to accompany me to Ridine, but it looks like neither of us can get out of it. Can we at least be friendly toward each other?"

"I didn't ask for a friend."

I stared, dumbfounded. "Have it your way, Your Highness."

"We're here." Mareleau tossed her hair over her shoulder as we came to a stop before a door opening to the palace gardens. "Walk straight. You'll find him."

"Find who?"

Mareleau ignored me and turned in the other direction. I frowned after her, then looked down the garden path.

I walked through the door and planted my feet on a flat circle of white marble. The stepping stones lined the way before me, weaving through rose bushes, shrubs, statues, and fountains. The marble stones branched off the main path to other directions in the garden. I followed the path straight, as Mareleau had directed. It turned slightly left and then opened into a circular courtyard with a shimmering marble floor surrounded by glowing lanterns. At the center of the courtyard was a raised pond.

At the edge of the pond sat Teryn.

5

FAREWELL

Teryn

I stood from my seat on the ledge of the pond but found myself unable to move any further. Cora stepped into the courtyard, and the sight of her took my breath away. I'd never seen her look more elegant. "You...look incredible," I managed to say.

Her rouge-painted lips stretched into a wide grin. She walked toward me, stopping a few steps away and turned in a circle. "Better than tangled hair and hunting pants?" The hem of her cloak and gown twirled around her.

When she was again facing me, I took her hand and pulled her a step closer. "I liked you even with tangled hair and hunting pants."

Cora laughed. "I find that hard to believe."

"It's true. I didn't realize it at the time, but I was fascinated by you from the first time I saw you, tangles, pants, and all." I smirked and acted out a sentimental sigh. "Even at knife point, I knew you were beautiful."

Cora rolled her eyes.

My face straightened into a more serious expression as I put my hand on her cheek. "Truly, though. I liked you from the first night we talked. I was drawn to your passion and your bravery. You are the strongest woman I have ever met, and beautiful in all your forms."

Cora swallowed hard, her cheeks flushing pink. Our eyes locked, and it felt like every inch of space between us was too much. My heart raced as I considered moving in for our third kiss. Why did each one feel like such a momentous feat to execute?

Sudden movement startled me. The two of us pulled away and turned toward the courtyard's entry as several hall servants filed in. Two brought in a modest table, two more brought chairs, and the remaining held covered plates.

"What's this?" Cora asked.

"Did you think I brought you here for a stroll?"

Her eyes went wide as our dinner table was set up in front of the pond and piled high with plates of food, candles, and two goblets of wine.

Once our dinner was set, the hall servants directed us into our chairs, then stepped to the perimeter of the courtyard.

Cora looked over the expanse of the table, then lifted her eyes to meet mine. "This is beyond anything I've ever experienced."

"That's a good thing, I hope."

"It is. I've just...I've never had a..."

I cocked my head to the side and watched her cheeks turn pink. "A what?"

"A courtship. I was very much at home with the Forest

People, but I only had one other person besides Salinda that I was truly close to. Maiya. She was like a sister to me. She was the only person I opened up to, yet I never let her know my secrets. I loved my people, but I kept them at a distance to protect myself. Before I was with them, I was a child. I've never had the opportunity to experience anything like this."

"So, you *are* impressed."

She laughed. "What I'm trying to say is, thank you. This means a lot to me."

"This means a lot to me too. I nearly lost my head when Verdian said I'd be leaving tomorrow. Nothing can change how soon we must part, but we can at least make the most of the time we have." My voice sounded calm and collected, but inside, the words made my chest feel tight. I still couldn't believe I'd be leaving her.

Cora lowered her eyes under my gaze, making me wonder how long I'd been staring.

I broke the tension. "I have another surprise for you."

"Another?"

"You'll be riding Hara tomorrow."

Her mouth fell open. "Hara? She's...here?"

I nodded. "Hara, your bow, saddlebags, quiver, arrows. I hadn't the chance to tell you before, but I made sure we brought her back with us from Centerpointe Rock."

Her eyes brimmed with tears. "Teryn, how do you keep doing this?"

"Doing what?"

A corner of her mouth lifted. "Impressing me."

"Just wait until you try the food. I can't take credit for making it, but I figured it was something you needed to try before you left."

She looked at the plates before her. "I can already tell this is a far cry from what they served me in the dungeons."

"Trust me, it's a far cry from anything you'll ever taste again."

~

Cora

Once we'd finished eating, the hall servants took our plates, cleared our table from the courtyard, and we were again left alone. The sun blushed behind the Verlot Mountains in a darkening sky.

Teryn picked up a lantern and extended his free hand to me. "Shall we?"

I placed my hand in his, feeling the warmth of his fingers entwined with mine as we left the courtyard. At first, I thought he was leading us back toward the palace, but after a few twists and turns down the garden path, it was clear we were heading deeper into the maze of greenery. *Good. I'm not ready for goodbye.*

With the summer sun no longer high in the sky, I was grateful Lurel had made me wear my new cloak. It was much lighter than my riding cloak would have been, but perfect for an evening stroll.

We walked along the path in silence, rarely meeting anyone else. I struggled to find something to say, but no word seemed more satisfying than our quiet closeness.

After many twists and turns, our path opened to another courtyard. This one was much smaller than the first, but with the same circular, marble floor. It was lined

with miniature, ivory statues in the likeness of forest crit-
ters. An immense white statue stood at center, towering
over the courtyard. I raised my eyes. Teryn lifted the
lantern, illuminating a unicorn with a golden horn,
rearing on its hind legs.

"There it is," Teryn said. "I knew we'd find it."

I was stunned by the beauty of the statue.

"It reminds you of Valorre, doesn't it?"

I nodded, eyes unable to pull away.

"You must miss him a lot."

"Every day."

"Do you know where he is?"

I looked toward the silhouette of mountains
surrounding the palace. "Close. He's somewhere at the
bottom of the Verlot Mountains."

"You'll see him soon, won't you?"

I smiled. "He says he'll follow me wherever I go. I can
feel his nearness every day. He's waiting for me. But
sometimes, I wonder if he'd be better off..." I lowered my
head, unable to finish my sentence.

Teryn set the lantern at our feet and folded me into
his arms.

I pressed my forehead into his chest and bit back
tears. "I'm still not sure I made the right choice. Coming
here, reclaiming my throne. Leaving the Forest People
behind without a word. Leaving Valorre."

Teryn tensed but continued to hold me close, and I
realized my words had brought him pain. I'd said I wasn't
sure I'd made the right choices, and *he* was one of those
choices. I could almost hear his thoughts as if he'd
spoken them out loud: *Are you uncertain about me too?*

I lifted my eyes and met his beneath a furrowed brow.

"I don't doubt being with you, Teryn. You know that, right? You've been the biggest, most surprising blessing in my life since Valorre."

His expression softened. "And you've been the same for me. I'm going to find a way to come back to you as soon as I can. You know *that*, right?"

"I look forward to it already." Our eyes locked. Aside from our quickening breaths, we were frozen. I wanted nothing more than to shatter the stillness by bridging the gap between us. Finally, I reached my hands toward his waist. Before I could press him closer to me, his lips were on mine. The sweetness of our first kisses was eclipsed by the fierceness in this one. His fingers ran thought my hair, sending pearls and clips clattering to the floor. My hands pressed into his lower back.

We stayed like that until I knew the experience would be etched into my memory forever, until the words *goodbye* seemed stripped of meaning.

6

CORONATION

Mareleau

I dropped to my knees before the altar in the Godskeep at Dermaine Palace and lowered my head. The hem of my white dress spread out before me in elegant, ivory folds. My hair draped over my shoulders and down my arms, grazing my hands folded in my lap.

Unlike my unceremonious wedding, a Godspriest conducted this ceremony, and Dermaine's court was welcome to witness our vows.

The old Godspriest placed his wrinkled hand over the top of my head. "May the Gods who watch over Lela cast favor upon Mareleau, daughter of King Verdian and Queen Helena, so she may rule Mena as queen through peace. May our land grow fertile, and may our people grow fruitful." He placed a finger under my chin and allowed me to meet his eyes. "Do you swear your obedience, your servitude, and your fidelity to the kingdom of

Mena and the land of Lela? To serve and protect her people?"

My arms trembled. "I do."

He lighted a hand on each of my shoulders, then kissed my forehead. I suppressed a grimace as his scratchy beard and wet lips grazed my skin. With graceful, deliberate steps, he turned to a pedestal that held a crown—a circlet of shimmering gold set with a glittering sapphire. He brought it to me, and I lowered my gaze as he placed it on my head. It was lightweight and not nearly as elaborate as my mother's, but it was mine. That's all that mattered.

"In the eyes of the Gods, Lela, and the people of Mena, I pronounce you Queen of Mena."

My heart raced as cheers rang out behind me. "Our queen, Queen Mareleau!"

The Godspriest bowed his head in a nod. "The queen may rise."

I stood on unsteady legs and turned to face the crowd. Unfamiliar faces shouted my name. I lifted my shoulders and chin, pressed my chest forward, and shined my smile upon the crowd. As much as I hated to admit it, I felt like my mother. Beaming. Beautiful. Fake.

Larylis came to my side. Upon his head was a wide band of gold engraved with vines, roses, and two soaring eagles, set with an enormous ruby.

"Our king, King Larylis, our queen, Queen Mareleau!" The chanting rose louder.

Larylis held out his arm and smiled. "My queen."

I put my arm through his. "My king."

We stepped down from the dais beneath the altar and began our procession through the Godskeep. The domed roof loomed high above our heads with thick wooden beams and intricate carvings. Although Dermaine's Godskeep was half of the size of Verlot's, and without the richness of white marble and towering statues, the room was intimidating nonetheless.

Our people bowed and whispered our names as we passed. Even though I kept my head high and my lips fixed into a smile, I couldn't help the sense of fraudulence that fought to crush my proud elation. In every face I passed, I saw my father's cold eyes. Every whisper of my name carried Father's condemnation: *traitor*.

I am not a traitor. I am queen. I deserve to be queen. The crown upon my head was proof enough. Wasn't it?

As if sensing my conflict, Larylis turned his head toward me and smiled. Beneath that, my distress melted. *I am* his *queen. That's all that matters.*

We stepped through the doors of the Godskeep and were met with a mild morning breeze. I closed my eyes and let it wash over me. It was a struggle to pry my eyes open after.

"You're tired, aren't you?" Larylis whispered. The court began to file out of the Godskeep behind us.

I nodded. Even though I'd only been awake for a few hours, I was already yearning for bed. I'd endured four days of speedy travel before arriving at Dermaine the evening before. Knowing I'd return to my travels the following morning was enough to make me tired. The fact that I'd be leaving Larylis behind was all it took to make my eyes burn continuously.

"At least we have today." Larylis pulled me closer and kissed the side of my head. We followed the path back to the main palace, and I soaked in every sight. Dermaine was so different from Verlot, but it carried its own beauty. And it was now my home, my palace. The walls, turrets, and gardens were mine. Its people were mine. And I had only one day to enjoy them.

OUR CORONATION FEAST WENT BY IN A BLUR OF RAUCOUS cheers, overflowing plates of food, and unfamiliar faces. The great hall was filled from wall to wall with people eager to see their new queen and congratulate their king. Despite the delicious food placed before me, I could hardly eat a bite. I even passed on wine, though my mother wasn't there to raise her brow at me.

Larylis, on the other hand, ate more plates of food than I imagined possible and drank enough wine for the both of us. I couldn't blame him. While we had different ways of expressing it, he and I were coping with the same pain.

I scanned the head table out of boredom and found one person who looked sullener than I felt. Teryn leaned back in his chair, pushing a full plate of food around with his fork while his glazed eyes seemed fixated on nothing. I couldn't help but smirk. Even though I was being punished the harshest, it was satisfying to see no one was benefiting from my father's wrath.

I felt Larylis' hand on my back, and I turned to him. His crooked, wine-stained smile made me erupt with laughter. Even his crown was askew. When I reached up to straighten it, he brought his lips to mine. I felt my body relax as he placed his hand behind my neck.

"Maybe we should sneak out of this feast early," he whispered.

I grinned. "That's the best idea I've heard all day."

A throat cleared behind us, and I jumped, pulling back from Larylis to meet the judging eyes of my uncle, Lord Ulrich.

Lord Ulrich was a head taller than my father, but with the same husky build. He was clean shaven with a double chin, and a head of brown hair cropped below his ears. His gray eyes were much like my father's.

Larylis seemed to sober in my uncle's presence. "Yes, Lord Ulrich?"

Ulrich stood tall with his hands behind his back, looking down his nose at my husband. "The feast must come to a close. You are needed on the council. Your councilmen await." He then turned to me. "You, Your Highness, must prepare for our journey north."

"What's there to prepare?" I said under my breath. "I've hardly had time to unpack."

Ulrich ignored me and wordlessly excused himself.

Larylis' shoulders dropped as he turned back to me. "I'm sorry, my love. I thought we'd at least have one day together before you left."

My throat constricted, and I fought the tears welling in my eyes. I forced a smile. "Don't worry about it. I'll see you tonight."

Larylis let out a shaking breath, then kissed me on the cheek. "Tonight."

When he left his seat, the entire room felt empty, drained of all color. Pain rippled through me from my gut to my throat, the beginning of a sob threatening to spew forth.

"Breah, Ann, Sera," I barked at my queensmaids. "I want to return to my room."

My ladies hurried to my side. I barely acknowledged the court as they stood to honor my departure from the great hall. I clenched my jaw as we made our way through the corridors to my room.

Once inside, I left my ladies in the study and closed the door to my bedchamber behind me. In the absence of sound, admiring eyes, and false smiles, I let myself crumble. I felt as if a wall was shattering around me, piece by piece. My face contorted, eyes turned to slits. I pressed my mouth into a pillow, let out a muffled wail, and began to pour all my sorrow, all my disappointment, all my pain into a flood of tears.

Larylis

The Godskeep looked much different in the candlelit dark than it had mere hours before when I'd had a crown placed on my head. The Godspriest knelt at the altar, whispering some incantation to the Gods, and paid me no heed as I entered. I walked swiftly through the main room to the other side where the tomb halls began. The hall of my most recent ancestors wound to my right. I followed it until I came to the newest tomb. The tomb of my father.

I placed my hands on the cold stone of his unfinished effigy. Through tear-filled eyes and the dim light, I could make out the lifeless features of eyes and face. Despite the talent of the stone carver, nothing could capture the true warmth of my father.

Footsteps sounded on the hall floor. I turned and saw a shadowed silhouette step into the light. *Teryn.*

I didn't bother to wipe my eyes; his were as red as mine. Without a word, he stood at my side, and we studied the effigy together. The silence stretched on until Teryn finally spoke. "Through all the chaos of the past weeks, we've hardly had time to mourn him."

He was right. "Today should have been in *his* honor. Instead, a celebration was held in mine. Instead, I was in his place at the head table, wearing a crown. Instead, I sat at his desk in his study, and signed my name on documents in lieu of his."

"Don't feel guilty about that. You're only doing your duty. None of this is your choice."

"You're right," I said with a bitter laugh. "I haven't made a single choice since he died. I've been nothing but passive, unclear about where desire ends and duty begins."

Teryn touched my shoulder and made me face him. "What are you talking about?"

I refused to meet his eyes, keeping mine on Father's tomb. "All of this. All these decisions. Becoming crown prince, becoming king. Mareleau..." I stopped myself, coming close to confessing her lie. I chose another angle. "I didn't fight for her when she was nearly forced to marry you. I didn't fight you when you abdicated to me. I've lost sight of what's right or wrong. I don't know where my place is in all of this."

"Brother, it's all right to feel confused and out of place. Do you think I completely understand what's happening?

What the consequences of my choices are? All we can do is our best. Sometimes that's following our duty. Other times it's following our hearts."

This time I met his eyes. "That's easy for you to say, because you've done both. I've followed neither. I'm being pulled by what's happening around me. What would have happened if you hadn't abdicated? Would I have let Mareleau go? Would I have spoken up if she hadn't?"

"It's impossible to know. Besides, it's in the past. You're king now. The choices of our kingdom are in your hands."

The muscles in my neck tensed. My hands clenched into fists as shame and anger filled my veins. "Don't you see? I don't deserve that responsibility. I couldn't fight for the woman I love, nor could I turn down a crown I don't deserve."

Teryn's mouth hung open for a moment. When he spoke, his voice was gentle. "So, you didn't fight for her. There's nothing you can do about that now, besides fight for her every day moving forward."

"How do I do that when we are all being controlled by King Verdian? How can I fight for her and keep her home with me when I don't yet know my rights as king? Can I defy the father of my wife?"

Teryn shrugged. "I don't know either. I know far less about being king than Verdian gives me credit for. He thinks I was well trained, but he's wrong. I'm just as lost as you are. But I know you'll learn in time. Your power and your influence will grow. Besides, Verdian can't stay mad at his daughter forever."

I sighed. "It doesn't change the fact that I don't deserve to be king in the first place." I looked at my brother. "This crown should be yours."

He looked at the band of gold with disdain. "No, it shouldn't. You are worthy of the crown as much as I ever was. When war came into our land, you acted. You protected our kingdom and our people with every opportunity you had. If I were in your place today, I would feel equally confused. Neither of us were prepared to lose our father so soon."

It was time to make my language clear, as awkward as it made me feel. "But if it weren't for you, I wouldn't have this crown. You abdicated because of something you think...because of something I did. I betrayed you with your own betrothed and was rewarded for it. I will never feel good about that."

"I didn't do it for you." Teryn let out a strained laugh. "For one, Mareleau should never have been my betrothed. I should have listened to you all those years you told me you and Mareleau loved each other. I betrayed *you,* refusing to believe your words."

I opened my mouth to interrupt, but he held a hand out to quiet me.

"For another, I don't love Mareleau, and I was crazy to think I ever did. I was more...obsessed. I attached a false significance to marrying her, thinking she was a prize that would make me worthy to be king. You see, I may have been crown prince, but I too grew up in Father's shadow, thinking I'd never be as good a king as he was. I thought Mareleau would change that, but I was wrong. You have no idea how relieved I was when I'd heard what the two of you had done. You freed me from a duty I no longer wanted to follow."

His words lifted a weight from my shoulders that

made me feel like I could stand tall for the first time in a week. "You mean it?"

"Yes. And most importantly, I love Cora. I wanted to marry Cora, and I saw only one solution to make that happen. Luckily, it was a solution that benefited all of us."

I felt the corners of my mouth involuntarily rise. "You really love Cora?"

He nodded, and his lips pulled into a smirk as he slapped me playfully on the shoulder. "How could you think me so unselfish? You really think I'd do all that just for *you*?"

"I did. The shame was eating me alive."

Teryn rolled his eyes. "Idiot."

It was my turn to punch him in the arm. With the air between us so much lighter than it had been before, we returned our attention to the tomb.

"I loved him so much," I said. "In his last days, he showed me how much he loved me too."

"We were lucky to have him as a father."

"He's no Verdian, that's for sure."

We laughed, echoes of it drifting through the hall until it faded into another long stretch of silence.

Feeling the freedom of my brother's forgiveness and remembering the love of my father sparked a fire in my chest. It started as a giddy compulsion and ended with the power of choice. I turned to Teryn. "You should go to her."

He looked at me with a blank stare. "What do you mean?"

"Go to Ridine and be with Cora."

His eyes went wide. "But Verdian...I'm supposed to help you..."

"You said so yourself. You'd be just as lost as I am if you were in my place. How can I expect you to help me?"

Teryn smiled. "Are you sure you want to risk the wrath of King Verdian?"

"He may be our ally, and he may be the father of my wife, but he is not King of Mena. I am. As your king, I order you to go to Ridine."

"What about Lord Ulrich? He'll never allow me to come with."

"Wait a day or two after they leave and then travel in secret. Once you're there, he cannot stop you."

Teryn beamed and pulled me into a crushing embrace. "Thank you, brother. You have no idea how much this means to me." He released me and turned away, his steps jubilant as he sprinted from the hall.

I followed, but at a slower pace. By the time I reached my room, it was past eighth bell. I quietly undressed and slipped into my bedchamber. Mareleau was under the covers, fast asleep.

My heart fell when I saw her, eyes closed, lips slightly parted. We'd had one day to spend together at Dermaine, and that day was already over. I sat at the edge of the bed, looking down at her while I etched her face into my memory. I stroked her golden hair away from her cheek and brushed her forehead with my lips.

I'll bring you back home to me, I silently promised. *Someday.*

7

HOMECOMING

Cora

"**W**e're approaching Ridine," Lord Kevan told Dimetreus in his gruff voice. With his stout build and stoic expression, he was a near spitting image of King Verdian. However, instead of silver hair and gray eyes, Kevan had piercing blue eyes and a head of golden-brown hair down to his shoulders and a thick beard to match. "We should arrive at the castle gates within the hour." Kevan rode back to the head of the line next to the other councilman from Verlot.

I lifted my hand to shade my eyes from the late afternoon sun. There was no sign of the castle, just dense forest, mountain peaks, and open road ahead.

"He acts as if we don't know how to recognize our homeland," Dimetreus said under his breath.

After two weeks of traveling, he was growing increasingly irritated with Lord Kevan's control. He and I hardly had a say in the plans of our travels. We were guarded at all times, stayed at the inns that had been prearranged for us, slept in the rooms we were assigned to, and kept to a schedule we weren't made aware of beforehand. We kept our composure and followed along with grace, but I was starting to wonder if this would continue once we arrived at Ridine.

That's not an option. I tightened my grip on Hara's reins and clenched my jaw. The thought of being watched and controlled in my own castle made my stomach churn.

I closed my eyes and turned my thoughts to more pleasant matters. Sounds around me amplified and then became a hollow echo from far away as I focused on the windblown leaves of the forest trees, the turning of aromatic soil, and the pounding of unfettered hooves dancing on the forest floor. I was elated with the joy of running free and unseen, at one with my surroundings.

I am here. I go with you.

I smiled, comforted by Valorre's words. While I longed to be where he was, I was satisfied knowing he was near. *Soon. I'll be able to visit you soon.* I stroked Hara's neck and returned my attention to my traveling party. The murmur of voices, the rhythmic hooves beating the road, and the screeching wheels of our traveling coach were a disappointing exchange. But it was the path I'd chosen.

I looked above the trees to the snowcapped peaks of the Ridine Mountains. It was a sight I'd seen many times as a child whenever I'd looked out my window. Thoughts of daily life with Mother and Father flooded my memory. I let them stay where they were, neither following them into sentimental mourning nor to the anger over their morbid demise.

I turned to my brother. "Is this strange for you? Returning home?"

He furrowed his brow and stared ahead of him. "I don't quite know what to expect. Last time I was here, I could hardly be called a man, much less a king. My memories are so jumbled, I can barely make sense of what has happened. I'm almost afraid that returning home will bring it all back. Everything I did. Everything I let happen."

My heart sank at his words. "That wasn't you. Besides, I'm here this time. We will figure this out together. We will find a way to make Ridine feel like home again."

"I think we'd have to raze it to the ground for that to happen."

I frowned. Perhaps it was the strain of travel and Lord Kevan's watchful eye that had my brother so on edge. It made me wonder if he'd wanted to return to his throne in the first place. Had I been fighting for something he didn't even want? But what would have been the alternative? Execution? A life of imprisonment?

Dimetreus looked at me, and his face melted into a smile. "I'm sorry, Coralaine. I don't mean to talk like that. This is going to take some time for me to adjust to."

I sighed. "Me too."

We continued down the road between the forest trees until they began to thin.

Lord Kevan slowed his horse in line with us. "We're here."

In the distance, Ridine came into view. I'd expected it

to look dark and menacing, the way it had under Morkai's ownership. However, beneath the fading light of the sun, it reminded me more of a lame animal, hunched and waiting to be put from its misery. Its walls were weathered stone, crumbling where Morkai had once pulled down a tower. The lawn surrounding it was wild and overgrown, nearly impossible to tell the landscape from the woods.

Upon further inspection of the lawn, I noticed movement—heads bobbing amongst the weeds and greenery throughout the field. More movement drew my eye ahead, and I noticed guards standing before the gatehouse.

"Has Lord Ulrich already come?" I asked.

Kevan shook his head. "We aren't expecting him for another two days, at least." He didn't seem surprised by the sight of guards or the workers in the fields.

I turned to Dimetreus and kept my voice low. "Where did these people come from? They obviously weren't left by Morkai."

He leaned toward me, eyes full of disdain. "Verdian seized Ridine as soon as the battle ended. He placed it under the control of his guards, stewards, staff, and who knows whom else."

While I'd been concerned about the process of re-staffing Ridine and how to manage in the interim, it had never occurred to me that it would already have been done for us. I could have considered it a favor from Verdian, but I couldn't help feeling betrayed. Strangers had entered my home before me.

As we approached the gatehouse, Lord Kevan nodded to the guards, and the portcullis began to raise.

My heart beat high in my chest as we rode beneath the gate.

Lord Kevan turned his head toward me and Dimetreus. I couldn't tell if he was smiling or scowling. "Welcome home."

~

WE ENTERED THE CASTLE WALLS AND MOVED INTO THE courtyard. As I dismounted, I raised my eyes to the turrets and massive stone towering above me, trying to remember how it must have looked when I was a child. I couldn't remember ever feeling like the walls were closing in so closely as they did now.

"Your horse, princess?"

I jumped at the voice, and whirled around to find a lanky boy a few years younger than I. He held out his hand for Hara's reins. "Of course." I steadied my breathing, surprised at how jumpy I was. With a wistful feeling, I handed him the reins and watched as he took her to the stables. I brought my attention back to my retinue as a dozen members of castle staff came to greet us and help unload our belongings.

An older man with a slim build and a kind face greeted my brother with a bow. "My king, I am Master Arther, and I am to be your Royal Chambermaster and head of staff until more appointments can be made."

Dimetreus nodded brusquely, giving no word of greeting.

Lurel clambered out of the traveling coach and came to my side, squealing as she tugged the sleeve of my gown. "We're here! This is your home!"

I tried to imitate some of her excitement. "Yes. My home."

She stretched her arms high above her. "I don't know how you can handle riding, Your Highness. I can't believe you didn't ride in the coach with me."

"I told you, I like to ride."

"Yes, well, riding is one thing. Traveling like that, though, is another. I thought I would die of boredom! I can't imagine if I'd been bouncing up and down on a horse the whole time."

"Lurel, bring the princess inside," Lord Kevan said.

Lurel curtsied, turning a more serious face to him. "Yes, Father." When she turned back to me, she was beaming again. "I can't wait to see your home. It's so...different from Verlot!"

"Different is right." I took a deep breath. "Shall we?"

Lurel linked her arm through mine, and we walked into the castle. The main hall was dimly lit but appeared to be freshly cleaned. However, a staleness hung in the air from years of Morkai's neglect. Would we ever be rid of it?

We continued until we stood outside the doors to the great hall. Bile rose in my throat as I remembered the nightmare I'd had last time I was at Ridine. In that nightmare, my parents had sat in the hall, the room bright and vibrant until everything turned to grim darkness. *It wasn't real. Breathe.*

We entered, and I found it resembled nothing of my nightmare, or of my childhood. It was neither vibrant and lively, nor dark and domineering. It was clean and empty, save for a newly built table where the head table used to stand.

"We'll have more furnishings built in the coming weeks." I jumped at Lord Kevan's voice. I turned to see him, Dimetreus, Master Arther, and a few other members of staff walking toward us.

"Was there nothing left of use in here?" I asked.

"Hardly anything has been worth saving here at all, from what I've been told." Kevan grimaced at the walls around us, as if he feared their prior filth would return. "Verdian ordered Ridine to be given a fresh start. However, in the brief time it's been re-staffed, only a handful of rooms have been tended to. There is still much to do."

"Yes, I hadn't been aware Ridine had been re-staffed in the absence of its ruler."

Kevan narrowed his eyes at me. "Lucky for you, my brother is so kind."

Behind him, Dimetreus smirked. "Again, we are ever grateful for his helping hand."

Kevan's jaw twitched. "Indeed. Now we should see you to your rooms." He strode away from the great hall, and the rest of us followed. "Modest arrangements have been made for staff in the servants' quarters, but most of the efforts have been spent on the rooms in the great keep. Isn't that correct, Master Arther?"

Arther nodded, increasing his pace to match Kevan's. "Yes, we have cleaned the most prominent rooms for King Dimetreus, Princess Coralaine, and Queen Mareleau. We also have appropriate accommodations for you, Lord Kevan, as well as for your brother, Lord Ulrich."

"Very well. Let's get our king and princess situated first."

Master Arther bowed his head, then took the lead.

We followed him up the steps of the great keep, toward the rooms of my childhood. The halls were bare and clean, and most of the doors we passed were closed.

"This is the third largest room we've found." Arther extended his arm to indicate the open door at our right. It didn't take long for me to recognize my old bedroom.

"This one is nice," Lurel said.

Dimetreus looked at me, frowning. I met his eyes and shook my head. This was the room I'd spent my tortured childhood in. This was the room where I'd awoken as Morkai's captive. There was no way I'd spend another night there.

Dimetreus turned to Master Arther. "Save this room for Queen Mareleau. As for me, I know what room I want to stay in. I'd like my former room, which I'd shared with my wife. I want no other room. I appreciate the efforts the staff has made in preparation for our arrival, but this is *our* home."

Arther shifted from foot to foot. "I'm sorry, Your Majesty. It's just that none of these rooms appeared to have been inhabited for many years."

"That's because they haven't been. I spent countless years sleeping in the servants' quarters. I'm eager to have my room back."

Lord Kevan made a grumbling sound, and I wondered if it was wise for my brother to admit so much.

"How about I show *you* where my chambers are?" Dimetreus said.

Master Arther folded and unfolded his hands, looking from my brother to Lord Kevan. Finally, he nodded.

Dimetreus strode down the hall, his pace demonstrating his agitation. At the end of the corridor was another open door. He paused, bringing his hand to his chin, then took deliberate steps into the room. I peered in behind him. Inside was an old four-poster bed with an elaborate headboard carved with *D L* in a trailing script. *Dimetreus and Linette's old bed.* The simple, wool bedding was new, and the only other item in the room was a desk.

Dimetreus turned toward me, eyes rimmed with red. He then looked past me at Master Arther. "This room."

"If you wish, Your Majesty, but we do have the master chamber ready. It is the only room we have appropriate bedding for a king—"

"This room will do." His voice was firm.

Arther nodded, brows knit tightly together. "Then perhaps the master chamber for Princess Coralaine?"

I swallowed the lump in my throat. The master chamber would be my parents' old room. I nodded and followed him in a daze.

"The master chamber! How exciting," Lurel whispered close to my ear. "You're going to feel like a queen."

If only queens fared well at Ridine Castle.

8

BROTHER

Mareleau

I rolled onto my side, wincing as the bed frame trembled and floorboards creaked in response to my movement. Ann mumbled in her sleep, Sera snored, and Breah's arm flew across my face. I sat up, crossing my arms over my chest as I glared at the three sleeping girls. *How can they sleep in accommodations like this? How is this appropriate for a supposedly pregnant woman?*

I wanted to scream, to stomp over to Lord Ulrich's room, pound on his door, and demand he find a private room for me. But after nearly two weeks of travel, and every night like this one, I knew it would do no good. At least we were finally nearing the end of our journey.

But what then? Would Ridine be any better?

I laid back down and found Breah had taken up more space in my absence. With a groan, I stood and grabbed my cloak, wrapping it tight around me as I crept from the room.

The hall outside was chilly and lit with a single lantern. I made my way down the stairs and into the empty dining room. Clanging pots and the giggling of scullery maids echoed from the kitchen. I went to the hearth and pulled a chair next to the dying flames. A shiver ran down my spine, and I pulled my cloak even tighter.

My eyes unfocused and I thought of Larylis. Anger and sorrow and tenderness all flashed through me in turn. *Damn you.* I'd hardly seen him before I'd left Dermaine. He'd been at his council meeting nearly all night, coming to bed long after I'd fallen asleep. *How could you?* In the morning, I'd barely gotten a kiss before we were interrupted and told to prepare for my departure. I'd held my tears as he embraced me at the gate, whispering farewell. But now—and every night since—I let them fall. *I miss you.*

I had but one thing to soothe my heart.

I reached into my cloak and withdrew a folded piece of parchment. The sight of it was enough to produce a heavy sob. I unfolded the paper and stared at the words that swam before my eyes.

> "If my lips are ever blessed with your kiss,
> I'll fall into the deepest bliss,
> And if your heart is ever my own,
> Forever will it have a home.
>
> My love for you will never be an ember,
> It will burn for you from now until forever,

For one could never extinguish the fire of
    love,
Its eternal glow shall rise above.

And you, my dear, are the one I adore,
You, my love, I could hold forever more,
You are the one I want by my side,
You, Mareleau, are the love of my life."

It was my song, the one Larylis had written for me,
the one he'd sang to me amid hay bales and stolen kisses.
He'd pressed the parchment into my hand as he'd given it
a final squeeze. Now it was all I had of him. *That, and his
heart.*

I read the words over and over until my eyes were raw
and my lungs were sore from silent sobbing. With a
heavy sigh, I refolded the paper, careful to press it neatly
along its worn creases, then tucked it back into my
pocket. I stood to return to my room but fell back into my
seat as the dining room door opened.

The old innkeeper entered, followed by a hooded
traveler. "What is your name, sir?" the innkeeper asked,
keeping his voice low.

"Tom."

I remained still as the two crossed the room and went
upstairs to the sleeping quarters. As queen, I was in no
danger of being reprimanded for my late-night wanderings. However, I was in no mood to converse with anyone,
much less a fidgety innkeeper and creepy night-traveler.

I waited until the old man made his way back through
the dining room and out the door into the outer room
before I stood from my spot. With silent feet, I tiptoed to

the bottom of the stairs, and came face-to-face with the stranger.

His eyes widened, and his mouth fell open.

I blinked into the lantern light, finding a familiar face staring back at me. My heart flipped, and tears sprang to my eyes. *Larylis!*

I nearly rushed forward to embrace him, but hesitated. The face became clearer the longer I stared. This was not Larylis. The face before me was more squared, and he was slightly too tall.

"What in Lela are you doing here, Teryn? Or should I say *Tom*?" My voice was a furious whisper. "You nearly gave me a heart attack."

Teryn hunched his shoulders as he looked behind him up the stairs. He skirted around me and pressed himself to the nearby wall. "Please don't tell anyone I'm here."

"Then you better answer my question."

He again looked up the stairway, then walked toward the hearth in the dining room. I followed. Away from the shadows of the stairwell, I could see Teryn in full. He was dressed in common garb with a heavy, hooded cloak around his shoulders. Nothing but his face could have given him away as the Prince of Mena.

He pulled his hood closer around his face, but he wouldn't meet my eyes. "I've been following you to Ridine."

"Just you? Alone?" I knew what his answer would be, but part of me held a flicker of pathetic hope.

"Just me. Larylis told me to go."

I clenched my teeth. "He told you to follow me? He couldn't have come himself?"

Teryn waved a hand in front of him. "No, not to follow *you*. I'm going to Ridine to see Cora. I'm following your retinue so I can arrive separately. I didn't expect to catch up so quickly."

"You're an idiot."

Teryn looked taken aback. "I'm sorry if I startled you. You won't tell anyone, will you?"

"Why shouldn't I? I was ordered to go on this journey against my will, and you were ordered to remain at Dermaine. Why should I, the queen, follow orders while you get to break them?"

His face softened. "Larylis didn't want it to happen like this. He doesn't know how to bring you home yet without invoking the wrath of your father. I, on the other hand, have less to lose by breaking the rules."

I pursed my lips and crossed my arms over my chest.

"He misses you already. Horribly. I haven't seen him in such a stupor since...well, since you banished him from your balcony at the spring festival." Teryn smiled.

My lips twitched at the corners, but I kept my expression hard. It wasn't easy to forget that the man before me once wanted me as his bride.

"So...do we have a deal?"

I narrowed my eyes at him.

"You kind of owe me."

"Oh, really? I'd say we're about even. I helped you with Cora twice."

He raised an eyebrow, smirking. "And I helped you marry the love of your life. I'd say you might owe me forever."

"You only had to help me because *you* tried to marry me first!"

Teryn held up his palms, and his expression grew serious. "I'm only kidding, Mareleau. I know you must resent me, seeing me as the person who stood between you and Larylis, and I regret pursuing you how I did. You're my sister now. I just want to be friends."

"Sister?"

"Yes, as wife of my brother, you've become my sister. I promise to always respect you as such and do whatever I can for you and Larylis. All I ask is the same respect in return. Please, don't tell anyone I'm here. I must see Cora again. At least until your uncles throw me out of the castle."

My shoulders fell. "Fine."

Relief filled Teryn's face. "Thank you, Mareleau."

I nodded, my jaw set. Everything in me wanted to hurt him, to betray my word and have him sent back to Dermaine. But there was something else growing within, something that began to bloom the moment I knew Larylis would be mine. I let my shoulders relax and forced a smile. "So, I have a brother now?"

He gave me a light pat on the shoulder. "Yes, you do."

9

RIDINE

Cora

"It's your first morning home, princess!" Lurel threw back the curtains of my bed, sending morning light streaming in through the tall windows. She laughed as I blinked into the brightness. "At least your bed has been curtained already. I've been awake since first light."

I'd experienced the opposite of Lurel; I'd tossed and turned all night, only able to sleep within the last few hours. It was strange being in my parents' old room with none of their belongings or furnishings. Everything from the bed to the bedding, blankets, and furniture had been made new. It was by far the most well-furnished room I'd seen at Ridine. "I'm sorry, Lurel. You could have slept in the bed with me."

Lurel put a hand to her chest. "Oh, I'd never complain, princess. The lounge was fine enough for me. I'm just grateful you didn't have me sleep in one of the dirty rooms. Now, what dress would you like to wear today? I sent your riding gown to be washed. The hem was filthy." She opened the wardrobe, displaying my three new gowns from King Verdian.

I pushed away the heavy covers and sat up, craning my neck to look into the wardrobe. My heart sank when my eyes fell on the sapphire-blue dress, reminding me of my last night with Teryn. With my simple wool riding dress being cleaned, the next most practical was a deep forest-green. "The green one."

Lurel wrinkled her nose. "Are you sure you don't want to wear the blue?"

The thought of a plunging neckline in a castle full of strangers made my stomach churn. Besides, I had a plan that didn't involve sitting pretty all day. "I'm sure."

She sighed and brought me the green dress. "What are we to do today, princess? I suppose there isn't much to do with so many rooms in disrepair. Is there a garden?"

"Not anymore." I pulled the dress over my head and turned for Lurel to tighten the laces.

"That's a shame. Perhaps we can take a stroll through the grounds?"

I bit my lip. "Lurel, I'm going to need to spend some time alone today."

She paused her work on my laces. "Oh, Your Highness?" The disappointment in her voice was clear.

"I...need time to adjust to being here. There is much about this place that you don't know. It's hard for me to be home."

Lurel resumed lacing. "I've heard many things about the sorcerer and the war. Even though I trust they are true, the stories sound too fantastic to be real. When I consider them as truth, it scares me."

"It scares me too, which is why I need time to be alone. These are my parents' rooms. They were murdered here in their own home by the sorcerer you've been told about. My brother's wife died in this castle. I was banished from here, only to return years later as a prisoner in the dungeons."

Lurel faced me, eyes drawn down at the corners. "Oh, Your Highness, I never knew any of that." She wrapped her bony arms around my waist and buried her face in my hair.

I patted her lightly on the back. "It's nothing to cry over, Lurel, but now you understand. I need some time before I will be ready to walk the grounds and lounge around doing needlework together."

She released me and nodded. "Whatever you wish, princess. I'll do anything you need me to do, even if that means staying quiet in a corner. I'm very much practiced at that."

"I'd never ask such a thing from you. Perhaps you can explore. Walk the grounds yourself. See what rooms need care for the most. Find a room you might like for yourself."

Her face brightened. "I can pick my own room?"

"Of course."

"What will I tell my father? He told me not to leave your side."

I clenched my jaw. "Of course he did."

"But if you are in mourning..."

"Yes, tell him I am in mourning and recovering from our lengthy travels. I will be in my room today."

"What about your meals?"

"I'll send for you if I get hungry, but I honestly haven't much of an appetite."

"Are you sure you don't want me to stay?"

"I'm sure. Now, run along."

Lurel sank into a curtsy, then skipped from my room out the doors.

I let out a deep breath I hadn't realized I'd been holding. My stomach sank with guilt for manipulating her. At least most of what I'd said was truth.

Once I could sense her distance, I put on my traveling cloak and stood behind my doors, closed my eyes, and extended my senses. I let my power flow through my blood, my veins, and my hands. It had been weeks since I'd last used my power to such a degree, yet it came back to me, as familiar as a lifelong friend. The fire within tingled from my head to my toes, tickling the tips of my fingers. I listened for voices, felt for movement, sensed if anyone was nearby.

All was clear.

I opened my doors and thought about the walls around me. Simple stone. Nothing to look at. I walked through the hall, one with the stone, one with the shadows. Down the stairs of the great keep I went, careful to think only of the stones beneath my feet.

At the bottom of the stairs I heard voices coming near. I breathed in deeply, bringing myself closer to the wall as I rounded the corner and slipped past the guards. *Stone. Shadow. Nothing to look at.* They ignored me.

I continued my silent travels through the castle until I found myself at a familiar door—the door that would take me to the charred field and the forests beyond. As I touched the handle, memories of wraiths, lifeless eyes, and a crumbling tower threatened to shake me from my glamour. I breathed them away and opened the door. The fresh air hit me like a welcome embrace. I looked from left to right for any sign of servant or fieldworker. Empty.

Like a rebellious child, a smile took over my face as I sprinted for the line of trees. My heart raced the nearer I came to their protective cover. Once beneath the leafy canopy, I closed my eyes, taking in the scents of soil, leaves, and animal. Birdsong flooded my ears, along with the pounding of hooves.

I'm here, Valorre.

I felt his joy as he pranced through the trees and made his way to me. Happy tears poured from my eyes as soon as I caught the first glimpse of white darting between trunks of trees. A moment later, my face was against his soft coat as he nuzzled my shoulder. I sobbed into his neck, sensing the same emotions flooding from him as well. "I missed you so much."

Missed you. Missed you. Missed you.

We stayed like that for what felt like an eternity, and I could have stayed an eternity more. The thought of returning to the castle after my first taste of freedom made my throat tighten. How could I ever go back?

Don't go back yet. Ride.

I looked up at Valorre, at his big, gentle eyes the color of ripe chestnuts, and felt giddiness ripple through us both. He lowered his head, inviting me onto his back like old times.

With a lightness of heart I didn't think I'd ever feel again, I sprang onto his back. Before I could even right myself, he took off into the trees. I laughed and squealed as we sped through the forest, no agenda, no rules. For the first time in our travels, we were running neither to nor from something. We were simply free. Tears continued to pour from my eyes, and I let them fall. I let everything go—my fear, doubt, loneliness, and anger—streaming behind me and into the wind.

THE TIME CAME WHEN I KNEW I HAD TO RETURN TO RIDINE. Valorre and I stopped where we'd met, and again I pressed my face against his neck. "I'm so sorry I have to leave you."

Don't be sorry. I stay here.

My bottom lip quivered. "Valorre, if you wanted to leave, you could. I would understand. Coming back to Ridine was my choice, and I'm not even sure it was the right one."

I sensed confusion in him.

"What I mean is, I don't know how often I'll be able to come see you. If I had my way, I'd come every day, all day, but things are different now. I'm being monitored. Some people still don't trust me. Besides, I don't want anyone to find you. Not that anyone would ever hurt you here, I just don't want to draw attention to you."

You were stuck before. I stayed. I stay now.

"That's just it. I'm not stuck this time. I'm here by my own choice." I nuzzled further into his coat. "I feel so guilty keeping you here because of a choice I made."

Valorre rippled with something close to anger. *I am not pet. I am unicorn. I am friend.*

I stepped back and looked at him, turning my head to the side.

I stay because you are friend. I don't need you. I don't need attention. I love you. I stay.

My lips melted into a smile and warmth flooded my heart. "You're right, we are together because we are friends, and you are perfectly capable of taking care of yourself. Friends don't rely on each other for survival, they lean on each other for strength."

No guilt.

"No guilt. I'll come back as soon as I can."

Valorre tossed his head up and down. *I'll be happy.*

I walked back to the castle feeling like a weight had been lifted from my shoulders. My breathing felt easy after filling my lungs with the air of the woods, and my heart was at peace.

I slipped through the door near the field and made my way back to the stairs beneath the great keep.

"There she is."

My eyes shot up at the sound of Lord Kevan's voice, realizing too late I'd forgotten to wrap myself in a glamour.

He stormed over to me. "Where have you been?"

I held my shoulders straight and looked him in the eye with an innocent expression. "I went out for some air, Lord Kevan."

"Why wasn't Lurel with you?"

"I told her I needed to be by myself. Returning to the castle has been hard on my nerves—"

"Well, she's dead now. My daughter died when she was supposed to be with you."

The breath caught in my throat as I struggled to

understand his words. "Lurel...is dead? What do you mean? How?"

Kevan heaved in front of me, his temples pulsing, eyes bulging with fury. "You tell me."

"There you are, sister." Dimetreus came toward us, releasing some of the tension between me and Kevan. "Lord Kevan, you should tend to your own personal matters. I'll deal with Princess Coralaine."

Kevan burned me with a withering glare before turning away.

"Dimetreus, what happened?" My words came out between ragged gasps.

Dimetreus pulled me close to a wall and lowered his voice. "Lurel was found near the high tower."

I furrowed my brow. "High tower..."

"Morkai's tower."

My eyes widened, and I brought my trembling hand to my mouth. "What happened to her?"

"She was found at the bottom of the stairs."

"She fell?"

He shook his head. "She appeared uninjured, as if she'd simply fallen asleep on the bottom stair, but she was cold to the touch and not breathing."

"What could have happened to her?"

"The guards searched up the stairs. The door to the tower room was ajar and a book—one of *his* books—was left open on the ground, as if it had been dropped."

"Morkai's tower has yet to be emptied, hasn't it?" The answer was obvious.

"No one has dared enter the room since Ridine has been occupied."

"No one except for Lurel."

Dimetreus nodded. "And if she touched anything of his..."

He didn't need to finish; I knew exactly what would happen. I recalled the two horns I'd taken from the hunters. I remembered the darkness they'd emanated upon touch before I'd cleared them. No one unskilled in the Arts would have been able to resist the consuming power they contained. Within my own castle, a room full of the same dark power awaited.

I slid against the wall into a heap on the floor, head in my hands. My heart felt as if it were being squeezed tight, and my mind spun, sending waves of nausea through my stomach. "Leave me, brother. Please."

Dimetreus hesitated before placing a hand on my head. "I'm here for you if you need anything."

Once he was gone, I wailed and screamed with abandon. Lurel was dead and I had no one to blame but myself. I could have taken her to visit Valorre, but instead I lied to get her out of my way. I'd told her to wander and explore. I'd told her to find a room for herself. She'd done exactly as told.

My sweet little friend, yet another killed by Morkai's darkness.

Fire flooded through me. I felt the temptation to set it free with my rage, to let it crumble the walls around me. Instead, I breathed it back in, let it fill my mind with clarity.

I wouldn't let Morkai, a dead man, destroy the people I loved. I wouldn't let him destroy *me*.

On unsteady legs, I stood and curled my fingers into fists so hard, my nails pierced my palms. *Lurel will be avenged.*

10

COUNCIL

Mareleau

I looked out the window of the traveling coach as we entered the courtyard of Ridine Castle. The smell of mold, dirt, and the stench of the stables invaded my senses, making my stomach churn. Breah, Sera, and Ann squealed their distaste.

"Ugh, this place is like a barn, not a castle," Sera said.

Ann snickered. "I bet they keep animals inside."

"Haven't you seen the princess? Of course they do." Sera burst into laughter.

We tumbled out of the coach, huddled together as we looked around us. I wrinkled my nose at the faded, crumbling stone. It was nothing like the white marble of Verlot Palace, or the modest comfort of Dermaine.

"Is there a piece of the castle...missing?" Breah pointed to a corner of the castle that appeared lopsided, bringing about a fountain of hissing laughter.

Lord Ulrich and the three councilmen from

Dermaine began to unload the horses and coach. "You may go inside, Queen Mareleau," Ulrich said. "No need to stand out here in the dirt."

"Will it be any better inside?" I muttered.

Large doors swung open and people began to file out of the castle toward us. All were strangers until I saw Lord Kevan, King Dimetreus, and Cora. The men bowed before me and then went to assist Ulrich.

Cora came forth and gave me a modest curtsy. "I'll show you inside. A room has already been prepared for you, although we are still in the process of preparing accommodations for your ladies."

I kept my head held high as we walked into the shadowed hall beyond the doors. My eyes darted from corner to corner of every ceiling and floor, wondering if a spider or rat would scurry before me. "Lovely," I said under my breath.

"I know it's not what you're used to." Cora's voice was flat. "I don't like seeing Ridine in such a state either."

As we walked up a narrow staircase and down a dim corridor, my ladies grasped my arms, whimpering at every shadow. We stopped at an open door.

"Here is your room, Your Majesty." Cora stepped aside.

I looked into the room, finding a tall window and sparse furnishings. "That's all?"

Cora put her hand on her hip, unconcerned. "New items are being brought in every day, and you are welcome to order whatever you wish to fill the room with."

I stepped through the doors. There was no study. No sleeping chamber. "Is there anything bigger?"

"You are welcome to choose any other room you like, and have it cleaned to your liking."

I narrowed my eyes at her, about to snap my retort when her face fell.

"Just don't go to the high tower."

"What's in the high tower?"

She sighed. "You probably haven't heard. Your cousin Lurel has died. She was found at the bottom of the tower steps."

The girls gasped behind me and began muttering. I felt numb. Lurel...was dead? She was the single most annoying girl I'd ever met, but to think her gone forever seemed impossible. I kept my voice level. "What happened to her?"

Cora's eyes unfocused. "The tower is a dangerous place, Your Majesty."

"I want to go home," Ann whined.

"This place is haunted," Breah whispered, pulling the sleeve of my gown.

I squeezed my eyes shut. "Quit your whimpering, you cows."

The girls were silenced.

I returned my attention to Cora. "Is there anywhere else to go? A ladies' quarters? A garden?"

She shrugged. "There is no garden, but the fields and lawn are being tended to. The great hall has been cleaned. Other than that, I'm not sure."

"Is this not your home?"

"It was, once. It has not been my home for many years. Now it is being made new. Perhaps one day it will feel like home again."

I resisted the urge to roll my eyes. She was more

dramatic than Larylis. I turned to my ladies. "Shall we find this great hall? Anything is better than being stuck in this cramped room."

Cora's jaw moved before she turned away. "Right this way, Your Majesty."

Once we were back in the main hall, the men from outside were making their way through the doors. Chests were hauled by and conversation escalated, sending a jarring echo through the bare castle.

We moved past the men toward a wide room with a single table.

"What are you doing down here?" Lord Kevan stomped toward us. His eyes were bloodshot, and his face was flushed, reminding me of my cousin's passing. "No women in the great hall. Now that Lord Ulrich and the councilmen have arrived, we need to assemble our first meeting."

"Where else is there to go? I can't stay in that tiny room all day."

Kevan shrugged, apparently forgetting my position as a queen. "The day is still early. Walk the grounds." He brushed past us into the room, followed by the men from Dermaine.

"Princess Cora, show us the grounds."

She turned to me. "Actually, I won't be able to join."

"What do you mean?"

She ignored me, looking over my shoulder and down the hall. "Dimetreus." She ran to her brother, whispering something to him. He nodded, and she fell in step alongside him.

I crossed my arms as they walked past us into the

great hall. "You can't go in there. My uncle said no women allowed."

Cora smiled. "Your uncle isn't king."

Dimetreus bowed to me before they turned and joined the table of men.

I stomped my foot. "What am I to do, then?"

Lord Ulrich came forward with two men. One was a skinny old man with graying hair and a heavy mustache.

"This is Master Arther, Your Majesty," Ulrich said. The old man bowed. "You can help him choose linens."

I felt heat rise to my cheeks. "Linens? Princess Cora gets to sit on the council while I choose linens?"

"We'd trust only a queen to do such important work." Ulrich smirked before entering the hall and closing the doors behind him.

"Linens," I said through clenched teeth. I turned to Master Arther. "Well, then. Show me the most hideous linens I can choose from."

Cora

Dimetreus and I approached the table where Lord Kevan, Lord Ulrich, and the four other councilmen sat. I looked above the table where a purple banner hung bearing Kero's black mountain sigil. It made me smile to see our sigil return to its rightful place in Ridine after Morkai had changed it to his black moon.

Dimetreus followed my gaze. "None of our old banners remain. This one has been made new, and more will come shortly."

Kevan stood and placed both hands on the table, bringing our attention to him as his eyes burned into me. "Did you not hear me? I said no women."

In one step, Dimetreus was in front of me, reflecting Kevan's stance. "And I, King of Kero, invited her to the council."

Kevan paled slightly as he returned to his seat, although his jaw remained set. "And why is that, my king?"

"As it is our first meeting, we likely have topics to discuss that involve her. Since she is Lady of Ridine, I want her here for this meeting."

Kevan grumbled, eyes flashing toward Lord Ulrich. Ulrich, however, said nothing. "Very well, Your Majesty. Let's begin."

Ulrich cleared his throat. "Perhaps we should begin with the matter about Princess Coralaine, then?"

Kevan studied me with a cold gaze. "Fine. What have we decided to do about the princess being brought back from the dead? Lord Marcus, have you begun to circulate anything?"

The man at Kevan's left spoke. "Here's what the people are being told so far. King Dimetreus knew a sorcerer wanted his throne and was secretly killing his family, although he didn't know whom it was. To protect his one living heir, he sent Princess Coralaine to live in safety, only to return once the threat had been destroyed."

"Very good," Kevan said. "What is being said to clear King Dimetreus' name?"

Lord Marcus continued. "To protect his people, as well as his own life, King Dimetreus closed down court and kept to himself while he investigated the identity of the sorcerer. When he discovered the sorcerer had been living in disguise as his Head of Council, he fled to Sele to gather allies. During this time, the sorcerer posed as king. The three kingdoms fought the sorcerer and won, and King Dimetreus was able to reclaim his throne and bring Princess Coralaine back from hiding."

"My people are accepting this as truth?" Dimetreus asked.

"Indeed," Marcus said. "Some may suspect otherwise, but most are eager for a reason to trust their king and feel at peace."

"Won't the truth get out?" I asked, speaking for the first time. "There's nothing to explain the Roizan, the wraiths, the ensorcelled men who served Morkai without consent. Everyone who fought that battle—"

Lord Kevan held up a hand, stopping me short. "Everyone who fought in the battle knows why this story is safer than the truth. The common people of Ridine will accept this lie, especially since the truth is closer to a fairytale. Your people don't want the truth. They want to feel safe."

I looked from him to Marcus. "What about the men who fought for Morkai? The men he controlled the same way he controlled my brother? What has happened to them?"

"We are taking care of that," Kevan said.

"How?"

Kevan remained silent.

I looked down the table, waiting for an answer.

Finally, my brother turned to me and spoke. "Many men surrendered after the battle. Those who did were questioned about their loyalty. Some are still being questioned. Those who prove they were working under Morkai's control, as I did, will be held under oath and sent back to their families."

"And those who can't prove it?"

Dimetreus maintained a stoic expression. "You know what needs to be done."

I swallowed hard and let my eyes fall on the table, wondering how many men were too confused to prove their innocence.

"Next related topic," Ulrich said. "What have we decided to do about the fighters who joined the battle, the ones Princess Coralaine and Prince Teryn referred to as the *Forest People?*"

My eyes shot up. "What about them?"

Ulrich raised an eyebrow at my outburst. "They are unknown to us."

"They helped us fight Morkai and his Forces, what more do you need to know?"

Kevan spoke. "While they did fight with us, they made no contact with anyone from the three kingdoms before or after the battle. We don't know who they are, where their loyalties lie, or what their motives are."

"The Forest People raised me," I said, eager to clear their name. "They were my family for six years. They fought at my side because I convinced them to."

"What did you promise them in return?" Ulrich asked.

"Nothing. They knew it was their duty to protect the land from dark magic."

"Yet, as people of Kero, it is also their duty to serve the crown," Kevan said. "Do they pay taxes to our king?"

My mouth fell open as I searched for the right words. "They are a peaceful people, practicing the Ancient ways.

They live in the woods, they take only what they need from the land, and they do no harm."

Lord Kevan leaned forward. "If they live on this land, if they take even one hair from a rabbit, then they owe something to the crown." He turned to Ulrich. "I say we send men to find them and question them."

"No!"

Kevan's face turned red. "Excuse me, Your Highness?"

I turned to my brother. "Please, Dimetreus. Let them live in peace. They mean no harm."

"Harm or no, they owe the crown," Kevan argued.

I kept my eyes locked on my brother's.

Dimetreus shrugged, turning to Kevan with a neutral expression. "Lord Kevan, a group of uncivilized forest-dwellers is the least of our worries."

I bristled at his words but knew they were just for show.

"These forest-dwellers wield weapons, Your Majesty," Kevan said through his teeth.

"And so far, they've only used those weapons to our aid. I consider their debts to the crown paid. In time we will find them, but for now, let them be."

I let out a shaking breath. An uncomfortable silence settled over the room like a fog.

Ulrich broke the tension. "Next topic."

The meeting continued with far less strain as more neutral issues were discussed. I kept quiet, biding my time and waiting for the perfect moment to bring up the one thing I was determined to discuss. The longer the meeting went, the quicker my heart raced, and not once did I find an ideal moment to speak.

"If that is the last item to discuss, we can conclude," Ulrich said.

It was now or never. I wrapped my fingers around the edge of my seat. "I have one thing to discuss before moving on."

Each man on the council froze, eyes burning into me.

Kevan ground his jaw. "Have you not spoken your share today, Your Highness?"

I kept my voice level. "I appreciate your kind welcome to this council, yet there is one important matter you have yet to discuss."

"And what would that be?"

"The high tower."

Kevan paled. "What about it?"

"It needs to be cleaned like all the other rooms in Ridine. As the most dangerous room in the castle, it needs to be taken care of before anything else."

"We have closed off the wing to the high tower and sealed the door. No one will be going in there again."

Irritation rippled through me. "You can't simply close the door on dark magic. The items in that room are powerful. Who knows what kind of damage they could do if left alone too long."

Ulrich leaned toward Kevan. "This is the room Lady Lurel was found in?"

Kevan's chest heaved as he turned to his brother. "Yes. She died while Princess Coralaine slipped out of the castle unattended."

My fingernails dug into the wood of my seat. "She died because Morkai's tower is brimming with dark magic that needs to be controlled."

Ulrich cocked his head, looking at me as if I were a

child. "I take it my brother is already doing all he can, Your Highness. What more do you expect?"

"I agree. He is doing the best he can, but it is not the best that can be done."

Kevan stood and leaned across the table toward me. "You, Your Highness, are out of line. I am doing everything that *can* be done. It is not your place to question my authority, as you know nothing about running a castle."

I felt the fire burn through me as I stood, keeping my chin high. Even standing, I had to tilt my head to look into Lord Kevan's stony eyes. "You may know everything about running a castle, but you know nothing of magic."

"And you do?"

I kept my eyes locked on his, my voice soft, my lips curled into an innocent smile. "Yes, I do."

Kevan's eyes widened, and he opened his mouth to speak.

"Let us hear her out." Dimetreus' voice was strong, making Kevan flinch. Kevan moved back into his seat, and I returned to mine.

Lord Ulrich squinted as he studied me. "Go on, then, Your Highness. What do you know?"

I folded my hands on the table and allowed my words to carry the fire still burning within. "Dark magic must be released and destroyed. Keeping it in the dark will only allow it to grow."

"How can the magic be released and destroyed?" Lord Marcus asked. "Simply touching an item from the tower may have brought death to Lady Lurel."

"It needs to be done by someone trained in the Arts."

"The Arts?" Ulrich echoed.

"Magic."

"Are you saying we bring in a sorcerer to clean up another sorcerer's mess?" Kevan threw his hands in the air. "That's preposterous! We'll find ourselves in another magic war in no time."

I looked at him with another sweet smile. "Not another sorcerer. Me."

It sounded as if every man at the table held his breath. Lord Ulrich broke the silence. "What do you mean, you?"

My throat tightened as I prepared to admit a dangerous truth. "I told you, I know about magic. The Forest People trained me in the Arts."

"I thought you said the Forest People were peaceful!" Kevan shouted.

"They are."

"You're a sorceress, then?"

"The Arts are nothing like the sorcery Morkai practiced." I settled my gaze on each councilman in turn as I chose my next words carefully. "The Arts simply allow me to detect evil and work to destroy it."

"What do you mean?" asked a man whose name I'd yet to learn. He leaned back in his seat as if he feared I might touch him with my power.

"The Arts allow me to come into contact with dark artifacts without being destroyed by them. I can then separate the darkness from the item and dissolve it completely."

"You think you can do this to the high tower?" Lord Ulrich asked.

"I can. It will take a long time to go through each item, but it's a task I'm willing to take for the safety of this castle."

Lord Kevan spat a laugh. "You think we are going to allow you to work magic here, when magic is the very thing that nearly destroyed our land?"

"Magic is the only thing that can stop the high tower from hurting anyone ever again."

Kevan mumbled something under his breath.

Ulrich looked to my brother with an uncertain expression. "We await the word of our king."

Dimetreus turned to me, smiling. "She has my permission and my trust."

Lord Kevan shook his head at the table, face nearly purple.

"Thank you, my king. I will begin my work tomorrow." I looked back at the table of councilmen, some faces curious, others suspicious. Lord Kevan's was filled with rage. However, he was the least of my worries. A greater challenge had just begun.

11

CLEANING

Cora

I stood at the bottom of the stairs leading to Morkai's tower, looking into the expanse of black that awaited me ahead. I couldn't help but wonder how Lurel had the nerve to ascend these stairs to begin with. *What was she thinking? Anyone can sense the darkness lurking ahead, can't they?*

I placed a foot on the first step and felt a shock run from my toes to my scalp. Death. *This is where she died.*

I closed my eyes. Sweat beaded on the back of my neck. *Breathe in, breathe out.*

I bent down and placed my hand on the step, feeling the cold stone beneath my palm. Fear and confusion flooded my senses. In my mind's eye, I saw Lurel coming down the stairs, eyes darting from wall to wall. She paused and looked back up the stairwell, trembling. Her chest heaved, and she ran down the remaining stairs. As her foot touched the bottom step, she put her hand to her forehead, her skin pale. Her eyelids fluttered. She took one more step, and with that she collapsed.

I opened my eyes and blinked back tears. The vision fueled my fire, increasing my determination to destroy Morkai's tower with every ounce of the Arts I held within me.

"Would you like us to accompany you up the stairs, princess?"

I turned toward the two guards behind me. Their eyes were terrified as they looked from me to the dark stairwell. "No. Remain here. I will call if I need your assistance."

The guards nodded, and one handed me a lantern. I ascended the stairs, extending my senses with every breath, anticipating any possible danger. With my free hand, I pulled my cloak close to my body.

At the top of the stairs stood a closed door. I took a deep breath and pushed it open.

The lamplight illuminated the circular room, filled with endless bookcases and mysterious objects. I walked the perimeter, watching for movement, sensing darkness. As light fell on one portion of the room after the next, I was surprised to find a lack of threat. Without Morkai's ominous, red, glowing lights, the room appeared how Ridine itself had looked upon my arrival—lame, empty, broken.

I moved to the center of the room where Morkai's table stood, piled high with books. Near one of the table legs, a book laid open. *The book that killed Lurel.* Bile rose in my throat, and I wanted nothing more than to set fire to its pages immediately. *Breathe. Not yet.*

With a seething glare, I turned my back on the book

and set the lantern on the desk. I then moved to the walls and began to tear down every tapestry, bringing dust spilling forth with the hazy sunlight that came through the narrow slits of windows that hid between book-shelves. *How long since this room has seen light?*

My eyes adjusted as sunlight began to touch the many cracks, crevices, and shadows in the room. I nodded with satisfaction. "Not so scary now, are you?"

I returned to the book, kneeling next to it with deliberate, careful motions. I held my hands over it and immediately sensed the darkness within. It expanded and surged toward my hands. I thought of Valorre, Teryn, and Lurel, everything that made my heart feel warm until I sensed the darkness retreating away. I could almost hear it screeching as I pursued it, let warmth and fire flow out of every fingertip, tearing the darkness bit by bit until it was like a wisp of smoke. Then it was nothing.

I opened my eyes, unsure how much time had passed. The book lay innocent before me. Pain tugged at my heart. *If I'd done this before, Lurel would not be dead.*

I gritted my teeth, held my chin high, and lifted the book in my hands. "What about you had Lurel so curious?" I thumbed through the pages, finding recipes for spells, potions, and poisons. Some I could decipher, while others were written in foreign languages. Words flashed by with nothing to catch my eye until I came across a chilling illustration. It was a towering, hairless creature that appeared to be made from two different animals. Next to it stood a man. Above the illustration was one word I could understand. *Roizan.*

I studied the illustration closer. Something resembling a mass of black threads were coming up from the ground and into the creature. Between the creature and the man, one thin, black thread was drawn. I understood what the illustration was conveying. *The Roizan is a channel between the magic and the sorcerer.*

I turned back a few pages to find more illustrations. A cat and a mouse in a battle of teeth, hair, blood, and claws. A cat and a mouse dead. An animal resembling both a cat and a mouse, yet at the same time, showing likeness to neither. *The Roizan is created from death.*

I shivered and slammed the book shut. It was one thing to know Morkai used necromagic; it was another to see it illustrated before me.

I stood in the doorway and called out to the guards. After a moment, one timid head bobbed into view in the stairwell. "Princess?"

"The first item is clear. Bring me two chests. One for items we can burn, another for items that must be locked away."

The guard hesitated and looked at the book in my hands. He nodded.

"When you return, this one can be burned."

BY THE TIME THE SUN BEGAN TO SET, I'D FILLED THE BURN-chest twice, and filled the lock-chest halfway. Most of what I'd found could be burned once cleared. The only things that couldn't were potions too volatile to pour out and too beyond my powers to destroy.

I looked around the room, and my shoulders sank. Despite how many chests I'd filled, I'd only managed to go through Morkai's table and half a bookcase. The work ahead of me would take weeks. *I knew this going into it*, I reminded myself.

I brushed the dust from my skirt and went to retrieve the cloak I'd left draped over the now-empty table. As I secured it around my shoulders, I felt a weight brush against my thigh. My eyes widened as I reached into my cloak pocket and pulled out Morkai's purple crystal.

In my eagerness to begin my work, I'd forgotten the reason I'd brought my cloak with me in the first place. I set the crystal on the table and considered whether to leave it for my next day's work. *No. It needs to be destroyed.*

With the crystal between my hands, I sank to my knees and closed my eyes. *Breathe in. Breathe out.*

Just like the first time I'd held it on the battlefield, I expected darkness to expand from it. But as before, nothing came—nothing like the other dark items, that is. There certainly was something there, but I couldn't comprehend what it was. A weight. A sorrow. Pain. Light. If darkness hid within, it was hiding well.

I sat motionless until I could bear it no longer. With a grumble of frustration, I held the crystal into the fading light of the setting sun. "What are you?"

I studied its many facets, its shimmering color that appeared more fluid and less solid the longer I looked. Sudden movement caught my eye. A trick of the light? I brought the crystal closer to my eye and held still as stone. I could have sworn I'd seen something moving within. The purple grew brighter and brighter, yet I couldn't look away.

Then all I saw was white.

Blinding white light surrounded me. There was neither sky, nor wall, nor ground. I pressed my hand beneath me, feeling something solid, yet nothing like the stone floor of the tower room. It was smooth and glassy yet took no shape beneath my hands. I stood and looked around.

"Hello? Guards?" My voice echoed in a way I'd never heard before. I pulled my cloak tighter and took a step. But where? There was no sense of direction, only light.

My heart began to race. "Guards?"

"What are you doing here?" I spun around as I felt something grasp my elbow. At first, all I saw was a shimmer of purple through the white light, but then a face came into view. I blinked at the contrast of the unusual light with the beautiful, female face before me. She looked a few years older than I, with rich, brown skin, dark-brown eyes surrounded by heavy lashes, and hair as black as a raven's wing, worn in a mass of curls cropped above her shoulders.

"Who are you?" I asked.

"You need to get out of here." Her voice held an unfamiliar accent.

"How?" I backed away from her, but she closed the distance, keeping her hand firmly on my elbow. I noted that her touch felt strange, as if my skin had lost some of its feeling.

"Keep your voice down."

"Where am I?"

The woman looked from side to side, eyes wide. She brought her face close to mine. "How did you get in here?"

"I don't know. I was just holding a crystal and then—"

The woman put her hand over my mouth just as I heard a muffled sound, like shuffling footsteps behind a door.

I pushed the woman aside. "Guards! I'm in here!"

"I said to keep your voice down!"

The shuffling stopped.

"Run." The woman took my hand and we ran to nowhere I could see. All around me was blinding light.

"What are we running from?"

"Do you have any idea what he'll do to you if he finds you? What he's been dying to do to you all along?"

"Who are you talking about? What's going on?"

The woman continued to pull me forward. I followed her, wondering how she could see anything. She looked over her shoulder and then pulled me to sitting. "Where are you?"

I looked around me. "I don't know."

"Not here. Your body. Where were you last?"

"In the tower room."

"Picture it. See it around you."

I tried to do as told, but my mind wouldn't steady.

"Calm. Picture the room."

Her words reminded me of Salinda, and I felt my muscles relax. I closed my eyes and imagined the room exactly as it had been. I was on the floor near the table. The crystal was in my hand.

"Good. Keep going."

I opened my eyes and jumped. The white light was fading, mixed with a hazy view of the tower room.

"Don't open your eyes in here. Open your eyes *there*."

My hands trembled. "I don't know what you mean."

"Just focus on the room."

I did as told, breathing away my confusion and trying to ignore the sound of muffled steps drawing near. I saw the room. I felt the floor beneath my knees and shins. I smelled the stone.

"Now open your eyes."

I tried to, but my eyes were unwilling. "I can't"

"You must."

The footsteps came closer.

"Open your eyes."

My eyelids fluttered but felt stuck shut. *Where am I? Where am I?*

"The tower, Coralaine. Think about the tower."

I was frozen with an inner chill deep in my gut. I opened my eyes into the white light with the woman still sitting across from me. "How do you know my name?"

The woman's shoulders fell. She opened her mouth to speak, but her eyes darted to her left. "It's too late."

Darkness crept forth, spilling into the light as if coming from behind an opening door. A bony, white hand reached forward.

I stifled my scream and squeezed my eyes shut.

A warm hand fell on my shoulder. "Cora."

I opened my eyes and blinked into the dim light of the tower room. My breathing came out in ragged gasps. The crystal fell from my hand, rolled down my knees, and onto the floor, stopping beneath the table. My body convulsed as I stared at it.

"Cora." The hand still held my shoulder.

I turned and looked into the eyes of my rescuer. "Teryn."

12

REUNION

Teryn

I pulled Cora into my arms. She sobbed into my chest while I stared wide-eyed at my surroundings. I didn't need to ask whose room I was in; it was clear it had belonged to Morkai. The question was, why was she there? And what had happened to her?

Once Cora calmed, she pulled away from me and looked into my eyes. Her brow furrowed. "What are you doing here?" Suspicion hung in her tone, and I felt her grasp loosen around my waist.

"I came here to surprise you."

She took a step away from me, eyes darting from me to the walls, to the floor, and then back again. "You did not arrive with Mareleau and the councilmen. You are supposed to be at Dermaine."

The fear in her face sent a chill down my spine. I was careful to keep my voice calm and my expression gentle.

"Larylis allowed me leave to come see you. I followed Ulrich and Mareleau, maintaining a day's distance."

"That doesn't make sense. Verdian ordered you to stay at Dermaine."

"Cora what's wrong?"

"I can't tell if you're really here...if I'm really here."

"Where else would you be?"

She looked toward the table where a large crystal laid.

I took a cautious step toward her. "Cora, I'm here. You can even ask Mareleau. She caught me following them but promised not to tell."

She crossed her arms in front of her, clasping each elbow. "If no one knows you're here, how did you find me?"

"They know I'm here now. Lord Kevan's head nearly exploded, but he can't send me away. I'm sure he'll write to his brother."

Cora's shoulders relaxed.

"Your brother told me where I'd find you. Two guards were at the bottom of the stairs but didn't seem too keen to accompany me."

She let out a heavy sigh and closed her eyes, dropping her arms to her sides. Tears streamed down her cheeks. "I'm sorry, Teryn. I was so confused."

I brought her back into my arms. "What happened to you? You were sitting still as stone when I found you, and you didn't respond until I touched you."

"It was the crystal."

We both turned toward the table. "What is it?"

"It's from Morkai's staff. I never told you, but I found it on the battlefield at Centerpointe Rock. It was the only thing of his that didn't turn to ash. I took it so I could destroy it, but I hadn't had a moment to try until now."

"It couldn't be destroyed?"

She shook her head. "I don't understand it. It's not like Morkai's other things, where the darkness is obvious. Within the crystal, there is something very dark, but the crystal itself is neutral. And there's...a woman in there."

It took me a moment to know I'd heard her right. "A woman? Inside the crystal?"

"I don't even know if she's real. She tried to help me get out from where I was trapped."

"You were trapped?"

"It may have been my imagination, some trick of the mind, but it felt so real. She knew me by name, which frightened me. I've never seen her before, not in life or dream."

"Perhaps it was a mind trick."

"Either way, it needs to be destroyed, and I don't know how to do it."

"Is that why you're up here? Are you trying to destroy Morkai's things?"

She nodded. "Someone has to do it. Someone trained in the Arts."

"Your brother is allowing you to do this alone? Why aren't the guards in here helping you?"

"No one else dares come near this room. Especially since..." Her eyes went unfocused.

"What?"

"My chambermaid, Lurel, is dead. She came up here, touched one of Morkai's spell books, and died moments later.

"All the more reason why you shouldn't be alone in

here. What would have happened to you if I hadn't found you just now?"

She shivered. "I don't know."

"You're determined to do this, aren't you? Stubborn as the day I met you." As worried as I was, I couldn't help but smile. "You'll take on an entire room of evil objects by yourself if you have to."

She nodded.

"Then let me help you."

"Teryn, what could you possibly do? I told you, only one skilled in the Arts—"

"I don't care what I have to do, but I can't let you do this alone. Let me stay while you work. Let me break down book shelves and transport the magic-less items away."

Cora frowned and put her hand on her hip. "You won't take no for an answer, will you? Reckless as the day I met you."

I laughed and brushed my hand along her cheek. "See, we're already getting to know each other so well."

She smiled. "Fine. Just don't touch anything until I tell you it's safe."

"I'll behave, I promise."

Cora turned from me and went to the table, crouching beneath it. She wrinkled her nose as she stood with the crystal in her hand, then placed it in the middle of the table. "I'll save you for later."

As she returned to my side, I realized how pale she looked. "Have you eaten anything today?"

She pursed her lips. "I...was brought a plate of something."

"How long ago? You're still shaking."

She nodded. "You're right. I could use a meal."

I offered my elbow, which she accepted. "I'd take you to dinner, but I have no idea where I am."

She let out a weak laugh. "I'll take you to the kitchen."

Cora

We neared the kitchen, sounds of lighthearted gossip growing louder. As we entered, the talking halted. Two women—one large and middle-aged, another thin and in her teens—froze and stared at us. After a moment of shocked hesitation, the two women sank into clumsy curtsies.

"My princess," said the older woman, "I'm so sorry. We weren't expecting you. Is something wrong?"

I smiled to put her at ease. "Not at all, and I'm sorry to intrude. Can I have your name?"

"Sadie, Your Highness."

"Sadie, has dinner been served yet?"

Her face fell. "Yes, Your Highness. Were you not fed?"

"It's not a problem, I assure you. I was kept busy until late. Is there anything left for Prince Teryn and I to eat?"

"Of course, princess. I'll bring a full feast just for you in the great hall."

I looked to the crooked wooden table in the center of the kitchen. "Do you mind if we eat here instead? I'd feel more comfortable. Besides, we don't need a full meal."

"You are the Lady of Ridine, princess. You may eat where you insist, but this kitchen is no place for a royal."

"It will be fine. Please, don't go to too much trouble. We simply want a small meal in private."

Sadie nodded. "All right, then, Your Highness. Beca, you heard our princess, get moving."

The two women got to work warming our meal, and Teryn and I sat at the table on opposite sides. The room was lit by the flickering light from the stove and hearth and was filled with aromas of pungent herb and smoke. If I closed my eyes, I could almost imagine I was at the cook fires with the Forest People.

Teryn reached across the table to grasp my hand. "I'm sorry about your maid. Aside from that, has being home treated you well?"

I shrugged. "As well as it can, I suppose. How about you, how were your travels?"

"Much easier than trekking through the forests of Ridine. I never had to sleep in the dirt once."

"And you said Mareleau found out you were following them?"

He nodded. "I caught up with them too quickly one night. She saw me checking into the inn."

I tried to ignore the irritation tickling my heart as I raised my eyebrow. "I'm surprised she didn't turn you in then and there."

"She isn't so bad."

"I wish I held the same opinion," I muttered under my breath.

"I'm sure the two of you will get to know each other. When we're married, you'll practically be sisters."

I blushed, but the heat was quickly cooled at the thought of being related to Mareleau. It was impossible to imagine her in such a position. Linette had been my sister. Maiya had been my sister. Mareleau would never be.

Sadie and Beca set plates of food before us. As soon as the aromas reached my nose, my stomach began to growl, and I realized how hungry I was.

Teryn tore off a piece of dark bread. "I'll be making sure you eat from now on."

I smiled with my mouth full. "Deal."

"When do we resume our work in the tower?"

"Tomorrow morning."

"After breakfast, right?"

I rolled my eyes. "Yes, after breakfast."

We finished our meal and lingered long after, enjoying our quiet conversation until the sound of footsteps interrupted our peace.

"There you are, Princess Coralaine, Prince Teryn." Master Arther entered the kitchen with one of Mareleau's ladies. "Prince Teryn, we have arranged a room for you to stay in. Princess Coralaine, until more appointments can be made, Lady Sera will act as your chambermaid."

Sera had a round face, an upturned nose, and straight, black hair that brushed her shoulders. Her lips were drawn into a pout as she assessed me from head to toe. "I'll fetch your bath and prepare your bed, princess." Her high-pitched voice lacked enthusiasm.

While I wanted nothing to do with one of Mareleau's ladies, especially while Lurel's loss was still fresh in my heart, I had to admit a bath sounded pleasant. "Very well, Lady Sera. Thank you."

Sera curtsied and left the kitchen, while Arther remained. "Prince Teryn, if your meal is over, your chamber awaits."

Our privacy was at an end, and with our plates empty, we had no excuse to stay. As we stood, it took everything within me not to pull Teryn close and kiss him goodnight.

Teryn's smile was warm and full of regret as he bowed to me. "Goodnight, princess."

I returned the formality. "Goodnight, Your Highness."

We went our separate ways, he to his room, and I to my room where a warm bath and a scowling maid awaited.

Knowing Teryn was close and would be closer yet the next day was enough to send me to sleep with a smile. However, no smile of mine was wide enough to ward off dreams of a dark crystal, a blinding light, and a wisp of trailing, black smoke calling my name with a sinister hiss.

13

OLD WOUNDS

Mareleau

I paced at my window, hands clenched into fists within the folds of my gown. "For the love of Lela, I am so bored."

Breah and Ann murmured their agreement. Breah wrinkled her nose at her needlework while Ann stared blankly ahead, wrapping strands of her curly, red hair around her finger.

"Why am I even here? Why are we sitting around, doing hideous needlework and choosing linens while Princess Cora does sorcery in some creepy tower? How is she allowed to do such a thing?"

My door opened, and my heart leapt. It was absurd that every distraction had become a welcome one. I frowned as Sera sulked into the room.

"My queen, will you please allow me to stay with you awhile?"

While Sera's whining voice was an assault on my ears, I couldn't subject her to the misery of being Cora's servant if I could help it. "You may."

Sera sank onto my newly acquired lounge next to Breah. "Day after day it's the same. All I ever do is wait at the bottom of the stairs—of the creepiest stairwell known to man, no less. I can't stand it! Then I have to watch as chests of vile things are hauled by. I shouldn't have to witness such evil!"

"It's awful, Sera," Breah cooed. "I can't believe you were forced to serve her."

I suppressed a laugh. It was Sera I'd chosen to part with when I was asked to make temporary leave of one of my ladies. She was a sacrifice I'd been willing to make. "Well, now that you're here, make yourself useful. Find chocolate. There must be someone who can import chocolate."

Sera crossed her arms. "I've already asked."

"Then ask again. We had chocolate at Verlot, and I'll be damned if I can't get it here too."

Breah raised an eyebrow. "Chocolate? Has Her Majesty conceived?"

My mouth fell open as I considered how to answer. I lifted my chin and turned back toward the window. "Isn't that what every queen wishes?"

The girls fell into a fit of giggles.

I closed my eyes and reminded myself of my plan. My moon blood would come any day now. When it did, no one would think anything of it, save for the few who knew of my supposed pregnancy. To them, I would break the news of my heartbreaking miscarriage in secret. *Then my lie will be over at last.*

"Is it strange having Prince Teryn here?" Breah asked.

I rounded on her. "Why in Lela would it be strange?"

"Well, because of your broken engagement."

"What do you know of my *broken engagement*? Our engagement was nothing. My father simply felt guilty Teryn had risked his life for my Quest and wanted to make it up to him."

Ann and Breah exchanged a glance. Sera looked down at her feet.

I narrowed my eyes at them. "Speak."

Ann twisted her hands in her lap. "It's just that...you never speak to us about such matters, so all we know is what we hear elsewhere."

Sera's face brightened. "You wouldn't believe the stories going around! They're fantastic."

Breah nodded. "They are beautifully tragic, Your Majesty, and so romantic."

"What stories are going around? And who do you hear them from? There's no one to talk to here."

Ann shrugged. "Word travels. Everyone seems to have something to say, even the common folk and the merchants."

"Then get on with it, what is being said about me and this tragically romantic broken engagement of mine?"

Ann clasped her hands to her chest, her auburn eyelashes fluttering over her freckled cheeks. "My favorite story tells how you gave your heart to Prince Teryn. However, your parents didn't approve and forced him to compete for your hand in the Quest. So you sent your three suitors on a lighthearted journey, knowing Teryn would come out as champion. But tragedy struck, and the prince was captured and tortured. He returned home,

feeling betrayed, thinking you had sent him and Prince
Helios into a trap so you could be with Prince Lexington.
Even after Prince Lexington forfeited the Quest, Prince
Teryn still didn't believe your heart had been true to him.
Your parents even thought you had turned the Quest into
a scheme. As punishment, they forced you to marry
Prince Larylis, brother to your true love. Even though
you'd never love Larylis, his love for you was strong. In a
fight for your honor, he battled Teryn, wounding him in
the ribs and stealing his right to the throne."

I burst into tears from laughing so hard. "That's the
most ridiculous thing I've ever heard!"

Breah nodded, a sheepish grin on her face. "Even I
can tell some of that isn't true. But don't you admit it is a
beautiful tale?"

"Beautiful? No!" I stomped my foot, feeling heat rise to
my cheeks. "These idiots are spreading rumors that are
completely untrue. I have never had even a thread of love
in my heart for Teryn. I've always loved Larylis. He's my
true love and always will be. And Teryn wasn't wounded
by Larylis, he was wounded at the Battle at Centerpointe
Rock and has healed without issue. There was no fight
for my honor. There was no punishment. I have won." My
last statement wasn't entirely true. I had won, but not
without consequence.

My ladies' eyes were wide as they tried to suppress
their smiles.

"Now what is it?"

Ann beamed. "We've never heard you talk like that,
Your Majesty. You've never spoken of love."

"You've hardly said a word about how you felt about

your marriage," Breah said. "It's good to know you truly are happy."

I lifted my chin. "Of course I am."

"I bet you miss your husband." Sera's eyes were filled with sympathy. It made my chest ache, followed by a fury that made my shoulders clench tight.

I put my hands on my hips. "Sera, did I not command you to find me chocolate, or are you deaf?"

The pity slid from her face as she curtsied. "Yes, Your Majesty."

I turned back toward the window and blinked tears from my eyes, begging them not to fall.

~

Cora

"That's everything for today, I think." I handed Teryn the last book from a shelf and stood back to admire our work. After three days, we'd cleared out half the tower room, including three full bookcases. Teryn's help had proved to be more useful than I'd imagined, and his presence wasn't nearly as distracting as I'd predicted. I thought I'd be nervous about using the Arts in front of him, but it never became an issue. If anything, his presence calmed me and allowed my powers to flow with greater ease. I was beginning to wonder how I would have fared without him.

Teryn stood behind me and wrapped his arms around my waist. "What should we do with the empty bookcases?"

I squinted at the three cases, large, dark, and looming in the room. While they were powerless, they carried the burden of having belonged to Morkai. "Burn them."

Teryn kissed me on the side of the head, then stepped around me to one of the bookcases. He put his hand on the side of it, testing its weight. "They're heavy. We'll need help from the guards."

"Oh, they'll love that," I said with a smirk. It was hard enough to get the guards through the door.

Teryn took one more look at the bookcase, then paused. He ran his hand along the wall next to it. "What's this?"

A feeling of apprehension weighed down my gut as I joined him at the wall and saw what he was referring to —a paper-thin crack running through the wall, almost as high as the bookcase. He pushed against the stone. It moved.

I jumped as an unseen door swung inward. Teryn and I exchanged a glance before he pushed the door open further. He placed a protective arm in front of me as a vast blackness was revealed to us. "Is this another room?"

"I've seen this door before." I swallowed the bile that rose in my throat. How could I have forgotten the unseen door I'd watched Morkai walk through mere months ago? "But I don't know what's beyond it."

Teryn took a step forward.

I grabbed his sleeve, making him pause. "Let me go first. I can sense if there's danger."

After a moment of hesitation, he reluctantly nodded.

I went to the table and retrieved one of our lanterns. The sun had yet to fully set, but whatever was beyond the door seemed untouched by the light of the room. With a trembling hand, I pushed the door open further. It was impossible to ignore the dark power lurking within. I took a step forward, finding the same solid floor beneath my feet.

The lantern illuminated a narrow room. In one corner was a cot covered in luxurious blankets and linens. Next to it sat a low table covered in parchment, ink, quills, and books. At the other side of the room was a bookcase full of potions, a table with a large, metal bowl, and more books stacked high against the walls. *This is where he slept. This is where he cast his darkest spells.*

I felt the blood leave my face. Even though this room was a fraction of the size of the main tower, it was teeming with Morkai's power, condensed in every scrap of parchment, every page of every book, every thread of every blanket. "This is going to take even longer to clear."

Teryn put his hand on my shoulder. "We should leave it for tonight. Return to it tomorrow."

I knew he was right. What progress could I possibly make before nightfall? My muscles tensed as I sensed the darkness swirling around me. It felt as if it were taunting me: *you'll never be rid of Morkai.*

I shook my head. "I'm sorry, Teryn. I need to do something. I at least need to clear the air. Its darkness is suffocating. I can't risk it moving into the rest of the castle."

He nodded, but the worry in his eyes was plain. "You should take a rest first. It's been hours since you've eaten anything."

I put my hand on his arm and smiled. "I'm fine. How about you take a break, go to the kitchen, and have something made for us. By the time you return, I'll be done for the night."

"I'm not leaving you."

"I'll be fine. I need to shift the air out of this room to clear it, and it will be a lot easier to do it if I'm not worried about it touching you. Make the guards stand outside the tower door."

I could sense his dilemma of whether he should argue or give in.

"This won't take long, I promise."

"Fine. Just don't do anything dangerous."

Everything I'm doing is dangerous, but I didn't say so out loud.

When he was gone, I opened the few windows I could reach and brought every lantern and candle I had at my disposal into the secret room. I could feel the darkness retreat from the light, screeching and scurrying into corners and shadows. I closed my eyes, held out my hands, and let the fire fill me. It spilled from my finger-tips, reaching toward the darkness, surrounding it, embracing it, drowning it, bit by bit until it had nowhere to hide. In my mind's eye, I saw it roaring, surging toward me with a vengeance. I kept my breathing steady and continued to let my power flow. I chased it from the secret room, herding it into the main tower, and surrounded it with my power. It revolted over and over, but still I pursued it until it was nothing more than ordinary air.

By the time I was through, sweat beaded at my fore-head and behind my neck. My limbs trembled as I walked to the tiny room. *There's still so much more to do.* The darkness may have left the air, but each item in the room still held Morkai's pulse.

I scowled from one side of the room to the other, assessing what I should destroy first in the morning.

The bed and blankets held memories of Morkai's flesh, so that was high on my list; the scraps of parchment held his vile spells, which I was eager to watch burn; the books that lined the walls held dark power but felt like the least of my worries. Then my eyes fell on the bookcase filled with potions. I walked toward it, scanning the vials. Some were covered in layers of dust while others seemed almost new. Most bottles were a dark-brown color, but a few others nearly glowed with vibrant hues.

I gritted my teeth, knowing it would be impossible to destroy all the potions. My only knowledge of potions involved herbs and tinctures, one of the simplest forms of the Arts. I was certain the vials before me held little in common with those.

I scanned the labels of the bottles, trying to decipher the inky script beneath smudges and dust. Most were unreadable, and those that were legible held words I didn't understand.

Until I came to one: *Coralaine.*

My breath caught as I stared at the letters clearly forming my name. With a racing heart, I reached forward, fingers trembling as they touched the dusty, brown, glass bottle. I took it from the shelf, clasped it in both hands, and closed my eyes. At once, I felt a surge of pain deep below my lower abdomen, followed by a hollow sensation. I opened my eyes and shoved the bottle back on the shelf.

So, he'd been telling the truth when he'd said he'd poisoned my womb. My head began to spin.

"Cora." Teryn's voice was a welcome interruption.

"You can come in." My voice sounded dry. I left the

secret room and met him in the outer room, wrapping my arms around his waist.

"Did you finish what you'd wanted to do?"

I nodded, swallowing the tightness in my throat.

"Good. Our dinner awaits."

I smiled up at him, but it didn't reach my eyes.

He put his hand on my cheek, and his eyes grew wide. "You look exhausted."

"I am, but I'm fine. Clearing the air was harder work than I'd thought."

Creases formed between his brow. "Why don't we take tomorrow off? We can spend the day just you and me. You can show me around Ridine. You know, the rooms *other* than the dungeon, the kitchen, and the tower."

I forced a laugh, which faded as my eyes fell on the bookcases, still full of items that needed to be cleared. "I don't know. There's still so much to do."

"It will be here the next day. One day away from this place can only help you keep your strength. I don't know exactly how the Arts work, but I've seen you exhausted from them before."

A memory of me sliding from Hara and into Teryn's arms after I'd drained my powers came to mind. I looked around the tower again, pausing when my eyes fell on the secret room. I shuddered.

Teryn placed his finger under my chin, bringing me to meet his eyes. "Did something happen while I was gone?"

My mouth fell open, but I was unable to speak. There were no words for the ache I felt in my heart. I would have to tell him. As my future husband, he needed to know I'd never provide him an heir.

Not yet.

I stretched my lips into a more convincing smile. "It's nothing. You're right, we should take a break tomorrow." My stomach churned as I swallowed my lie and left the tower room behind me.

14

BROKEN

Cora

I paced beside the doors in my room, waiting for the sound of footsteps or a knock. *I have to tell him today. I can't tell him. I must.* I brought a fingernail to my teeth and nibbled it.

"Surely, you don't need to fret, princess. The prince should be here any moment." Sera eyed me from the lounge.

I jumped, having forgotten her presence; she wasn't talkative like Lurel had been. I stopped pacing and put my arms at my sides. "Quite right, Sera. It's just a case of lovers' jitters." As soon as her eyes left me, I began to nibble my nail again. Not a moment later, a knock sounded on my door. I smoothed my dress, took a deep breath, and forced a grin. As I opened the door to Teryn's smiling face, my own expression became a genuine reflection of his.

He offered me a formal bow. "Princess Coralaine."

I laughed, feeling my prior tension slip away as I curtsied. "Prince Teryn."

He held out his arm, and I slipped my hand into the crook of his elbow. We walked away from my room and down the hall. "Where are we going?"

"Good question," he said, "but you'll have to tell me. We have the entire day together to do whatever we wish. What is it you'd like to do?"

Forget, just for a while, was my true wish, but I couldn't say that to him. I wanted to enjoy my time alone with him before shattering it with what I had to say. "Perhaps we should get out of the castle."

"Yes, why don't you show me the grounds?"

His words gave me an idea that brightened my heart. "I have just the thing." I took his hand and pulled him through the castle, down the stairs, and out the door near the charred field. We were met with the bright light of the morning sun.

"These aren't the grounds I had in mind."

I rolled my eyes with a smile and pulled him past the field toward the line of trees. I closed my eyes and sought the warmth that was never far from my heart.

Excitement answered, followed by the sound of prancing hooves pounding the forest floor in my mind. Valorre was near.

We entered the cover of trees and waited until the hoof-beats were audible to both of us. Teryn's eyes shot to mine, and his lips stretched into a grin. A moment later, Valorre stopped before us, throwing his mane up and down and side to side.

I went to him and caressed his muzzle. Teryn followed behind. "He's happy to see you."

Teryn reached out a hand to pat his back. "It's good to see you again, too."

Surrounded by the two beings that made me smile the most, I felt completely at ease, unburdened by what was yet to come. I put my hand in Teryn's. "Come. Now I can show you what makes Ridine beautiful."

We walked through the forest, listening to birdsong, feeling the crunch of twigs, leaves, and dirt beneath our feet, and the gentle breeze blowing through the trees. After some time, we came to a clearing and stopped. We were at the edge of a gently sloping cliff overlooking a valley filled with red and yellow wildflowers. At the other side of the valley rose the Ridine Mountains, towering in all shades of green and speckled with sunlight. The sky was a clear blue filled with streaks of feathery clouds.

Teryn squeezed my hand. "It's beautiful."

"This is the Ridine I remember from my childhood. Before everything happened."

"I can see why you wanted to return."

"I didn't think I'd *ever* want to return. Not until after the battle. After that, I knew it was what I had to do."

"But it's been much harder than you thought it would be."

I sighed. "I expected it to be difficult, but actually experiencing it is a whole other challenge. When you and I got engaged, I was able to forget what I was getting into. But now..."

He turned to me, squinting beneath the light of the sun. "I know it's hard now, and Ridine will never feel like your childhood home, but in a matter of time, Ridine will be new."

My heart grew heavy, and I could barely move my head to nod.

Teryn took a tentative step toward me and held both my hands in his. "Best of all, it's a new start together. I don't know how long I'll be allowed to stay before Verdian finds out, but I'm here with you until then. Even after that, we are making something new together. In one year, no one will be able to force us apart, as we'll be married."

My hands began to tremble. *I have to tell him.*

Teryn looked toward the wildflower meadow and the mountains beyond. "Just think, this will be *our* kingdom to rule together. *Our* mountains. *Our* forest." His eyes returned to me, and he put my face in his hands. "We'll grow old together here. Our children will grow up here."

My mouth went dry, and my heart hammered in my chest. My smile slid from my lips.

Teryn squeezed his eyes shut and pressed his lips into a tight line. "I'm sorry. That was too much, wasn't it?"

I shook my head but couldn't find the words to respond. I pulled away, crossed my arms over my chest, and faced the valley. "Is it important that we have children?"

"Yes, but it's not something we need to talk about now. I didn't even mean to bring it up. I got carried away." He put his hand on my shoulder. "I'm sorry, Cora. I never want to make you feel rushed. Our relationship is still new, and we have a year before we even marry."

"It's not that..."

"What is it?"

"Is having children important to you *ever*?"

He hesitated. "Well...of course it is. We will need an heir for our rule to remain safe."

"And if we don't have an heir? What then?"

He gently pulled me to face him. "That's not something we need to worry about yet."

My eyes met his. "Yes, it is. If I can't provide you children, I can't be your wife, right?"

He opened his mouth, but no sound came out.

That was all the answer I needed. Tears sprang to my eyes. Valorre tossed his mane, sensing my agitation.

Teryn looked from Valorre to me. "Why are you so worried about this?"

"Because I don't want all of this to be for nothing."

He put his hand on my cheek and gently wiped a falling tear with his thumb. "This could *never* be all for nothing. Cora, I love you."

My lips quivered between a smile and a frown as I let his words wash over me. *He loves me. He said it. Do I dare shatter this moment?* I closed my eyes. There was only one honest thing I had the nerve to say. "I love you too."

He brought his lips to mine and we kissed until we were out of breath. When we parted, his entire face was stretched into a smile. I, on the other hand, felt mine slip away. Outside our love, outside our kiss, I was again faced with a daunting reality. A reality where I could never be his queen.

I turned away before he could see my frown. "We should return."

We walked back through the woods in silence. The beauty around me seemed dulled by my swarming thoughts. *I still have to tell him.*

When we reached the tree line near the field, we said

our farewells to Valorre and headed back to the castle. Each step away from Valorre and the woods felt like a step into increasing darkness.

"What would you like to do now?" There was hesitation in Teryn's voice, no matter how he tried to mask it. I didn't need to use my power to know he could sense the tension in me.

"I'm going to return to my room for a while. Being cooped up in Ridine has made me unused to long walks."

Disappointment blanketed his face. "Can we have dinner together tonight?"

"Of course." My throat constricted as I turned away and entered Ridine, but I didn't let my tears fall. My pain was replaced by fury as my mind flooded with all the things Morkai had taken from me. *My parents. Linette. My own brother, for a time. Lurel. And now Teryn.* My limbs shook with rage as I ascended the stairs.

How could I be so stupid? How could I have thought I'd find happiness with the one I love? How could I think Morkai's influence would be that easy to end?

Once outside the tower room, I pushed open the door, feeling my anger nearly blow it off its hinges. I stormed toward the secret room and set to the one task that could channel my pain. Vengeance.

Teryn

"What do you mean she isn't here?"

Sera crossed her arms and cocked her head to the side. "Does it look like she's here, Your Highness?"

I looked past her into the room. There was no sign of Cora. "Was she here earlier?"

"Last I saw her, she left with you."

My eyes went wide. It had taken all the restraint I had not to seek her out before nightfall. I'd wanted her to get all the rest she needed before our dinner. "Do you have any idea where she might be?"

"If I were to guess—"

"The tower." My heart sank. *Why did she say she needed to rest if she was going to work instead? And why did she go without me?*

I sprinted down the hall and to the stairs beneath the high tower. As I climbed, a faint glow appeared ahead. I quickened my pace, taking two steps at a time, until I bounded into the tower room. A lantern sat on the table, illuminating the room. A secondary illumination shone to my right.

I ran to the hidden room and found Cora sitting cross-legged on the floor, unmoving, with a book in her lap. A chest filled with books and blankets sat on one side of her, and at the other was a chest full of vials.

"Cora."

She started, and her eyes shot toward mine, wide and terrified. Her expression calmed when she saw me. "Teryn, you scared the life out of me. I was in the middle of clearing something."

I was taken aback by the irritation in her voice. "Why are you even here? I thought we agreed to take a day off?"

She wouldn't meet my eyes as she got to her feet and brushed the dust off her skirt. "I know. I'm sorry I didn't keep our agreement. There's just too much for me to do to take a day off. I can hardly relax until this room is empty."

"There's plenty of time for that tomorrow."

"But look how much I've done today." She extended her arms toward the overflowing chests, a maniacal look of pride in her eyes.

"If you'd told me you wanted to work, I would have joined you."

"I wanted *you* to have a day off. You clearly wanted it."

I let out a frustrated sigh. "I only wanted it so we could spend it together. Besides, you shouldn't be up here alone. You don't even have guards stationed!"

She crossed her arms. "I'm fine. I know what I'm doing."

I wanted to argue, but I knew it would be of no use. Besides, I didn't find her to start a fight. My face softened with a smile. "You're right. You've done a lot. Really, I'm impressed."

Her shoulders relaxed, and her arms went to her sides.

I took a step toward her. "It's nightfall now. Let's have dinner."

Cora's face fell, and her eyes glistened with tears, making me wonder how I'd become so adept at making her cry lately. "I can't."

"Why?"

"I just..." Her eyes went unfocused. She brought a fingernail between her teeth.

"What is it?" I reached my hand to her cheek, but before it could land, she took a step away from me.

"I have a lot to do tonight," she said. "I never should

have taken the day off, because now I need to make up for it."

"That doesn't make sense."

"You wouldn't understand."

"At least let me help you."

Her lips trembled as her eyes met mine. "Not tonight. I want to be alone. Please, just leave me alone for a while."

I felt as if my heart had been pierced with an arrow. My lungs felt too small as I struggled to take shaking breaths. I opened my mouth to convince her otherwise but couldn't find the words. Instead, I nodded and took a step out of the room.

Cora's expression was full of remorse as tears streamed down her cheeks, but she didn't change her mind. "Goodnight, Teryn."

"Goodnight, Cora." I watched her disappear behind the door until I was sealed out completely.

On unsteady legs, I made my way through the room, stopping when I reached the table. *This is all my fault. I pushed her too far. I scared her away.* I closed my eyes, feeling heat rise to my cheeks as I replayed our conversation from earlier. *Why did I have to bring up our marriage? And children? Idiot!*

I slammed my fist on the table, as if that could rid me of my humiliation. Hearing an odd sound, I opened my eyes in time to see Morkai's purple crystal roll off the edge of the table to the floor. I sprang forward and caught it before it landed.

I stood, a chill running through me as it dawned on me that I was holding one of Morkai's dark objects. Torn between disgust and curiosity, I could do nothing more than stare at it. I expected it to burn my flesh, explode into a thousand tiny fragments, or fill me with dark visions. Nothing happened. I almost regretted that it hadn't. Anything was more welcome than the pain I felt inside at that moment.

I frowned at the crystal, remembering what Cora had said about it. *There's a woman in there.* I watched the light of the lantern catch on the crystal's shimmering facets, wondering why Morkai kept an item so beautiful. It was nothing like him.

I shook my head and went to set it down but felt an overwhelming urge to inspect it closer. Without a second thought, I brought it toward my face, closing one eye as I examined the largest facet with the other. I waited one tense moment after the next. Nothing. My shoulders fell. *There's nothing in here.*

When I opened my eyes and looked away from the crystal, everything had turned white.

15

DINNER

Mareleau

I put my hands on my hips, stood back, and admired my work. "It's perfect."

Ann grimaced and rubbed her shoulder. "All this hard work, though, and you don't even get to enjoy it, Your Majesty."

I lifted my chin. "I'm enjoying it right now, am I not? Would you prefer we'd spent all night cooped up in my room, instead?"

Ann looked at her feet.

"It's lovely. You have a knack for creating elegance," Breah said.

"It beats picking out hideous linens." I smirked and returned my attention to the tiny kitchen, illuminated by dozens of candles lining the walls. Vases full of fresh herbs and flowers decorated the table, adding their aromatic warmth to the less-pleasant smells of food and cooking grease. "Why Teryn insisted on having dinner in the kitchen is beyond me, but I suppose it will do."

The kitchen maids, Sadie and Beca, entered carrying armfuls of empty plates. They were followed by a few young boys, newly hired hall servants. "Dinner is finished in the great hall, so now is as good a time as any for Prince Teryn and Princess Coralaine to come."

Beca placed the dishes in the wash bin and dried her hands on her apron. "It's such a kind thing you are doing for Princess Coralaine, Your Majesty."

"I only do it because Teryn is my brother." In all honesty, I'd said no about five times when Teryn first asked me to help him plan a dinner for Cora. However, the thought of getting out of my room and ordering people about was too tempting to ignore.

"Whatever the case, I never imagined this old kitchen could look so beautiful," Sadie said with a gleam in her eye.

I brushed my hands together. "Well, I've done my part. I'm sure the two lovebirds will arrive any time now." I felt a squeeze on my heart at the thought. *Why them? Why not me and Larylis?* I turned around and snapped my fingers for Ann and Breah to follow.

We made our way down the dim hall toward the stairs. As we rounded the corner into the stairwell, a shadow fell over me. I leapt back and suppressed a shout while my ladies squealed like mice. As my eyes adjusted to the dark, I saw the shadow was that of a man standing motionless on the stair. His face turned toward me as he stepped into the light of the hall.

I let out a sigh of relief. "Teryn, why do you keep doing this to me? First at the inn, now this."

He cocked his head, staring blankly at me.

"Where is Cora? Your dinner is ready."

"My dinner?"

"Yes, the one you had me spend the best part of the day planning for the two of you." I ground my teeth, crossed my arms, and popped my hip to the side. "Don't you dare tell me all my hard work was for nothing."

Teryn sighed and put his hand to his chest. "Sadly, I fear it was all for nothing. Cora won't be joining me tonight."

I threw my hands in the air. "That's the last time I ever do you a favor, *brother*."

He tilted his head. "Perhaps we should make the best of it. Will you join me for dinner, instead?"

"How dare you ask me, a queen and married woman, to join you for dinner?"

Teryn laughed. "I'm not asking anything inappropriate. You said it yourself, I am your brother. After all the work you've done for me, the only way I can thank you is to invite you to reap the benefits of your labor."

I wrinkled my nose and considered his offer. I *had* worked hard. "Fine. Breah, Ann, you may return to my room and wait for me there."

My ladies whined as they stepped around me toward the stairs, demonstrating why I hadn't invited them to join us.

Teryn offered me his arm. "Sister."

I hesitated before accepting, feeling uncomfortable with our closeness.

Teryn's eyes darted from floor to ceiling as we strolled through the hall back toward the kitchen. As we entered the room, he froze, blinking into the soft candlelight. "I like what you've done to the place."

"It's as good as it gets for a kitchen." I released his arm and went to the bench, careful to sit fully on the plush cushion that had been placed there, keeping the hem of my dress from touching the floor. It was easier said than done.

Teryn sat across from me and stared at the plates of food before us. His eyes lingered on the bottle of wine, and a wide grin stretched over his face. He took the bottle and two goblets and raised his brows at me. "Shall I pour you one as well?"

I leaned forward with an eager *yes* on my tongue, before I remembered myself. I narrowed my eyes at him. "I'm not allowed to drink wine."

"Now, why is that?"

I looked around us. The room was empty, but I kept my voice low regardless. "Mother says it's dangerous. You know, for the baby."

His eyes strayed from my face down the front of my body. "Yes, you carry my brother's baby. However, a glass of wine can't hurt."

"Oh, and what makes you the expert?"

"Everyone knows it's an old witches' tale. Mere superstition. Wine is known to strengthen the womb."

I wasn't sure if I believed his logic, but if it allowed me a glass of wine...

"You won't report my actions to my mother and father if I drink with you?"

Teryn shook his head, looking at me as if I spoke nonsense. "Why in Lela would I begrudge a young woman—a queen, no less—for enjoying herself?"

"Fine, then. Pour me some." I watched as he poured me a full goblet, more than any hall servant had given me in all my days. I was bubbling with giddiness as I accepted the cup and brought it to my lips. The first sip sent my head spinning in a delightful way, and a warmth flooded my stomach. "I've missed this. I had no idea pregnancy would be so restrictive."

"Yes, what a joy children bring." His voice was flat and emotionless as he waved his free hand with a flourish. The way he sat, legs crossed to the side, shoulders stiff, made him look completely unlike his usual, carefree self.

"What happened with Cora? Why didn't she join you tonight?" I took another sip of wine, then reached for a fluffy, fruit-filled pastry.

His lips pulled into a frown. "She doesn't have time for me. Sometimes I think she cares more about that tower than she does our relationship."

"I thought the two of you were the perfect couple. You did come all the way here just to see her."

"I thought we were too. I'm afraid I was wrong to come here. However, I must make the best of it." His eyes met mine with a wink.

I grimaced at him and turned my attention back to my goblet. It seemed like no time passed before it was empty.

"Another?" Teryn offered.

I nodded, giggling at how fuzzy the movement made me feel. Teryn refilled my cup while I tore into another pastry. He handed me the goblet, and I froze, seeing his plate had remained empty. "Aren't you going to eat? I had this meal made specially for you."

"I appreciate everything you've done, but unfortunately, I find myself too heartbroken to eat."

I laughed. "You sound like Larylis. I didn't know you were the brooding type too."

"Perhaps we should get to know each other better. Tell me, sister. What is your deepest secret?"

I took a long drink of wine, eyeing him over the rim of my cup. "I have no secrets."

"Then what is your greatest desire?"

I needed no time to answer. "That Larylis were here, or that I was home at Dermaine where I belong."

Teryn's face was full of sympathy. "You've been treated so unfairly. You deserve better."

I held my head high but felt myself swaying in my seat. "I deserve to be...treated like the queen...I am." My words were slurred, which made me laugh. I covered my lips to hide my smile.

"You do. You're too beautiful and too strong to be stuck in this dark place." Teryn reached his hand across the table and placed it over mine. "My brother never should have let you go."

My hand trembled beneath his touch, sending ripples of nausea through my stomach. I pulled away. "My husband only did what he had to do."

"It must be so hard for you to be here alone. Without friends. Without family. All the while watching Cora get everything she wants. Her home, her lover. And what do you get?"

His words rang true yet sent a shiver down my spine. *Why is he saying these things?*

"At least you have me, dear sister. I'll always be here for you."

Nausea wrenched my gut again, and my dizzy head went from pleasant to painful. I stood on legs that felt like water. "I'm going to bed now."

Before I could take a step further, Teryn was at my side with an arm around my waist. "My dear, I think you've had your fair share of wine. Allow me to walk you back."

"I can walk myself." I darted forward and found myself clinging to the doorway, giggling as my foot caught in the hem of my dress.

Teryn joined my laughter and helped me to my feet. "Now may I help you?"

I couldn't remember why I'd refused him in the first place. This was my brother, and we were laughing together. What was wrong with that? I took his arm and let him lead me up the stairs and down the hall toward my room. He paused midway down the hall. "I don't actually know which room is yours, Your Highness."

I looked left and right, then pointed at a door that looked like mine.

He burst out laughing so loud, I thought he'd wake the entire castle. "This is your room?"

I stumbled into him and pressed my hand over his mouth. "Hush! You'll get me in trouble! If anyone sees I've had...hears me...the wine..."

Teryn took my hand from his mouth and grasped it between his fingers. He then pulled it to his lips and planted a kiss upon it. "Goodnight, sister."

The feeling of his lips on my hand was enough to sober me for a moment. I pulled away and again felt the nausea rise to my throat. This time, it couldn't be settled. I turned toward my room, stumbling into the wall next to my door. My hair hung over my face as I heaved onto the floor. I whimpered as I watched deep-red liquid flood the stone and seep into the hem of my dress.

Tears poured from my eyes. I heard my door open behind me, followed by the gasp and squeal of my ladies.

"Take good care of your queen, dear ones," Teryn said. "Call upon someone to clean the mess."

I scowled at his silhouette as he walked down the hall and out of sight. I squeezed my eyes shut, remembering the crawling of my flesh when his lips met my hand. It was all I could do not to hurl again.

"You heard him, you cows. Get me inside and cleaned up at once."

16

REPERCUSSION

Cora

With bated breath, I knocked on Teryn's door. I straightened my bodice to keep my hands from shaking and pulled my lips into an unsteady smile. *I have to tell him. Now.*

For moments I waited, but no answer came from the other side of the door.

"Teryn? Are you there? I need to talk to you. I need to...apologize." I knocked again. Still no answer. I hurried up the stairs to the tower room, heart racing as I imagined the worst. But when I opened the door, I found nothing but shadows fading from the early morning light that streamed from the windows. I went to the secret room. Empty.

My heart raced as I continued through the rest of Ridine—the great hall, the kitchen, the field—with no sign of him.

"Coralaine, what's wrong?" I turned to find my brother

walking toward me as I made my way through the main hall for a fourth time.

"Dimetreus, have you seen Teryn this morning?"

"No, I haven't seen him since yesterday. Why?"

Tears spilled over my cheeks. "I think he left, and it's all my fault."

"He doesn't seem the type to leave without saying goodbye." His voice was gentle. "I've seen the way he looks at you. I know what that look means."

I hid my face behind my hands. "I said some things I shouldn't have, when I should have just told him the truth. I told him to leave me alone."

Dimetreus pulled me into a hug. "Dear, dear, Coralaine." There was laughter in his voice. "This is simply the first of many fights you will have with your beloved. It's hardly the end."

I tilted my head and looked up at him, wrinkling my brow. "What do you mean?"

"Do you think Linette and I never argued?"

"Of course not, you were always so in love."

"Love and arguing are not exclusive from one another. When you begin to share your life with another person, you meet both the shadows of yourself and of the other. It's a learning process. Even if he did ride off in a huff, he will be back. Trust me."

I smiled through my tears and studied his expression. His words were light, but his face was creased with pain. "You miss her still, don't you?"

"How could I not? Coming back here, reclaiming my mind, remembering everything...it's brought all the pain that had been numbed from Morkai's control crashing down on me at once."

His words filled me with guilt. I'd come back to Ridine for him, to help him reclaim his kingdom, but ever since I'd begun my work in the tower, I'd spared no time for him. And after Teryn had arrived, I'd given my brother even less thought. "Dimetreus, I'm so sorry I haven't been here for you. I feel like I've become so selfish since I've been here—"

"Don't ever think that, Coralaine. Your work in the tower is the greatest service any of us here are doing. This is hard on both of us." He let out a short laugh. "However, being siblings, we are stubborn to no end, and don't ask for the help we need."

A sense of lightness filled my heart. "How can I help you, though? Be honest."

He took me by the shoulders. "Take some time to be happy. That's all I ask. Do your work in the tower, but don't forget what really matters."

"What's that?"

"Love." He kissed me on the forehead. "Don't let some silly fight be the end of your joy."

I nodded, wishing I was dealing with just some *silly fight*. But like he said, I was stubborn to no end; I wouldn't let him know the full weight of my worries. "You're right."

"Now I must go start *my* work. I've convinced the council to put some funds toward repairing the Godskeep. Linette and our parents deserve a better resting place. Not one filled with overgrown roots and dust."

"Brother, that's wonderful."

"We're working on Linette's tomb now." He squeezed my hand. "I must go. If you need anything, that's where I'll be."

I watched him walk down the hall and out of sight before I turned toward the stairs. With dragging feet, I made my way to my room. I knew I should start my day's work in the tower, but I couldn't bring myself to do so until I'd spoken to Teryn.

Maybe it's best if he really did leave. Perhaps he shouldn't forgive me for shutting him out. Then he never need know what I have to say. I shook the thought from my head. *No, I can't let it end like this without him knowing the truth. If he's gone home, I'll write to him...*

My thoughts were interrupted by the sound of whimpering. It was coming from my old bedroom—Mareleau's room. My first instinct was to move along and leave her to whatever ailed her, but I sensed an uncharacteristic distress coming from behind the door. I knocked. "Mare...Your Majesty?"

"Go away," came her voice, followed by a moan.

I knocked again. "It's me, Cora."

I heard muttering, shuffling, and more whimpering. A moment later the door slowly opened, revealing Sera's face. Her cheeks were blazing, and she wouldn't meet my eyes. "Your Highness, I apologize for not coming to you this morning."

I bit back a laugh, realizing the source of her shame. "It's quite all right, Sera." I looked over her shoulder, trying to see into the room, but she was much taller than I. "I'm sure you had your reasons."

She pursed her lips, her face relaxed. "Yes, Queen Mareleau required my assistance."

I raised an eyebrow. "Why is that?"

Her lips shifted, as if she were searching for words.

A blonde head, that of Mareleau's Lady Breah,

bobbed up behind Sera's shoulder, whispering into her ear. I heard the words *witch* and *help* clearly.

Sera's face paled as she stared at me. Then, she slowly turned her head and looked into the room. She sighed and opened the door all the way. "Can you help her, Your Highness?"

The room was now fully exposed, and I took in the scene before me. Mareleau was sprawled out over her bed, face pale and glistening with sweat, whimpering and moaning beneath the covers.

I went to her side and put my hand to her forehead, gagging at the smell of vomit. "What's wrong with her?"

Mareleau looked up at me, grimacing. "You can ask me myself. I'm not dead, you know."

I forced my lips into a smile and spoke through my teeth. "What's wrong with you then?"

"I've been like this all morning. It's awful. Make it stop. Use your spells."

I ignored her last statement. "What symptoms are you experiencing?"

"My stomach. It's...roiling nonstop." Her face wrinkled, and she began to sob. "I look and smell hideous. I can't stand it. I want to go home."

It took all my strength not to laugh. Instead, I took a step back and shook my head. "Mareleau, this is a common symptom of pregnancy. Don't you know that?"

Her ladies gasped and surrounded the bed. "Pregnant? Is Her Majesty really pregnant?"

My eyes widened as Mareleau shot me a seething look. I'd forgotten her pregnancy was supposed to remain secret for the time being. I turned back to the girls. "Yes, she obviously conceived on her wedding night. Isn't she blessed?" I returned my attention to Mareleau and lowered my voice. "Now is as good a time as any, Your Majesty."

Her face turned red as she raised herself off her pillow. "But I'm not..." Her words were lost, her eyes went unfocused, and the color faded from her face. "I'm...no. No, it can't be." She fell back onto the bed, covered her face with her hands, and let out a muffled wail. "I'm pregnant."

"This is all natural, Your Majesty. The nausea, the emotional turmoil. All healthy parts of being pregnant."

"What would you know?"

"I saw many children born amongst the Forest People."

Sera came to my side. "Is there anything you can do for her? You know, with your...magic?"

I clenched my jaw. "It's called the Arts, and I can help her even without it. Go to the kitchen and ask Sadie to brew fresh ginger tea. Have Queen Mareleau sip it throughout the day."

Sera nodded and hurried from the room. I followed her but paused in the doorway. "One more thing. Have any of you seen Prince Teryn since yesterday?"

Breah and Ann exchanged a glance, then looked at their feet. I looked to Mareleau.

She frowned. "Of course I have. I saw him last night, and it's all your fault I feel this way."

I cocked my head to the side. "Why is that?"

"I spent all day working on his stupid romantic dinner for you."

I swallowed the tightness in my throat. "He planned a dinner for me?"

"He planned nothing. I planned everything, but you refused to join him. I had to have dinner with him instead."

"You had dinner with him last night?" My voice trembled in a way I hadn't anticipated.

"Yes, and I ended up...eating too much. Hence my current pain."

"Mareleau, I told you. Everything you are experiencing is related to your condition."

She crossed her arms and looked away from me.

I took a step closer. "How was he? Was he upset?"

"Weird, is what he was. Don't spurn him, Cora. I don't like him when he's heartbroken."

Her words sent my heart racing. *He was heartbroken. He was being weird.* "And you haven't seen him since?"

"Not since last night."

I nodded and left her with a curtsy. I returned to my room with more anxiety and more questions than I'd had before. *Where in Lela is he?*

17

THE CRYSTAL

Teryn

I woke with a gasp, blinking into blinding white light. I tried to shout but all I could produce was air. Hands pressed softly into my shoulders. I heard a woman's quiet hushing.

"Calm, Prince Teryn."

I craned my neck back and looked into a beautiful face of smooth, dark skin surrounded by a halo of rich, black curls. I scrambled away but didn't know where *away* was. There were no walls, no floor that I could see. I looked back at the woman. "Who are you? How do you know who I am?"

Her face held a neutral expression. "My name is Emylia. I know you because I have seen you from afar many times now."

"Where am I?"

"Inside the crystal."

My mouth fell open. "How? No, I must be dreaming. I

have to get out of here." I closed my eyes to shut out the glaring light but could still see it burning through my eyelids. A memory flashed through my mind—the bright light, the woman's terrified face, a hand coming toward me from behind an invisible door.

I opened my eyes, but the memory continued to seize my mind—a figure entering the light, surrounded by darkness. A familiar, terrible face laughing as he charged forward. His hands grasping my shoulders. Me screaming as pain seared through my skull. Then nothing.

Emylia put her hand on my arm, and my eyes snapped to her face. "You need to remain calm."

"How long have I been here?"

She shrugged. "Hours. Days. It's impossible to tell the passing of time from within."

"I need to get out of here."

"I know, but you never will if you lose hold of yourself."

I blinked again and again, but no matter how I tried, I couldn't adjust to the light. "Why is it so bright in here? Why are there no walls?"

"The crystal is made of light. That light holds great power. You can use it, if you know how."

I clenched my teeth. "If you know, now would be a good time to show me."

She seemed unaffected by the edge in my voice. "I do. I can create what I want to see." She stepped a few paces away, held her hand high in the air, and closed her eyes. With slow, circular motions, she waved her hand through the air and circled me. As she did so, waves of color began to spread out to become walls, a floor, tapestries, and furnishings, as if I were watching a watercolor painting come to life.

Once she was again in front of me, she lowered her hand and smiled at her surroundings. We were now in a modestly-sized, square room with wide windows that held no glass. Tapestries in vibrant colors of saffron, ruby, and indigo decorated the walls in strange patterns. Books were piled high around the room, and in one corner sat a pile of patterned quilts and fluffy pillows.

I approached one of the walls and pressed my hand against a tapestry. At first, the wall felt like any other, solid beneath my touch. However, the longer I kept my hand in place, the more I realized *solid* had taken on new meaning. There was resistance between my hand and the wall, but it was more like a thick buzzing sensation than an actual barrier. "What is this place?"

"You are still in the crystal, but I have shaped the light into the likeness of my old room at Temple."

"Temple? Is that like a Godskeep?"

"You could think of it like that, I suppose. It was where I lived for many years."

I turned away from the wall and looked back at Emylia. Now that I was no longer blinded by light, I could see her fully. Her dress was unlike anything I'd seen before, sleeveless, closer to what I'd call a nightdress than a gown, lightweight and gauzy, and in a deep purple that faded to lavender toward the top. It draped with many folds and tied at the waist with the same material, as if it were made with one endless piece of cloth.

I averted my eyes and felt my cheeks tingle. "My lady, are you in a state of undress?"

A corner of her mouth lifted. "No, this is what I

always wore back home. I forget how modest your people are on this side of the world. If it makes you more comfortable, I can put on a cloak."

I returned my eyes to her face, careful to keep them above her neck. "Never mind that. I need to get back to the tower room. Please, can you do this," I extended my arms toward the walls, "to put me back in the tower?"

Her face fell. "If I did, it wouldn't be real. You wouldn't really be there."

"Then how do I get back? Cora got out, and she said you helped her."

"She got out because she wasn't yet lost."

"What do you mean *lost*? How am I lost when she was not?"

"He...touched you."

"He?" The memory took hold of my mind again, and I saw him. I stepped back until I felt the energy of the wall buzzing against my back. My heart pounded in my chest. "I must be dreaming. Morkai is dead. I watched him die on the battlefield."

"Yes, he is dead," Emylia said. "His body is forever gone."

"Then what did I see in here? Is he a wraith?"

Emylia folded her hands at her waist and walked toward me. "He's more than a wraith, but less than a man. He's tethered his ethera to the crystal."

"Ethera?"

"You would call it his soul."

I narrowed my eyes at her. "Morkai has a soul? I find that hard to believe."

"He has a soul wrapped in darkness and the power of

necromagic. Nothing more than his own death was needed to bring him back here."

I looked around the room. "Where is he now?"

Her expression softened. "He is where you no longer are."

"What does that mean? Am I dead?" I looked down at my hands and arms, opening and closing my fists, and then rubbing my hands together. With a shudder, I realized every sensation representing physical movement or touch had been replaced by the gentle buzzing resistance I'd felt with the wall. Even what looked like my body had taken on a shimmery quality. "Is this my...soul?" I lifted my eyes to Emylia, realizing her form carried the same shimmering essence; none of her edges looked truly solid.

"What you see is the outer layer of your ethera, your non-physical essence. You are not dead in the same way Morkai is dead. Your blood has not been spilled, your heart has not stopped beating, and your lungs still pull in air. Your ethera is linked to your body. Your body, however, is no longer linked to your mind. Morkai has caused a split using your own fear. From there Morkai invaded, creating a link from the crystal to your body."

I swallowed the lump in my throat. "Are you telling me Morkai is...in my body?"

She nodded, her face a stone mask. "Yes, but you must stay calm about this."

"Calm? You expect me to stay calm? Morkai is in my body!"

She walked over to me and put her hands on my shoulders. I noted the buzzing between our touch. "That fear is what Morkai feeds on. You need to let it go."

"How?"

"Close your eyes and focus on your breath. Relax."

I wanted to do anything but what she was telling me. Rage and fear filled every part of me, and I could think of nothing else but Morkai invading my flesh.

"You aren't relaxing."

I suppressed a shout of frustration and attempted to follow her instructions.

"Can you feel the air moving through your lungs?"

"Yes," I said through clenched teeth. As I focused more on the feeling of expansion and contraction in my chest, my jaw relaxed.

"Can you feel the beating of your heart?"

I nodded, feeling the rhythmic pumping.

"Good. Keep feeling into what makes you feel alive. The pulsing of your blood. The workings of your heart, lungs, and other organs. That is your *vitale*. It is your life-force, the part of your body your ethera is attached to."

Her voice had become calming to me, and the more I let myself feel the rhythms of my body, the more clarity I received. I opened my eyes and met hers. "Thank you."

She nodded. "That is your greatest weapon against Morkai right now, but fear will strip it from you in an instant. Never lose touch with your vitale."

"Will that help me get my body back?"

Emylia shook her head. "I don't have an easy answer, but I will help you in any way I can."

I furrowed my brow as I studied her face. "What are you?"

Emylia gave me a blank look.

"Are you dead? Or are you like me?"

She lowered her gaze, frowning slightly. "I am dead and have been a very long time."

"If you've been dead for such a long time, then how do you know who I am? And how did you know Cora?"

"Like I said, I've been watching you from afar. Wherever Morkai takes the crystal, he takes me too. And trust me, he's hardly let it leave his side. I saw you in the dungeon when he captured you. I witnessed the battle unfold. I've watched Cora working in the tower room."

"You are able to see outside the crystal? How?"

"With the same power I use to create this room, I can create a window to the world around me."

"Show me."

She opened her mouth, but hesitated. "I don't know if you're ready for that. The things you might see…"

I felt heat rise within me, but I pushed it away, focusing on the beat of my heart instead. "Emylia, please. I need to know what he's doing with my body."

She sighed. "Fine, but you must do your best to remain calm. No matter what you see, focus on your vitale."

I nodded. She stepped away and again circled her palm in the air. The temple room shifted and melted away into shadow. I blinked to adjust to the darkness that surrounded us. When she was finished, I found myself in a narrow hallway.

I looked to my right where Emylia stood, and studied the dimly lit walls of stone covered in cobwebs. Everything my eyes fell upon seemed to be swimming behind warped glass. Nothing was as crisp or clear as what I was used to.

I turned left to take in my other surroundings and

froze, seeing a shadowed figure, head pressed against a wall. There was only one candle-filled sconce near us, and he stood outside its light.

Afraid to move, I remained where I was. I felt Emylia come up next to me.

"That's him," she whispered.

I started, expecting the man's face to shoot forward. "He can't hear us?"

"He can neither hear, nor see, nor sense us."

I looked back at my surroundings. "These look like servants' halls. Are we still at Ridine?"

Emylia approached the figure. "I believe so." She stood closer to him than I dared, mirroring his stance as she too pressed her head against the wall. "He's listening to a conversation. Sounds like a council meeting."

I crept closer, keeping to Emylia's side. The figure suddenly looked up, and the candlelight touched his face. *My* face. I held my breath as I saw my own eyes stare back at me. My heart raced, stunned that he could see me. I tried to recall Emylia's instructions to stay calm, to sense my vitale, when Morkai—wearing my body—took a step forward. It was then I realized he wasn't looking at me at all but staring down the hall behind me.

I released my breath, wondering if he too could feel what was happening in my body—the air pressing from my lungs, the pounding of my heart that now began to slow. If he did, he paid it no heed. He turned and hurried down the hall. I felt compelled to follow, and found Emylia keeping up at my side.

"We are bound to the crystal," she said. "Even when we look outside it, we are pulled wherever it goes."

"Where does he keep it?" I looked at Morkai, seeing no obvious sign of it.

Emylia held a hand toward Morkai as we walked. Her palm hovered near his chest. "I believe he's wearing it."

Shadows moved past my vision, interspersed with flickering candlelight as we moved through the halls. Finally, Morkai came to a stop. Light crept under the doorway ahead, while a dark staircase loomed to our left. He reached a hand toward the door, but his legs gave way beneath him. At the same time, I felt my breathing grow labored, and my heart began to slow.

Morkai crouched on the ground a few moments before he stood on trembling legs. He turned away from the door and made his way up the staircase instead. We followed him up flight after flight in darkness until Emylia grabbed my arm.

"Let's go."

The staircase shifted back into Emylia's room. I fell to my knees. "What's happening to me?"

"Your vitale is slipping, isn't it?"

"How? I was trying to do what you said." Even my words came out heavy.

"It wasn't your fault, Teryn. He's overused your body."

"What do you mean?"

Emylia crouched at my side. "Morkai's ethera is linked to your mind—your cereba—from which he controls your body. But you maintain the link to your vitale. He cannot sense when his actions from the cereba overexert the vitale."

It sounded as if she were speaking another language, but I nodded along and did my best to comprehend.

"This is good news. He has a weakness—he can't use your body forever without rest."

I looked up at her. "How do you know so much about these things—the vitale, the ethera, and the cereba? I've never heard nor read about anything like it."

"I studied great mysteries, including the mysteries of human life, when I was at Temple."

"And the crystal? How do you have so much power over it, yet you remain stuck?"

Her lips pulled into a sad smile. "This crystal belongs to me. At least it did once, long ago. It responds to me. Yet it was not I who trapped me here, therefore I remain."

"Why are you here in the first place?"

She turned away. "Morkai has plans for me."

I wanted to ask her more, but I was distracted by a shuffling sound in the distance. The room around us vanished and burned into the bright, white light. We looked toward the sound and saw darkness slowly spilling into the light like wafts of smoke. It formed a mass of undulating waves of black and gray, loosely resembling human form. At the top of the form was Morkai's face.

His eyes were heavy and rimmed with purple, and his shadowy limbs dragged low, longer than his physical arms had ever been. He paused and turned his face toward us. "Showing him his new home, are we?" His familiar voice sent a chill through me, yet it sounded undoubtedly fatigued.

I opened my mouth to shout at him, to argue, to insist he face me like a man and put me back in my body. But what good would it do? What power did I have here? I pursed my lips and scowled instead.

He turned his head and shuffled away until his darkness dissipated from view.

I turned to Emylia, keeping my voice low. "Where did he go?"

"Resting his ethera, I imagine. Allowing your body to regain strength. You should do the same. While he's resting, you should be strengthening your connection to your vitale."

I ground my teeth, bristling at the lack of physical sensation it caused. "He'll be back at it again, won't he?"

"Yes, but so will we."

18

TENSION RISING

Mareleau

With my forehead cradled in one hand, I brought a piece of bread to my mouth and took a bite. I closed my eyes, feeling my stomach alternate between lurching and settling.

Breah brought a mug near my face. Wafts of warm ginger filled my nostrils. "More tea?"

I grumbled but accepted. As much as I hated to admit Cora was right about anything, her witches' brew of ginger tea was the only thing that had cleared my ever-present nausea.

Breah sat next to me on the lounge and placed a hand on my back. "My mother felt this way with every one of my brothers and sisters, Your Majesty." I felt her warm palm through the loosened laces of my gown. Even the tightness of a fully-laced dress was enough to send my stomach roiling.

I slowly turned my head and glowered until she placed her hand back in her lap.

"It goes away, though. Mother always said the nausea only lasted a moon or so."

I took another bite of bread. "Why does no one ever mention this? How does one survive pregnancy if it feels like such torture?"

Ann clasped her hands from where she sat in the chair across from me, a dreamy look in her wide, dopey eyes. "It's all worth it when you think about the baby! Their tiny hands, their cheeks. I cannot wait until I'm wed and become a mother."

Breah nodded in agreement. "You won't even remember this part once you have your son."

I shot her an icy stare. "Son? Why would you say it's a son? For all I know it's a girl."

She shrugged. "Every woman, especially a queen, wants a son. A kingdom needs an heir. My mother always called my siblings *son* while they were in the womb. Then when my sisters were born, she pretended not to be disappointed."

Ann laughed while I fumed. I knew too well what it was like to be a disappointing daughter.

"Have you written to King Larylis yet? He'd love to know he has a son on the way," Breah said.

Ann sat upright in her chair. "Maybe he'll even bring you back to Dermaine! We could get out of this place."

Despite my ever-growing collection of new furnishings and luxuries, Ridine was still far from comfortable. Perhaps if Larylis knew my pregnancy had become a reality he'd stand up to my father's wrath and summon me home.

Thoughts of being where I belonged, in my quaint castle with my loving husband, filled me with warmth. I pictured us side by side, he with his handsome smile and tousled, sandy-brown hair beneath his gleaming, gold crown, and I with a shimmering gown and my golden circlet on my brow.

My thoughts turned sour when the image of me became bloated at the belly. I no longer looked like a regal queen in my mind, but more like a haggard peasant, breasts drooping while tiny brats pulled at my skirts. Could I really succumb to such a life so soon? Was I ready for that? Besides, my father already thought I *was* pregnant and had the power to keep me away from my husband. What difference would it make if my lie had come true?

"I don't think I should tell him just yet," I said. "I've heard most pregnancies end before a moon or two. I'd hate to disappoint him if this comes to nothing."

Ann wrinkled her nose. "That's awfully grim, Your Majesty."

I stood and snapped my fingers at her. "Life isn't all babies and butterflies, Ann. Real life is grim. Why else do I find myself in this awful place?" I stormed past her and collapsed on my bed, eyes filling with tears as I pressed my face into my pillow. I cursed myself, hating how often my emotions had been sweeping me away lately. It was so unlike me—the me I'd spent years cultivating, the me who'd survived every obstacle with a fierce strength. What was happening to me?

The silence of my maids spoke louder than their gossip ever could. It grated on my nerves to know they were aware of my emotional turmoil, watching their queen fall apart before their eyes. Nausea boiled through me again, and I let out a wail, stifled by my pillow. *A queen doesn't wail.*

I thought of the monster growing in my belly, stripping me of my pride, forcing tears from my eyes, and tearing at my guts. How could something so small have so much power over a queen? *I will not let you destroy me.*

Teryn

I looked down at the bed and at my body upon it. It lay motionless, aside from the rise and fall of its chest, and I felt that same rise and fall mirrored in my own. I breathed away the sick feeling that came from watching myself. You'd think after growing up with a twin, I'd be used to such a sight. Yet there was a significant difference between a man with my features, and a man with my very own body.

I looked at Emylia, and she nodded. With a deep breath, I lowered myself onto the bed, feeling a thick buzzing as I sank into the space of my body. The resistance felt almost painful at first, but after a few moments, I was used to the sensation.

"Now look around the room," Emylia said.

I took in the familiar sights of the room around me—the same room I'd been staying in while at Ridine. It was just as I'd left it the morning I'd last seen Cora. I wasn't sure if I was relieved or terrified that Morkai was still at Ridine, still close to the woman I loved. My eyes wandered to the walls, watching the morning sunlight streaming in through the windows.

Emylia kept her voice slow and gentle. "Now close your eyes and feel the sensation of the blankets against your back. Feel the pillows cradling your head, brushing against your cheek."

I followed along, noting the various levels of resistance and buzzing each object seemed to contain.

Emylia continued. "Notice your vitale. Your blood. Your heart. Your lungs. Now, again, notice your surroundings, what you feel against your body."

On and on we went through the exercise. At times following her instructions made me feel like I was one with a gently flowing stream. Other times, I felt like I was fighting against thrashing waves.

"You're doing well."

I smiled and returned my attention to my breathing. A buzzing resistance surged through my chest, and I felt my heart quicken. I watched as my body sat up and looked from side to side. I caught Emylia's eye, and she slowly nodded. Keeping my eyes on my now-awake form, I rolled on my side and slid off the bed.

"You were great," Emylia said as I went to her. "We will practice again next time he rests."

My breathing began to slow. "What do we do now? Are we going to follow him?"

"Of course."

We watched as Morkai stretched and dressed, allowing us to catch our first glimpse of the crystal, wrapped with gold wire and hanging from a chain around his neck. When he dressed in my undershirt and tunic, no sign of the chain could be seen. I wondered what would happen if it was removed.

Morkai left the room and entered the hall. We

followed him as he went through an unremarkable door and into the darkness of the servants' passage. He continued his wanderings, listening at walls, hiding in the shadows when a servant would pass.

"Are you keeping touch with your vitale?" It was likely the third time Emylia had asked since second bell.

I nodded, closing my eyes as I felt the strong beating of my heart. When I opened my eyes, Morkai still hadn't moved from his place behind a closed door in the passage. "What do you think he's doing?"

She stepped toward Morkai. "Gathering information. A lot has happened since his death. If he's going to convince everyone he is you, he's going to need to know everything you know—and more. I'm sure his plans for your body far outreach what you'd had in mind for yourself."

I remained calm, even though her words threatened me with panic. "What does he want this time?"

"He always has and always will want one thing—to become Morkaius of Lela."

"But his plan failed. His Roizan is gone, his war was lost."

"Think about it Teryn. With your body, does he even need a war to get what he wants?"

The thought chilled me. Before I could ponder it further, Morkai turned away from the door and hurried to the end of the hall. He paused outside another door before turning the handle and stepping into the light of the castle. He brushed off his—*my*—tunic and walked on ahead. It was the first time I'd seen Morkai in the main part of Ridine, and now that I could see him fully, I was certain his posture looked nothing like my own. His neck and torso were stiff, and his steps were too calculated. How was he expecting to fool anyone?

"Teryn?"

Cora's voice froze me mid-step. Morkai whipped around before I did. His eyes were narrowed, and his lips were pressed tight. It took him a moment to transform his grimace into a wide smile. "Cora, my dear." His voice came out in a crude semblance to my own.

Cora's expression made my heart ache as she shifted between relief and confusion. I stepped closer to her, wishing I could wrap her in my arms and press my lips against hers.

Emylia put her hand on my shoulder. "Breathe, Teryn. Stay calm."

I closed my eyes and realized I was trembling.

"Don't lose touch with—"

"I know." I winced at the irritation in my voice. "I'm sorry. I just..."

"It's all right. But you can't help her or yourself if you lose touch."

I put all my effort into steadying my breathing and focusing on my vitale before returning my gaze to Cora.

Cora took a step toward Morkai. "Where have you been? I've been so worried."

Morkai's face fell with mock-sympathy as he strode over to her and put his arms around her. "I'm so sorry I worried you. I just needed some time to clear my head."

I focused on the air pressing in and out of my lungs to keep myself from lashing out.

Cora's arms wrapped around his waist, but her grip appeared loose. When they parted, she furrowed her brow. "So, you aren't upset?"

He smiled. "Of course not. I love you. I could never be upset with you."

"I want to explain why I acted the way I did."

He waved a dismissive hand in the air. "There's nothing to explain."

"There is." Cora's voice was firm, and her jaw was set. "It is important to me that I tell you what I need to say."

Her serious expression sent a chill through me. I was torn between hope and dread that she was going to end our relationship. *At least if she ends it, she might be safe from him.*

Morkai put his hands on her shoulders. "Not right now, my dear. I have much to do."

She looked taken aback. "What are you doing?"

His jaw moved back and forth while he hesitated. "It may not have been the best choice to leave my brother at the beginning of his reign. Since I'm here with you, I need to make sure I am still serving him. I need to send a few letters, make some inquiries here and there. Don't you worry, I'll be here the whole time."

"When can we talk? Tonight?"

He squeezed her shoulder. "Yes, tonight." He turned to leave but paused. "You know, my business would be completed much easier if I could speak to King Dimetreus. Do you know where I can find your brother?"

"He's been working in the Godskeep for days. I doubt you'll find him anywhere else for very long."

His face broke into a wide grin. "Of course that's where he is." Without another word, he turned on his heel and continued down the hall.

I kept my eyes on Cora, feeling my heart break with every step the crystal pulled me away.

19

FRIENDSHIPS GROWING

Cora

I ascended the stairs to the high tower, unable to shake my encounter with Teryn. He'd seemed so different. I never thought he'd leave for days, only to return and not seek me out. *Perhaps he's trying to give me the space I asked for.*

I was also surprised he'd made no mention of our work in the tower, voiced no concern over whether I'd resumed my duties without him. I had continued my work in his absence, but I thought he'd be furious when he found out. However, he'd apparently found new employment. *Since when does Larylis need his help?*

My eyes were unfocused when I entered the tower, nearly missing the movement coming from the hidden room. I jumped and turned toward the scuffling, seeing light from a lantern flicker in the space of the half-open door. My heart pounded as I crept closer, making as little noise as possible as I pressed open the door.

Mareleau's face shot toward mine, her eyes wide as she stifled a scream and put a hand to her chest.

I let out a deep breath. "What in Lela are you doing here?"

She looked from me to the box her hand was still in—the box full of the discarded potions. Her jaw moved back and forth as her cheeks began to redden. A hint of guilt passed over her face but was lost when she met my eyes. She rose to her feet and placed her hands on her hips. "Are you not going to address me as queen?"

I narrowed my eyes at her. "Not when you are rifling around where you shouldn't. Are you trying to get yourself killed? Have you already forgotten your cousin?"

She glared back at me. "Of course I haven't. But you forget, as queen I can go wherever I choose."

"*You* forget that you aren't queen of *this* castle. I'm starting to wonder if anyone taught you how to be queen at all."

"Oh, and who taught you to be queen? The woman who was raised by wolves has no right to speak to me on such matters."

"Perhaps wolves would have done you well, as they may have taught you some manners."

Mareleau's lips peeled back, and I steeled myself for her backlash. However, instead of fury, she erupted with laughter, doubling over as she gripped her stomach. "Wolves!"

My mouth hung open as I stared at her. "What is so funny?"

"I was just picturing wolves...teaching me manners..." she said through bursts of chortling. Just as quickly as her laughter had begun, it was cut off. Her cheeks were pink when she looked at me, the corners of her mouth twitching up and down, and I wondered if she was about to start laughing again. But down and down her lips curled until tears sprang from her eyes.

Again, I could do nothing but stare as Mareleau fell into a fit of sobbing. I looked from her to the box of potions. It took minimal effort to comprehend what she wouldn't say. My shoulders fell as I realized the source of her turmoil.

I considered making her leave so I could get on with my work, but a gentler reaction took over. I put my hand on her forearm. "Come, Your Majesty, it isn't safe in there. At least come into the main room for a moment."

To my surprise, she listened, face in her hands as she took trembling steps forward.

I kept my voice soft. "Why don't you want to have this baby?"

She tore her hands from her face and stared daggers at me. "You know nothing."

"I know you were looking through potions, although *poisons* would be a more apt description."

She turned away from me and crossed her arms. "I heard my ladies exchanging rumors they'd gleaned from the guards. They say you can cure or create anything your heart desires from the chests that come from this room."

I clenched my jaw, wondering which of the idiot guards I had to thank for that. "That is so far from the truth. Those potions do nothing but harm. The man who created them sought only to create death."

Mareleau didn't flinch at the word.

"Which is what you want."

She rounded on me and brought her face close to mine. "I hear the accusation in your voice, and I know what you're thinking. I'm spoiled. I'm vain. I'm a terrible person. Maybe all those things are true, but I..." Her face fell, and her eyes went unfocused. "I'm just not ready. I can't be a mother."

"You really want something that will get rid of your baby?"

She pursed her lips and wouldn't meet my eyes. "Perhaps."

I stormed into the secret room, retrieved a vial, and brought it to her. "Here."

She took it from my hand, turning it over in her palm. Her eyes met mine. "It says your name on it."

"You may not be ready to have a baby now, but I sure wasn't ready to have my womb destroyed when this potion was forced upon me."

Her eyes widened. "Your womb?"

"I'm barren. Morkai decided to end my bloodline while still allowing me to live. He's robbed me of the ability to give life, the ability to produce an heir." My eyes filled with tears. "The ability to marry the man I love."

Mareleau looked back at the vial in her hand. "I didn't know."

"Neither did I until recently. You want a poison? There it is. I can't promise your body will ever be the same afterward."

With a trembling hand, she slid the potion onto the table. "Fine. I get it. I shouldn't have even considered going through that box. I just...why must this be all we are worth as women? Why are we here to produce sons, heirs? Why is that all we are good for? Why can't we just love and let that be enough?"

"I don't know, Mareleau. I wish it was enough that we simply love whom we love, and nothing more. Yet you and I were born into royalty. I'd forgotten what a burden it is to be royal, or perhaps I never knew in the first place. I think I'm about to lose both the burden and the privilege, once I tell Teryn."

"He doesn't know?"

"Not yet. My future hangs on this horrible secret I bear. You, on the other hand, hold the safety of your title, your kingdom, and your marriage, all in one."

She placed her hand over her abdomen, her eyes glazing with tears yet again. "That's too big a burden to bear. What if she's a girl? What if I want more time alone with my husband?"

My hand curled into a fist. "I would give anything to be afflicted as you are. To be able to provide a child. To be able to marry the man I love without fear of being set aside."

"Set aside? Are you threatening me?"

"No, Mareleau. This isn't just about you—"

"Of course this is about me!"

I opened my mouth to argue, but snapped it shut. What good would it do? We were both buried too deep in our own pain for words to sway either of us. I let out a heavy sigh. "I'm not here to judge you. What you do is none of my business. However, I can't stand by while you put your body in danger. If you truly don't want this baby, you'd be safer finding your remedy in the kitchen."

"More ginger root tea?"

"Herbs." While it wasn't something I had any personal experience in, and the very thought sent my stomach churning, I knew of the remedies made in secret amongst the Forest People, by those who needed to hide an unfavorable night's transgression. "If you are so determined, I will help you."

She raised an eyebrow. "You would do that? For me?"

"I have a feeling you will do whatever you can to get your way, whether I help you or not. At least if I help you, I know the remedy will be relatively safe."

A corner of her mouth twitched into a smile, but quickly disappeared. Again, her hands went to her abdomen.

"Although you must decide soon, it isn't something you have to choose today. Whatever you do, I am here for you."

Her head tilted back, and she looked at me as if my words had been spoken in another language. "Thank you." She looked equally perplexed at the words that came from her mouth.

"In the meantime, I do need you to get out of here. I have work to do and this truly is a dangerous place."

She looked around the room, flinching as if she were taking in her surroundings for the first time. A shudder rippled through her. "I don't know what I was thinking coming here."

"Desperation can make you do crazy things."

"Yeah, like befriending you."

"Oh, so we're friends now?"

Mareleau rolled her eyes, held her head high, and

brushed past me. With her back facing me, she paused in the doorway. "I hope it goes well with you and Teryn."

I swallowed the lump in my throat. "Me too." Without another word, she walked on, leaving me alone in the dismal room with plenty of work to do, while I awaited the conversation that could change everything.

20

IMPRISONED

Teryn

What does she want to tell me? What is she going to say? It was all I could think for the rest of the day as Emylia and I continued to follow Morkai. Seeing Cora and him together had given me a sinking feeling I couldn't ignore. I had to find a way to keep her away from him. But nothing we'd seen during Morkai's sneaking and hiding had given me any reason to believe I could stop him.

The change of the light brought my attention back to our surroundings. Morkai had stepped out of the castle and into the courtyard beneath the light of the darkening sky. Emylia and I paused, watching him close his eyes and lift his face toward the setting sun.

After a few moments, his head snapped back to center, his eyes opened, and he strode forward. We approached a building I'd never seen before. Its outer walls were crumbling and marked with patterns that looked like ivy had recently been removed. The door was open, and outside stood two guards. They looked at Morkai and moved aside when they recognized my face.

"Is the king inside?" he asked.

The guard at the right nodded.

My stomach dropped. *What does he want with the king?*

As we entered the building, I realized it was Ridine's Godskeep. It was much smaller and darker than Dermaine's, with no bright tapestries, no domed ceiling, no stained-glass windows. It resembled a dungeon more than a Godskeep.

The main room looked as if it had been recently cleaned. A bright red carpet ran from the doorway to the dais, where a long table stood. The table acted as an altar, bearing candles, statues of the gods, and bowls for offerings. At the foot of the dais knelt Dimetreus.

Dimetreus turned toward Morkai as he approached. Emylia and I exchanged a glance and followed.

"Teryn," Dimetreus greeted.

"Your Majesty." Morkai bowed. "May I join you?"

Dimetreus nodded and Morkai knelt at his side. "Am I even doing this right?" Dimetreus asked with a crooked smile. "I haven't knelt in the Godskeep since I was a boy."

"I say you're doing it right." Morkai turned his head toward the king. "Why are you kneeling, anyway?"

"They say it's what a king does."

"They?"

"Ulrich, Kevan. The council." Dimetreus grimaced. "Sometimes I think they'd rather I stepped aside so they can show me how to be king themselves."

"I have no doubt of that."

Dimetreus met Morkai's gaze, creases forming between his brows.

"They are ambitious men, my king. It's obvious to us all."

Dimetreus turned back toward the altar. "We don't even have a Godspriest yet. I honestly don't know what good this will do. Am I supposed to pray?"

Morkai shrugged. "If you did, what would you pray for?"

Dimetreus' shoulders fell. "I would pray for things that can never be."

"Linette?"

Dimetreus tensed, eyes steely. "Yes. I would give my own life to bring her back."

Morkai looked around the room. I followed his gaze to the clean walls lined with new-looking lanterns. "At least you've been able to make this a suitable resting place for her."

Dimetreus held his chin high. "She's even being built a proper tomb with an effigy. She was never awarded that respect before. Even though she's gone, I'm determined to honor her with every breath I take."

Morkai put his hand on Dimetreus' shoulder. "I know how you feel, my king. I too have lost someone I love dearly."

Dimetreus sighed. "Your father. I'm so wrapped up in my own pain, I wasn't even thinking what a Godskeep must remind you of."

I felt a lump rise in my throat, followed by a burning fury as I watched Morkai don a mask of my own pain. "Death is such a tragic thing."

Dimetreus frowned and turned toward Morkai. "I'm

sorry I didn't stop him, Teryn. I should have. I could have ended the war then and there if I'd been of the right mind to kill Morkai before your father reached him."

"I can't blame you."

"Even though my mind was coming back to me, I still wasn't my full self. It wasn't until I saw Morkai with his blade at Cora's throat that I remembered a piece of who I am. In that moment, it was like ice was melting from all around me, and I was finally able to see and hear in a way I hadn't for many years."

"Cora saved you, then."

Dimetreus smiled. "Without a doubt, yes. If I were to pray, it would be her I would pray for."

"You're ready to let go of your original wish so soon?"

Dimetreus' smile faded. "What do you mean?"

"For Linette."

"Such wishes will keep me stuck in the past."

"Not if you can make them come true."

Dimetreus clenched his jaw, brows lowered, as he turned his head toward Morkai. "What are you saying?" His voice held an edge I'd never heard before.

Morkai brought his face close to the king's and kept his voice at a whisper. "I can help you bring her back."

Dimetreus' eyes widened as Morkai stared back with a smug expression. Emylia and I exchanged a glance, and I felt as if the air around us had grown tense. "What is he doing?" I asked.

Emylia's mouth opened, but no words came out.

"What are you playing at, Teryn?" Dimetreus said through clenched teeth.

Morkai twisted my face into a maniacal grin I was sure I'd never worn before. "You know I have the power."

Before the last word was out of Morkai's mouth, Dimetreus leapt to his feet and unsheathed his sword.

Morkai cried out, my features morphing into terror as he cowered away from the king. "Guards! Help!"

The guards paused when they entered the room, shocked as they took in the scene unfolding before them.

"He's Morkai!" Dimetreus flung forward, sword swinging toward Morkai's face.

Morkai scrambled back, chest heaving. "He's gone mad. Help me!"

The guards were on Dimetreus before he could charge again. The king's face was red, spittle flying from his lips as he screamed and shouted, struggling with the arms that bound him. "Release me! I'm your king!" The guards ignored him as two more stormed into the room to help subdue him.

Morkai followed the guards as they pulled Dimetreus out of the Godskeep. "Where are you taking him?"

"To the dungeon," a guard said through gasping breaths. "Lord Kevan has directed us to detain the king if he falls out of line."

"Lord Kevan isn't your king," Dimetreus shouted. "Let me go so I can rip Morkai's head off!"

Morkai frowned at the guard, angling away from the thrashing king. "Verdian thought this might happen. Thank Lela Lord Kevan was prepared. However, the king isn't of the right mind. If you must put him in the dungeon, be sure to give him all the amenities he needs."

The guard nodded, and the men pushed Dimetreus into the castle. Morkai paused in the courtyard and let them continue without him. With no one else around to see, a wide grin spread over his face. His chest heaved with suppressed laughter.

My limbs trembled, and I felt a roar bubble in my chest, filling every part of me. As I let it escape my throat, I no longer felt the beating of my heart, the rush of my blood, or the air in my lungs. I felt nothing.

Cora

The sky had grown dark in the tower, signaling it was time to finish my work in the secret room. I discarded the newly cleared objects into the chests and closed the lids. My hands trembled as I did so.

I'd been able to remain distracted from my approaching conversation with Teryn, but now that my work was done, the weight of what I must say pressed heavy on my heart. I opened the tower door and descended the stairs. The lower I went, the more I sensed something wasn't right. The air was heavy, thick with turmoil and confusion. It made my skin crawl.

I made my way to the great keep and found Mareleau's ladies standing outside her door, whispering. Sera's eyes widened when they met mine. She parted from the group and came toward me. "Your Highness, have you heard?"

"Heard what?"

"Your brother attacked Prince Teryn."

Her words made no sense. There was no way I'd heard her right. "That can't be. Where are they?"

"King Dimetreus has been taken to the dungeon. Teryn is recovering in his room."

My eyes darted left and right, and I was torn between rushing to the dungeon or Teryn's room. I clenched my fingers to stop them from shaking and ran to Teryn's room. Outside his door, I called his name. No answer. I knocked, pounding my fist again and again to no avail.

I looked over my shoulder to find Sera watching me. I'd never seen her look concerned for me before. "Are you sure he's in here?"

She nodded. "Everyone is confused and scared, but we saw him go inside."

"Was he wounded?"

"I don't think so."

Just then I heard rustling from behind the door. "Teryn, are you in there?" Uneven footsteps approached, and a moment later, the door was pulled open. Teryn blinked back at me. I rushed forward and threw my arms around him. "What is going on?"

He hesitated before returning the embrace. I pulled away, worried I'd hurt him. "Are you injured?"

"No, I'm fine." His voice was weak and hoarse. "I'm just disoriented. I had to sleep after what happened."

"Teryn, I need to know everything. Sera said my brother attacked you."

"I don't know what came over him. I've never seen him like that before." He met my gaze, his eyes regaining their focus. "We knew this could happen, Cora. We knew coming back here might be too much for him."

"Too stressful, yes. But to the point where he attacks another person? I don't understand it. How did this happen?"

"We were in the Godskeep. I was joining him to pay respects to his wife. I told him I too had lost someone I love, and he pulled his sword on me. I wasn't trying to negate his loss with mentioning my own, but..." Tears pooled in his eyes. "I'm so sorry. I know you'd hoped he would remain of sound mind."

His words grated on my ears; I could make no sense of them. I turned to leave, but he took hold of my wrist. "Wait, didn't you have something you needed to tell me?"

I looked down at the hand grasping me, and it loosened.

Teryn moved it to my shoulder and brushed it along my arm. "I'm here for you, my dear. You know that, right?"

For one strange moment, I felt repulsed at his touch. I shook the feeling away. "I have to see my brother." Without another word, I raced down the hall. My heart quickened as I followed the all-too familiar path to the dungeon. I paused at the top of the stairs and took a deep breath. The last time I'd been on these stairs, I was fleeing for my freedom. I never thought I'd have to set foot there again.

The nearer I came to the dungeon hall, the more perplexed I felt. Waves of sound, like dozens of voices, echoed ahead. I opened the door, entered the hall, and gasped. Rows and rows of the usual cells were filled from wall to door with men. Faces looked up as I passed, voices quieting when they saw me. I pressed myself along the far wall as I walked, seeing every cell filled with the faces of strangers. Most wore clothing that seemed nothing more than soiled rags. Others wore clothes that nearly resembled a familiar shade of indigo.

"Is it you?" I looked toward the voice and saw a young

man with his face pressed against the bars of his door. I came to a stop before him.

"Who do you expect me to be?"

"It is you! You're the unicorn princess!" A rumble of exclamation echoed behind him, and men pressed toward the door to get a look.

"The unicorn princess?" I echoed.

"The lost princess who gathered the unicorns. You saved me."

"How did I save you?"

The young man pressed himself closer to the door and lifted a corner of his shirt. "Do you see anything here?"

I saw nothing but filthy flesh over his protruding ribs. "I see a man who is severely underfed."

"True. But there's more." He pulled his shirt over his shoulder. "What do you see there?"

"Nothing."

"Right. Nothing. Once there was a gaping wound." He pointed at his collar where a dark stain had spread from neck to elbow. "At one moment, I was fighting to my death. Then a unicorn came toward me and impaled me with his horn." He again pointed to his shirt, this time to a stain over his ribs and abdomen. "Blood spurted out everywhere. It should have led to my dying breath."

"I don't understand."

"Neither do I." He tapped the side of his head. "All I know is when I woke up, my mind was free."

I looked at the faces staring at me from within the cell, some nodding along with his story. "Why are you here?"

The young man shrugged. "Ask the men with the white rose."

"The white rose?" Sele's sigil came to mind. "Men from Sele brought you here?"

The man opened his mouth to speak, but another voice shouted over him. "Cora, is that you?"

I looked toward the sound at the end of the hall. "Dimetreus?" After running past more over-packed cells, I found my brother in a solitary cell of his own. He reached between the bars, and I clasped his hands, scanning him from head to toe for wounds. "What happened? Why are you in here?"

"It's Morkai. He did this."

His words pulled my own from my mouth. My throat felt dry. "Morkai?"

"He was in the Godskeep with me."

"Dimetreus, Teryn was in the Godskeep with you. Everyone is saying you attacked him."

My brother shook his head, teeth grinding. "He isn't Teryn, he's Morkai."

My jaw went slack as my eyes bore into his. I searched for reason, for truth. I let my power loosen, let it flow into my brother's mind, let myself feel what he was feeling.

I was struck with terror, conviction, and fury, and quickly pulled my power away. Whatever had happened, Dimetreus thought what he'd experienced in the Godskeep was the truth. He really had gone mad.

"You need to kill him. Kill Teryn."

I pulled away from the door. "You can't talk like that. I will not kill Teryn, and he is not Morkai. Morkai is dead."

"Coralaine, listen to me! That man is not Teryn." His

eyes were wild as he shouted, making my heart climb into my throat.

"What are you doing down here?" I turned and saw Lord Kevan coming my way, flanked by guards.

I ran to him. "Lord Kevan, my brother cannot be held in the dungeon. He is king."

"Oh? And where would you have me put a man who tried to murder your own betrothed?"

"In his room, heavily guarded. Anywhere but here."

Kevan ignored me. "For your own safety, get away from him and get out of here. Guards, escort her out."

I fought the hands that sought to guide me away, frantic as I tried to think of something to defend my brother. But what could I say? Could I promise he wasn't dangerous? After six years apart, was it possible I knew nothing of the damage to his mind?

I hung my head, tears streaming from my eyes as the guards urged me forward. Even the echoes of thanks I heard whispered from prisoners in one cell after the next couldn't lift my heart as I left the dungeon.

21

DECISIONS

Cora

I stormed into the great hall to find the council sitting at the head table. "Why are there men in the dungeon?"

Lord Kevan lifted his eyes from a stack of papers, a corner of his mouth lifting into a snarl. "Good of you to join us, Your Highness."

"Who are they, and why are they here?" The venom in my tone was obvious, yet Kevan remained unaffected.

"That's not why we called you to this meeting, Princess Coralaine."

"Did you think locking me in my room all night and morning would render me mute?"

Kevan continued to scan the papers before him. Lord Ulrich spoke in his stead. "We kept you there for your own well-being, Your Highness. It was clear what happened with your brother had you greatly distressed. We didn't want you to do anything that compromised your safety." While Ulrich was the gentler of the two brothers, I knew his kindness was merely an act.

I crossed my arms over my chest to calm the fire that burned through my limbs. "If you don't want me to endanger myself by seeking my brother, then you better answer my questions here and now."

Kevan's eyes met mine with a glare. "The men are prisoners of war, Your Highness. It is common after a battle to take hostages for questioning."

His condescending tone made me grind my teeth, but at least he was finally giving me answers. To show him my gratitude, I uncrossed my arms and took a seat at the table. "What is to be done with them?"

"We are questioning their loyalty. Those who prove loyal may return to their families. Those who prove to be what I *know* them to be will be executed."

I gripped the sides of my seat. "And what is it you know them to be?"

Kevan leaned toward me. "Traitors. Agents of evil. Is that not obvious?"

Ulrich clasped his hands and placed them on the table. "These were men from Morkai's Royal Force. We can't simply assume all of them were acting under mind-control as Dimetreus was."

"And with the most recent developments, I'm starting to doubt even that excuse is enough," Kevan muttered. The councilmen nodded their agreement.

I felt heat rise to my face as the back of my neck prickled with sweat. "These are men's lives you are talking about. Many of them are likely innocent!"

"Innocent?" Kevan spat. "You were on the battlefield, were you not? Would you call men who slaughtered your allies *innocent*? Would you call men who sided with Norun, calling your betrothed a murderer *innocent*? Would you call men who rise from the dead with sorcery *innocent*?"

I frowned. "What do you mean they rose from the dead?"

Kevan averted his gaze as if he'd said too much. I looked to his brother.

Ulrich let out an irritated sigh. "Many of the men in the dungeon were mortally wounded. They should have died. They appeared dead on the field. Yet they rose."

"And without any sign of a wound." I said the words under my breath and leaned back in my seat.

Kevan's head shot up. "How do you know about that?"

"I spoke to one of the men in the dungeon last night. But it isn't what you think. It isn't Morkai's magic that did that. I think it was the unicorns."

Ulrich and Kevan laughed, followed by mild chortling from the councilmen.

"I'm serious. I think the men who were wounded in battle by the unicorns were healed by the magic of their horns."

Kevan laughed even harder, tears pooling in the corners of his eyes. "That's the most ridiculous thing I've ever heard!"

Ulrich put his hand over his mouth to halt his laughter. "Come now, you must see how fantastic that sounds."

I looked from brother to brother. "Everyone knows unicorn horns hold great magic."

Kevan dabbed his eyes dry. "And what a convenience it is that the unicorns scattered and ran once the battle ended, leaving not even one to prove your theory."

"But it's true." I wanted to kick myself for how weak my voice came out.

"I'll tell you what, Your Highness. You find me a unicorn to test what you believe is true, and I will set the men free."

I felt the blood leave my face. There was no way I'd put Valorre—or any unicorn—in danger by exposing him to the uncles. But how else would I know if my theory was correct?

"Am I late?" I turned to see Teryn enter the room, surprised at the jovial expression he wore. Was I the only one concerned with what was happening in my castle?

"No, we were only speaking of light fare," Kevan said.

I shot him a scowl, which he returned with a smile. Teryn sat next to me and planted a kiss on my cheek.

"Let's get started, shall we?" Kevan said. "The urgent matter we must discuss is King Dimetreus' abdication."

"Abdication? What do you mean?" I asked.

Kevan paused and looked at me as if I were an aggravating child. "It was agreed upon that if Dimetreus proved unfit to rule, he would be forced to abdicate."

I looked at Teryn, whose face fell with sympathy. He placed his hand over mine. "It's true. It was one of the conditions we agreed to with King Verdian. Don't you remember?"

My heart sank. He was right.

Kevan continued. "However, the agreement was made with the assumption Princess Cora would already be married to Prince Teryn, which means we must proceed with your marriage contract immediately."

My mouth fell open as I sprang to my feet. "What? We were supposed to have a year!"

"A year if nothing went wrong," Kevan argued. "If you want to uphold the alliance with Sele and Mena, you will need to act according to the agreement you made."

"I don't understand. Why must we marry for the agreement to be valid? Can't I act as heir to Dimetreus? Rule Ridine as queen? Then in one year when Teryn and I marry, he will join me as king."

"That's not what you agreed on."

"But it makes sense. Verdian has made Mareleau his heir."

Ulrich cleared his throat, bringing my attention to him. "Verdian made Mareleau his heir for the sole reason that rule will pass to her husband, Larylis—a man she's already married to. Your situation cannot be compared to hers."

"Not to mention, a woman should never be made heir," Kevan said with disgust.

"That's uncalled for."

"That's the truth, Your Highness."

I opened my mouth to argue, but Teryn touched my shoulder. He stood and turned me so I was facing him and brought his face close to mine. "He's right, Cora. Making a woman heir is not common, and it could put your kingdom in danger. Not only would it break the agreement with Verdian, but it could make Kero vulnerable to outside kingdoms who wish to invade."

"Invade? Who would invade?"

"Have you forgotten Norun already, princess?" Kevan asked.

I ignored him and kept my eyes on Teryn. My chest felt tight. "We were supposed to have a year."

Teryn pressed his forehead to mine. "I know. I'm so

sorry this is happening faster than we wanted. Look at it this way, a year would have passed either way. Now it will pass with us being married. No one can tear us apart now. I never have to leave."

As much as I wanted his words to comfort me, they didn't. Everything was going wrong.

Teryn stepped away from me. His wide smile was in stark contrast to the turmoil I felt within. "I'm so happy to spend the rest of my life with you, starting now." He took another step away from me and bent down on one knee. "I know we are being forced to marry, regardless of whether I ask you or not, but I will anyway. Princess Coralaine of Kero, daughter of King Jeru and Queen Tiliane, will you marry me?"

My breath caught in my throat, and a sudden wave of sound and feeling pounded through my mind—agitated mutterings from Kevan, distracted thoughts from Ulrich, impatience from the councilmen. Thought upon thought crowded and grew, as if each man were screaming into my ears. Then there was Teryn. As I looked into his eyes, I awaited his thoughts of love and promise to flood my mind and send the rest scattering. Nothing came.

Teryn reached for my hand, and his lips pulled into a frown. "Cora, please say something. Don't you love me?"

I pulled my hand from his and fled the room.

ONCE OUTSIDE THE CASTLE, THE SOUNDS RECEDED FROM MY head and loosened their hold on my body. I breathed in deeply and let all the air escape my lungs. On feet that flew like the wind, I raced past the castle and into the forest beyond. Valorre came not a moment too soon, and before long we were racing between the trees as the tears dried from my cheeks.

Hours passed with me and my companion, and I relished the lack of words that were needed between us. With Valorre, I didn't need to explain myself, my fears, my pain, or my confusion. He was there for me either way, accepting me with all my flaws.

We'd come to rest on the cliff where I'd shown Teryn the view of my homeland, but I tried to keep my thoughts on anything else. It was easier said than done. "Valorre, I am to be married to Teryn."

Good. You love him.

My brows knit together. "I do, but...I feel like we still have much to learn about each other. Not to mention, I haven't told him the truth yet."

The truth you were hiding last time we were here.

Of course Valorre had been able to tell. "That's the one."

Tell him. He will understand.

"That's just it, I know he will understand, but what will he do about it? He was raised to be a ruler. The ways of royalty and succession are in his blood. He may love me, but if I can't provide him an heir, I can't be queen."

Silly rule.

"I know." I fell back on the sun-warmed grass and inhaled its fresh aroma. "If I tell him now, I'm not sure what will happen to Kero. Rule only passes to Teryn through his marriage to me. My brother has been cast aside. What would happen if I am too? Will Teryn be allowed to remain King of Kero without me as his wife? If not, then who will rule in our stead?" A vision came to me of Kevan and Ulrich, licking their lips, hungry for power. I shook the thought from my mind.

What will you do?

"I don't know. I wish more than anything that I could talk with Salinda. I miss her so much. And Maiya. Maybe I never should have left them."

An aching filled my chest. I sank into my pain of longing, imagining their faces. I let thoughts of the Forest People's camp fill my mind and senses, until it was as if I were there, walking past tents and cook fires, breathing in the scents of roasting meat, the gathering of aromatic herbs, the turning of soil, and brewing of tinctures. I imagined I saw a familiar tent, patterned scarves blowing in the warm, gentle breeze. A smile took over my face, and I raced to the tent and peeled the curtained door aside.

Salinda turned to me, eyes wide and lips turned up in a smile. "Well, this is new."

I cocked my head to the side. "You can see me? Am I really here, or am I imagining this?"

"You tell me."

I looked around the tent, so familiar, so reminiscent of the word *home*. Even more deserving of the title was Salinda herself. I gathered her petite frame into my arms, realizing how long it had been since I'd hugged someone smaller than I, and cried into her shoulder. "I missed you so much."

She stroked her hand along my back. "I missed you too."

"I'm so sorry I never came to find you after the battle. I never thanked our people. I never made sure you were safe. I never helped tend our wounded or bury our dead."

She pulled away. "Cora, you don't need to thank us. We knew what we were doing. Don't think for a moment we'd hold it against you that you didn't come back. Of course you didn't!"

I wiped the tears from my cheeks. "I could have chosen to come back. I could have left my royal life behind."

"You made your choice long before the battlefield. You will always have a home here, but your duty and your destiny lie elsewhere."

I lowered my head. "I'm not sure about that. Sometimes I think I never should have left you to begin with."

Salinda motioned toward her cot. "Come, tell me your pains."

We sat side-by-side, and I laid my head on her shoulder. I felt like I was ten again, seeking comfort with the woman who'd rescued me from my lone wanderings.

"I'm being forced to marry a man I love, but I'm afraid our marriage won't last."

"Why would you think that?"

I raised my head and looked into her dark-brown eyes. "Morkai took something from me. Something I can never get back."

Salinda remained silent and waited for me to explain.

I looked away, eyes unfocused. "When I was a child, he poisoned my womb so I couldn't have children. He has stripped me of my womanhood."

"Is that the truth? Since you cannot have children you are no longer a woman?"

I hesitated. "Not in a true sense."

"Is Nalia less than a woman because she can no

longer have children? What about me? I've had only one child, and it's safe to say I am fertile no longer."

Heat flushed my cheeks as I lowered my eyes to the floor. "I understand what you are saying. But you and Nalia have gone from maiden, to mother, to crone. How can I go from maiden to crone and still feel like a woman?"

"It isn't every woman's fate to become a mother. I can name plenty of us who have lived full lives from maiden to crone, never taking on the task of mother."

Her words calmed the tension in my shoulders, but there was still so much she didn't understand. "Salinda, these principles work amongst the Forest People, and even with the common folk. But I was born into royalty and am to marry a man who will be king. Since I cannot have children, I cannot provide him an heir. Therefore, I cannot be queen in the first place. Everything I've done has been for nothing."

"Has it truly been for nothing? Was it worth nothing to stop a sorcerer from taking over Lela? Was it worth nothing to fall in love?"

Again, I was embarrassed at the ignorance of my words.

She continued. "And what about these rules? You may have been born into them, but you weren't *made* under them. You were made to love and to be loved. If your love isn't enough, then that is a flaw in the rules, not you. Never let the rules of the world break your spirit or define your worth."

My eyes met hers and filled with tears. "I feel so split in two. Everything you're saying makes sense, but when

I'm at Ridine it's like none of that matters to anyone but me."

Salinda took my hands in hers. "You have to remember why it matters to you and let that be strong enough. Why did you go back to your old life? Answer from your heart."

I closed my eyes and took a few deep breaths. "To serve my kingdom and the land of Lela. To help my brother."

"Yes. You felt you had a service to give. You followed that service from a space of love, and you must always follow that."

"What if it isn't enough for the people I serve?"

"Our acts of service aren't always met with the responses we desire, and it isn't up to us how we are received. We follow the path we feel in our hearts we must follow and give where we feel called to give. Not all our gifts are accepted or rewarded, and that isn't the reason we give. We give because it is our way to bring light into the world around us. If the world answers you with darkness, don't respond with darkness. Respond with more light."

Her words lifted a weight off my heart, and it felt as if I remembered who I truly was. A piece of me that I'd somehow buried after the battle was now glowing bright within. "Thank you, Salinda."

"Always remember why you do what you do, and never forget how your power grows."

I wrapped her in a hug, trying not to squeeze her tiny bones with the force of my gratitude. When we parted, I kept my eyes on her face, studying every curve, color, and crease. It was all I could do to keep from admitting it was time for me to return.

Salinda seemed to know the truth without my confession. "I'm so happy to see how you've grown. I love you, my dear child."

"I love you too." I closed my eyes on the pool of happy tears, and thought about the grass on my back, the rush of air through the Ridine Mountains, and the breeze through the dense forest. I opened my eyes and found Valorre standing over me, and I wondered if everything I'd just experienced had been a dream. *Does it matter? Dream or no, it held a truth I needed to hear.*

I stood and pressed my face into Valorre's neck.

You feel better.

I nodded. "I'm ready."

22

PROMISES

Teryn

I woke with a gasp into blinding white light. I closed my eyes and thought of Emylia's temple room until I no longer felt the light burning behind my eyelids. The sound of footsteps brought my attention to Emylia, who knelt at my side.

"What happened?"

"You lost touch with your vitale." Her face was stern, but her voice was soft. "You've been resting ever since."

I sat up, swaying side to side with every move. "How long ago was that?"

"I don't know. I've been at your side the entire time, making sure you get the rest you need." I opened my mouth to ask another question, but she held up a hand to quiet me. "First, you need to check in with your vitale."

Her admonition sent a ripple of irritation through me, but I forced myself to breathe steadily while I sought contact with my outer functions. My heart beat steadily, air filled my lungs, and blood rushed through my veins in smooth rhythm. Once I'd fully connected to my vitale, I let my mind wander to what I last remembered. *Morkai in the Godskeep wearing my face. Dimetreus kneeling. Morkai taunting. A sword unsheathed. Dimetreus arrested.*

The memories made my heart quicken, but I willed myself to calm. "What has Morkai done since?"

Emylia gave a slight shrug of one shoulder. "Like I said, I stayed with you the entire time."

"Why? I'm the least of my worries. Morkai is following some dark plan. What if he's done something worse?"

She put a hand on my arm, and I felt the familiar buzzing resistance that had come to replace touch. "You need to remain calm."

I stood and stepped away from her. "What good will that do? I've done nothing but try to remain calm, to stay in touch with my vitale, to lie in bed within my own body. What have I accomplished? You said you were helping me."

"I am. It will take time. Once you can connect both to your vitale and your cereba—"

"Why are you helping me, anyway? I've been doing everything you say yet I'm still powerless. I don't know anything about you. How do I know you're really trying to help?"

She crossed her arms. "If you don't know anything about me, it is only because you've hardly asked. I'm helping you because I wouldn't wish my fate on anyone else. I don't need to know you to want to help you get out of this place."

I rubbed my hands over my face and felt the tension

begin to melt away. "I'm sorry. It's just that I'm terrified for the people I love."

"I understand."

"I need to get out of here. I must get my body back."

She turned away and began to pace across the room, hand cupping the bottom of her chin. "Instead of following Morkai around and trying to figure out his plans, maybe we should try to get you more practice connecting to your cereba instead."

"Yes, I'm ready to do something. *Anything* but wait around. Can we start now?"

Her eyes met mine. "We can try. Morkai is awake, which will make it nearly impossible to gain control over your cereba, but you can at least practice."

"I don't care about impossible. I want to *do* something."

"If you lose touch with your vitale again..."

"I won't. I promise I'll stay calm."

Emylia studied my face, as if trying to decide if she could trust such a promise. "Fine. But don't you dare get irritated at me when I remind you to check in with yourself."

"Agreed."

I kept my breathing steady as the temple room melted into the more muted canvas that was Ridine's great hall. The darkness outside the touch of lantern light told me it was night. At the head table sat the men of the council. Morkai was walking toward them with a leisurely sway in his steps. "She has accepted."

"Good, where is she?" Kevan asked.

"She's getting ready. A queen deserves to dress her best for her wedding night, am I correct?"

"Her wedding night will consist of signing a contract and retiring to her wedding bed, nothing more. She best not have expectations for fanfare."

Morkai waved his hand dismissively. "Of course not." He approached the table and smiled at Kevan. "By the way, when will Princess Coralaine be crowned? I suppose, while we're at it, when will I?"

Kevan narrowed his eyes at him and then looked away. "The people of Kero must not know what has happened between you and the king. It is peace we are trying to bring them, and trust in their rulers. Anything less could mean chaos."

"Which means," Ulrich said, "your marriage to Princess Coralaine must come before we announce Dimetreus' abdication, so that it seems a natural progression of events. We want to give the people no reason to fear what happens in Ridine. Once you are married and Dimetreus' abdication is made public, we will reopen court in celebration of your and Coralaine's coronation ceremony."

Morkai's jaw shifted back and forth. "When will that be, might I ask?"

"Within a month's time, I'm sure." Ulrich's words gave me no relief as Morkai's plan became clear. He was going to marry my betrothed and inherit Kero through her.

I felt Emylia's hand wrap firmly around my arm. She didn't need to say a word for me to realize I was getting worked up and losing touch with my vitale. I reconnected and turned to her. "What's the plan?"

"This isn't going to be easy. The only way you can try to connect to your cereba is to step into place with your body like you do when he's sleeping."

Wasting no time, I stepped toward my body. Fighting the buzzing resistance, I pushed forward until I was aligned. I put my hands where my body's hands were and planted my feet within the space of my shoes.

"You must do your best to move as one, to feel your surroundings, to be aware of the lantern light warming your skin, the rough surface of the table beneath your palms."

I did my best to follow her instructions, but each time I found myself in alignment with my body, Morkai would shift, and even the slightest movement was a challenge to keep up with.

"There she is. Let's get on with this." Lord Kevan's words distracted me.

Morkai turned and walked toward the other end of the hall, leaving me behind. I found myself unable to move as I watched Cora enter dressed in her blue gown—the one she wore when we had dinner in the gardens at Verlot. Her face showed no emotion as Lady Sera escorted her toward Morkai.

Emylia walked alongside Morkai, and I found myself pulled forward as well.

"You look beautiful." Morkai stopped before Cora and lifted a hand to her cheek. Cora responded with a smile that didn't reach her eyes. He looked past her face and down to her toes. As his eyes lifted and hovered over her chest, I found my blood racing. Emylia shot me a knowing look.

"I love this dress on you," Morkai said.

"It may not be a wedding gown, but it's my nicest dress."

"It suits you." Morkai held out his arm, and Cora took

hold. Remembering my mission, I fell back into step with my body, feeling heat flood my chest as my own arm linked through Cora's. The buzzing between our touch was stronger than anything I'd felt with my ethera before.

Cora's chest heaved the nearer we came to the table. She looked my way, and I looked back at her, the movement syncing perfectly with that of my own body. Her face flooded with a smile that made her entire face glow. My own smile mirrored hers, and I wondered if she could see it.

We approached the table, and Morkai turned forward before I did. I watched as Cora's face went pale, the smile falling from her lips as she looked at the contract with wide eyes.

My own movements became jagged as I struggled to stay in line with my body. Morkai leaned across the table, grabbed a quill, and hovered over the bottom of the document.

As he paused, I took my chance to catch up, breathing deep as I felt the smooth quill between my fingers, the weight balancing between the nib and feather. I felt the rough parchment beneath the palm of my other hand, and followed as my fingers lowered, bringing the nib closer and closer to the paper. As it made contact, I watched the ink spread from one tiny droplet into a flowing line. I felt the ease of control as I slid the nib straight down. Then I lifted it and moved it back to the top on the line, preparing to drag it diagonally to form the second line of the letter *M*—the letter that would reveal the identity of the man who wore my body.

I brought my hand down in a smooth motion and

froze. The hand of my body remained where I'd left it, at the top of the inky black line, trembling.

"What's wrong, Teryn?" Cora's voice shook my attention, and in that moment, Morkai crossed the nib over the top of the line and formed a *T,* quickly followed by the remaining letters in my name.

Morkai looked at Cora. "Nothing, my dear, just savoring this wonderful moment." He handed her the quill. "Your turn."

I didn't have the heart to return to my body as I stared down at my name, a near-perfect imitation of my true signature. Cora bent over the contract and placed hers next to it. As much as I'd anticipated the day I'd see our signatures side-by-side like this, now I wished we'd never been promised in the first place. I would have taken back every moment of joy we'd shared over our engagement just to save her this fate. Cora was now married to a man with my name and face, but with Morkai's dark soul.

And I couldn't do a thing to stop it.

Cora

My hands trembled as I paced back and forth in my room. With no better space available to serve as my wedding chamber, we'd be spending our first night as husband and wife in the master chamber—the room that would now become *our* room.

A knock sounded on my door, and I jumped, gripping a hand over my chest. I felt the blood leave my face and sink to my toes, leaving me with weak knees as I opened the door. A breath of relief escaped my throat as Mareleau greeted me from the other side.

"What are you doing here?" My voice held an obvious tremor.

"I'm helping you undress on your wedding night."

I looked down at myself, almost surprised to see I was still fully dressed, then let her enter the room. "Why you? Why not Sera?"

She looked around, assessing her surroundings with a wrinkle of her nose, then returned her eyes to mine. "Well, Kevan came to fetch Sera. I was appalled to hear you'd denied a procession to your wedding bed."

"Why would I agree to such a thing? It's ridiculous."

Mareleau put a hand on her hip. "I thought the same thing but was forced into it regardless. Needless to say, I was jealous to hear you'd gotten your way where I had not." She motioned for me to turn around so she could work on loosening my laces. "However, I realized your wedding was just as pitiful as my own. You didn't even get a feast afterward!"

"A feast is the last thing on my mind."

"I know. Even with the one you love, this is still a strange experience. So I figured I'd come along and make it worse for you."

I tried to laugh but could find no spirit to do so. "I know how you feel now."

She paused. "What do you mean?"

"About the baby. You aren't ready. Neither am I."

She sighed and resumed her duty. "I had almost ten years to be in love with Larylis. Even after knowing him that long, I was still nervous on our wedding night. I can't imagine how you must feel after only mere months. Besides, it's *Teryn*."

The disgust in her voice was enough to make my lips curl up slightly. "Why do you say that?"

Mareleau slid my loosened gown over my head and began to take down my hair, brow furrowed. "I don't know. Sometimes I really like him. He seems like someone I'd enjoy calling my brother. Other times...he's really touchy, isn't he?"

"Touchy?"

"I don't like being hugged or touched by strangers, especially men. Maybe that's all."

I looked up at her, feeling like I was seeing her for the first time. We'd never spoken more than a few tense sentences before, and never with so much honesty. In that one simple statement, I saw the wounded girl she was hiding inside, felt the pain of betrayal, and the fiery instinct of survival. I pulled my power away, realizing how far my empathy had reached.

My mind shifted back to what she'd said about Teryn being *touchy*, and I felt my stomach churn. Once I was undressed to my nightgown and my hair was in loose waves down my back, Mareleau left.

I sat on the bed and looked down at my hands. *Tonight is the night I tell him the truth. This can go no further.* I'd tried to tell him the truth when I had returned from the forest, but it did no good.

The door opened without a knock and in walked Teryn carrying two goblets and a bottle of wine. He was dressed in nothing but trousers and a white, un-tucked undershirt, with a hint of gold chain peeking above the collar. I'd never known him to wear a necklace, but my unshakable awareness of my own state of undress over-rode my curiosity.

Teryn didn't seem concerned as he gave me a wink and began to fill our cups with wine. He handed me one, and we drank in silence. I remained focused on the wall ahead of me, trying to ignore Teryn's burning stare. It suddenly occurred to me he may already be adept at what happened on one's wedding night.

He took my empty cup, and I shook my head when he asked if he should refill it. After draining a second goblet for himself, he set it down and sat beside me on the bed. His hand reached behind my neck and his lips darted toward my face.

Before he could make contact, I stood and stepped away from the bed. "Teryn, I have to tell you something before this goes any further."

His shoulders fell, and he looked at me as if I were a silly child. "Dear Cora, all talk can wait. We have a marriage to proceed with."

"That's what I want to talk to you about, and you promised you'd listen."

He stood and came toward me with open arms. I put my hands between us, and he paused, frowning. "This is our wedding night, the time for us to express our love. You agreed—"

"I agreed to sign the contract. Our wedding isn't final until we..." I swallowed hard before finishing my sentence, "consummate. And I won't do that until you hear me out."

Teryn returned to the bed and patted the space next to him. "Come, my dear."

With a shudder, I sat next to him. "I'm barren." The

words came out in a rush, but once they were out of my mouth, I felt the tension slip away. I sat straighter and met his eyes. "I can't provide you an heir. Morkai made it so when I was a child."

Teryn's face remained still as I waited for his reaction. He tilted his head to the side as his expression melted into sympathy. "You poor thing. No wonder you wanted to tell me so badly. You must have been worried I wouldn't want to marry you."

"Do you?"

"Yes, of course. I love you." He leaned in again, his breath smelling heavily of wine. My head swam from my own cup as I felt his lips touch mine. I tried to enjoy it, tried to burn with the desire I wanted so badly to feel. Instead, I felt my stomach sink as every inch of my body revolted against his touch. I stood. "I can't do this."

Teryn closed his eyes and clenched his jaw. "What more do you need from me? I told you I love you. I told you I accept you as you are, barren and all."

"I need more time. I'm not ready."

He stood and brought his face close to mine. "If you loved me, you would do this."

I felt fire move down my arms, tingling my fingertips. "If you loved me, you wouldn't ask me to."

He brought one hand to my cheek and the other wrapped around my waist. Before he could pull me closer, my hands struck his stomach, power radiating from my palms as I sent him back onto the bed.

He lay still, and I felt torn between anger and concern. *I used my power on the man I love.* As I approached the bed, I saw the gold chain had spilled over his collar, making me wonder what hung from the end still tucked within his shirt.

Teryn's eyes shot open and found my face. "You have to go. Now. Run." His voice sounded strained, and his body remained immobile.

I jumped back. "What are you saying?"

"Go! Get out of here!"

I turned my back on him and ran from the room, hearing his laughter behind me as he called me back to him. "I'm kidding," he shouted. "Come back, my love. I thought we were playing."

I closed my eyes and pressed his voice from my mind, instead focusing on the walls and shadows in the hall. My power wrapped around me easily as I stormed away. A sudden thought made me pause and look down at myself, realizing I was still in my nightdress. My dresses and cloaks remained in my room with Teryn.

Without a second thought, I went to Mareleau's door and knocked. I heard Mareleau curse as Breah opened the door. "Your Highness?"

I brushed Breah aside and found Mareleau on her lounge. She stood when she saw me. "What in Lela—"

"I need to borrow your riding cloak."

Her mouth fell open. "Why mine? You have your own."

I ignored her and went to a table where I found a quill, ink, and parchment. After scribbling my list, I handed it to her. "I said I'd help you. There are the herbs you need for the problem you have. Now, please, help me too."

A moment later, I was back in the hall, creeping into

shadows with Mareleau's gray, wool cloak and a promise of silence. Once outside the castle, I ran for the trees, seeing a flash of white reflecting under the moonlight. Tears clouded my vision as I mounted the unicorn and looked back at the castle looming against the night sky. This would be the last time I'd flee Ridine. "I'm done here. Take me home, Valorre."

23

MEMORIES

Teryn

I slid to my knees, gasping for shallow, shaking breaths. My heart raced, and no matter how much I concentrated on it, my connection to my vitale felt weak.

Emylia put a hand on my shoulder. "You did well, Teryn. As much as I doubted the possibility, you were able to control your cereba at least twice. I saw what you did with the quill."

I shook my head. "It did no good."

"If she listened to your words, it got her to run."

I stood on trembling legs. "What if she didn't? What if she only left to clear her head? What if he's going after her right now?"

"You did your best. That's all you can do. There are so many things you have no control over."

"Like what he did to her? Making her barren? No wonder she got upset when I brought up children." I pressed my fingers over my eyes, suppressing the frustrated moan that threatened to spew forth. "Why would he do that to her? She said he did it when she was just a child."

Emylia's face went blank, and she turned away from me. "I know exactly why. It was my fault."

"What do you mean?"

She turned her head to look at me, a shimmering tear running down her cheek, but gave me no answer.

My chest heaved with the effort it took me to keep my voice level. "Tell me what you know."

Her eyes were wide and empty. "It's better if I show you."

THE TEMPLE ROOM FELL BENEATH A SHEER BLANKET OF FOG. When it dissipated, the tapestries and furnishings had become muted in color and clarity, while the light coming in from the windows seemed to shift between mid-day and early evening, then back again. I couldn't tell the season, as I felt no warmth, wind, or chill in the air.

Emylia squinted at her surroundings as she paced the perimeter of the room. "Memories are hazier than real things outside the crystal, or things I shape within it." She put her hands behind her back, then moved to stand in front of a wall. I joined her.

The door opened and in walked another version of Emylia. She appeared to be a year or two younger than the Emylia I knew, but perhaps it was her carefree smile, the light in her eyes, and the buoyancy of her steps that made her seem so youthful. Her hair and dress were similar, although more subdued than the Emylia who stood next to me.

I turned my head and saw longing in Emylia's eyes as she watched the memory of herself walk into the room, arms full of books. I turned my attention back to the door as a tall, older woman with brown skin and dark-brown, short-cropped hair entered behind the girl.

"He says he's from Syrus. Seems to be about the same age as you," the older woman said. Her accent was like Emylia's. "He has been at the library every day this week, brimming with questions. An intelligent young man with insatiable curiosity."

The Emylia of memory set her books next to her bed and turned back toward the woman. "What would you like me to do, Mother Calla?"

"I don't think this young man's answers can easily be found in books, yet he spends all day in our library. He needs a channel, I need him out of our library, and you need to hone your skills."

Emylia's eyes brightened. "You mean I can practice channeling for someone outside of Temple?"

"Yes. I believe you are ready. As curious as this young man is, his search seems harmless, yet will provide you a challenge."

Emylia cocked her head to the side. "What is he asking about?"

"The Ancient Realm."

Her mouth fell open and her eyes bulged with dismay. "I want to discover great mysteries of our existence, speak to the spirits of the soil and air, not muse over children's tales."

Mother Calla smiled. "Perhaps you will prove the Ancient Realm isn't a tale after all."

Emylia pushed out her bottom lip and crossed her arms over her chest.

Mother Calla continued. "To become a Temple Priestess, you'll need to hone your skill. I won't have you practicing on strangers if you can't start small."

Emylia rolled her eyes. "Fine, I'll see him."

The image stilled, and the fog swirled around the room and began to reshape it. It formed a cobblestone street lined with narrow homes and storefronts, bathed in shadow and moonlight. There a hooded Emylia walked, feet silent despite her hurried pace.

The image shifted again to show her entering the door of an inn before the fog swept it away and formed a candlelit room. Here the image remained, as it took clearer shape, showing a filthy cot in one corner next to a tiny desk. Emylia entered the room, tossing back her hood as a young man closed the door behind them. She turned toward the man. "I'm Emylia, Temple Maiden."

The young man looked to be my age with porcelain skin, dark eyes, high cheekbones, and black, shoulder-length hair. "I'm Desmond. I see they sent me a Maiden instead of a Priestess."

Emylia's eyes were hard. "You must not have paid enough. Shall I go?"

Desmond looked down his nose at her. "You'll do for now. Take a seat and we can get started." He extended his arm toward the chair at the desk.

Emylia circled him, burning him with a piercing stare, before sitting down. With no other chair in the room, Desmond knelt at the opposite side of the desk.

I looked to the Emylia at my side. "Why are you showing me this? Who is Desmond, and what does this have to do with Cora?"

She turned to me slowly, as if she longed to keep her eyes on the memory. "You'll see." We turned back to the scene before us and watched as the Emylia of the memory reached into her cloak pocket and brought out a purple crystal that nearly filled her palm.

"What's that?" Desmond asked, eyes brightening.

"It helps me channel. It was a gift from my mother, who was a Temple Priestess."

"Was?"

Emylia scowled. "Was. Many years ago. Now what is it you want to know?"

Desmond took a deep breath. "Where is the Ancient Realm?"

Emylia smirked but resigned to closing her eyes. She breathed deeply and steadily for a few moments, grasping the crystal in both hands. "Where is the Ancient Realm?" she whispered. Her lips and eyelids fluttered while the rest of her remained still as stone. When she next spoke, her voice came out in a strong, emotionless tone. "All around. Here but not here."

She sat in silence a few moments more, then opened her eyes with an exasperated grumble. "I'm not getting anything more than that. I feel...things, but I don't understand what they mean."

Desmond's eyes were wide, a glint of excitement in them. "Keep going."

She shook her head. "I need more information from you first. I never knew of the Ancient Realm as anything more than a fairy tale. What does it mean to you?"

His face went blank. "I can't say."

Her expression softened. "Look, I can only help you if you trust me. I'm surprised I got as much as I did, considering my skepticism. But what I'm seeing is taking me in too many different directions. I need to know what *you* know if you want me to find answers."

Desmond opened his mouth, then snapped it shut. At a raised eyebrow from Emylia, he said, "You can't tell anyone what I tell you."

Emylia nodded.

"Fine. My father sent me. He's the one looking for it, not me. He says it has another name, but all he can remember is the Ancient Realm. I think he's under some kind of curse that is keeping him from it."

Emylia's eyes went unfocused. "That's it. There are multiple realms that are called *ancient*. I need to know the one your father is looking for."

"The realm of the Elvan and the Faeran. That's all I know."

She stood, stuffing the crystal back in her pocket. "I'm sorry. I wish I could have done more."

He rubbed a hand over his face, showing a previously hidden exhaustion. "I'll keep looking in the library. I'll find out what the Ancient Realm is called."

She brushed past the desk and reached for the door. Desmond stood and grabbed her other hand. His face looked less severe than it had before, almost gentle. "Will you help me?"

Emylia's brows knit together. "You want me to come back?"

"And perhaps you can join me in the library?"

Her lips twitched, as if fighting against a smile. "All right."

The fog flooded the room once again, forming image after image in rapid succession, as if representing the passing of many days. I saw Emylia and Desmond reading in the library, followed by another scene of them sharing a smile from across a long table. Then they were elbowing each other playfully as they walked side by side down the cobblestone street. Finally, a kiss was exchanged over the desk in the bedroom at the inn.

I averted my eyes for a moment, feeling as if I was viewing something far too private. When I looked back at the memories, they had shifted yet again.

Emylia flung open Desmond's door and found him at his desk inspecting a book. He jumped and slammed the book shut. Emylia wore a puzzled expression as she looked from Desmond to the book he was shoving beneath a stack of papers. "What are you reading?"

"Nothing," Desmond said. "What is it? You look like you're in a happy mood."

Emylia seemed to forget the book as she came to Desmond's side, taking his face in her hands. He wrapped his arms around her waist as he stared up at her, a crooked smile on his lips. "I found it," she whispered.

"Found what?"

"I know what the Ancient Realm is called. It's El'Ara." Her voice shook with excitement.

Desmond stood and took her by the shoulders. "Are you serious? Should we try again?"

"That's why I came here, isn't it?"

"That, and because you love me." Desmond leaned in and kissed her. Emylia giggled as she pulled him away from the desk and took his place in the chair. Like before, Desmond knelt on the other side.

Emylia brought her crystal between her palms, closed her eyes, and breathed deep. "Go ahead, Des."

Desmond kept his voice low and steady. "Where is El'Ara?"

"All around. Here but not here."

His jaw twitched. "How does one get to El'Ara?"

Her eyelids fluttered, eyes rolling side to side behind them. "So long as the veil remains, the blood of Darius cannot enter El'Ara."

"The veil? What is the veil?"

Emylia remained silent.

He tried a different question. "Can the veil be destroyed?"

"Where the veil abandoned its heart, one will be born that will stop the blood of Darius. Only then will the veil be torn."

A sheen of sweat spread over his forehead. "Who is this you speak of? Who will stop the blood of Darius?"

"The blood of Ailan will unite the land by royal birth and magic right and return El'Ara's heart."

His hands began to shake. "Who is the blood of Ailan?"

Emylia paused, head bobbing slightly side to side. "You will know him by his mother."

"Who is his mother?"

"Beauty of Satsara. Right by magic and blood. The unicorn will signify her awakening. Foreigners will flood the land. The heart of El'Ara will unite as one. Her son will be born under the house of the black mountain."

"What is the house of the black mountain?"

"A black mountain over a field of violets."

Desmond stood and paced back and forth. His face was red, and his eyes were bulging. "Where can I find the mother? When will her son be born? Where is this field of violets? Who are Satsara and Ailan?"

Emylia began to tremble, and her voice came out weak and strained. "Desmond, that's too much."

Desmond stopped pacing and stared at her, tapping a finger on the side of his chin while his foot pounded an echo on the floor. When he stilled, an icy calm passed over his face. "It isn't El'Ara he needs," he muttered. "Not for what he needs to do. It's the power of the Morkaius."

He returned to kneeling at the desk. "Can one claim the power of the Morkaius without entering El'Ara? Can one become Morkaius of *this* world?"

Emylia shifted in her seat, shaking her head. "I don't like this. The answer feels like it's coming from darkness."

"Tell me."

She shuddered, and her voice regained its steady tone. "To gain the power of the Morkaius, one must first become Morkai by right of magic and blood. One must rule the land that was once El'Ara's heart and harness the magic that seeps there."

Desmond's face broke into a grin. He grabbed paper, ink, and quill from the desk and began to write. "Rule the land by right of magic and blood," he said under his breath. "Harness the magic."

"He who harnesses the magic will be destroyed by it."

His eyes shot to Emylia, and he pursed his lips until they nearly turned white. With a roar, he got to his feet and swept his arms across the desk, sending books, ink, and paper flying. Emylia opened her eyes and let out a cry, backing away from him as he stood, chest heaving, surrounded by the last of the fluttering papers. Silence enveloped the room while the two remained motionless.

"What's wrong with you?" Emylia finally shouted. "You could have hurt me, forcing me out of a channel like that!"

As his eyes met hers, his face twisted, and a sob escaped his throat. Emylia ran to his side as he fell to his knees. "I'm trying. I'm trying to do what Father asked of me."

Her face softened as she knelt next to him and let him put his head in her lap. "You did your best. Perhaps he will be able to make more sense of the answers."

Desmond's breaths were wracked with sobs. "He has to. My father must become Morkaius."

"Why? What does that even mean?" Emylia brushed her hand over his hair.

"It's the only way he can bring my mother back."

"Your mother?"

Desmond turned his head in her lap until their eyes met. "She's gone, like yours."

Emylia paused, her hand hovering over his head. "Desmond, no one can bring someone back from the dead."

He sat up and faced her. "The Morkaius can as ruler over Ancient magic. My father promised me he will."

Emylia's eyes were wide as she leaned away from him. "But how? You heard the words. He who harnesses the magic will be destroyed by it."

"Father will find a way. Either that or he will find this mother of prophecy and end her." Desmond's eyes were wild as he stared unblinking at Emylia. "Whether of this world or El'Ara, my father *will* become Morkaius."

The image dissipated like smoke drifting into the wind, bringing us back to the temple room within the crystal. I pressed my fingers against the sides of my head, trying to comprehend everything I'd witnessed. "I don't understand. Are you trying to tell me Cora was supposed to be this mother of prophecy? How? Those words could have been about anyone."

"*Right by magic and blood.* What does that mean to you?"

I shrugged.

"It means she will be both magic and royal. Sound like anyone you know?"

I nodded and thought of what else Emylia had channeled. *The unicorn will signify her awakening. Foreigners will flood the land.* Valorre and the Battle at Centerpointe Rock came to mind. Even the part about *the heart of El'Ara uniting as one* could have referred to the Tri-Kingdom Peace Pact, if I were to believe the *heart* represented Lela. "I can see where Cora fits in, but how could Morkai have known these things in order to hurt her before the events even happened?"

"One simple statement was all he had to work with, and it took him years to puzzle over. However, it shouldn't be hard for you. Think, Teryn. What is the black mountain over a field of violets?"

"I've never seen such a place."

"But you've seen such a sigil."

A flash of purple struck my mind—a banner hanging over the head table in Ridine's great hall. *The black mountain of Kero.*

24

EL'ARA

Cora

Stillness grabbed my attention, prompting me to open my eyes. I lifted my head from Valorre's neck and blinked into the early morning light. The movement made me wince; my body was sore from sleeping while riding.

I slid from Valorre's back and looked around, finding us in a lush, grassy area surrounded by towering willows with twisting branches and waterfalls of leaves swaying in the warm breeze. A sea of vibrant, green grass came nearly to my knees, and flowers of every shade I could imagine freckled the landscape. Other than that, the place was empty. I turned to Valorre. "Why have we stopped? I don't see any sign of the Forest People."

Valorre seemed agitated, although it wasn't at me. *Confused.*

"What are you confused about?"

You said take us home. I tried.

I sighed. "It isn't your fault. If I hadn't been crying like a baby all night I would have been better help in finding them. We can rest here and try again now that I have my wits about me."

Valorre's ears began to twitch.

I put my hand on his side. "What's wrong?"

My mistake.

"I told you, it's not your fault."

I took us home.

I wanted to say something to soothe him, but I couldn't understand why he was so upset. Every muscle in his body began to quiver, and his gaze seemed locked somewhere beyond the willow grove. I followed the direction, peering beneath branches, until I spotted a pair of watching eyes.

My breath caught in my throat as I saw a tiny frame with sun-browned skin, long, dark hair, and dark-brown eyes staring back at me from under a tree. *Salinda!* But the longer I looked, the more unsettled I grew. How could I see such dark eyes from so far away? With a shudder, I realized the eyes locked with mine were unnaturally large.

Still, I made no move. *Who are you?* I projected my power, let it seep toward the figure, probing around her and sensing whether friend or threat awaited. I received a feeling of warmth mixed with something I'd never experienced before, followed by a jolt of surprise coming from the figure.

The tiny form came forward, and I looked at Valorre. "Do you know who this person is?"

Familiar, was all he said.

As the figure neared, I realized my first instinct wasn't too far off. It appeared to be a petite woman, much like Salinda in terms of hair and skin tone, yet with huge, almond-shaped eyes the color of cinnamon over a tiny nose, and lips like a new rosebud. Her forehead was wide and round, while her chin was dainty. I'd never seen anyone like her.

My heart quickened as she stood just steps away from me, her head falling below the height of my chest. "Hello," I said with a slight tremble. "My name is Cora. I think we may be lost."

She responded in words I couldn't understand, but her voice was gentle.

"I'm sorry, I can't understand you."

She gave me a knowing look, tapped the side of her head, then pointed at me.

She wants to talk. Like you do with me, Valorre said.

I looked from him to the woman, a rush of excitement and apprehension spreading over me. "How does she know I can do that?"

She felt your power when you used it on her.

I took a deep breath, extended my power, and addressed the woman. "Can you understand me?"

This time when she answered, I heard both the words in her strange language and the meaning behind them. "Yes. My name is Illian."

Proud satisfaction swelled in my chest. "I didn't know I could do that."

"You are human with human magic. Very strange. How did you get here?"

"I don't even know where we are. Valorre brought us."

She furrowed her paper-thin brows as she looked from me to the unicorn. "Valorre? He is from your world?"

I tilted my head to the side. "My world?" I turned to Valorre. "Do you know what she means?"

Again, he rippled with agitation. *My mistake. I brought us home.*

The meaning behind his words dawned on me, making my chest feel tight. "You mean *your* home?" I looked back at the woman. "Where am I?"

"El'Ara." Her words brought no double meaning to explain what they meant.

"I've never heard of such a place." Sweat began to pool under my arms. "Valorre, I thought you didn't remember where your home was?"

I didn't. I don't understand.

Illian's face softened. "He's come a long way from home. He's the only one who made it back so far."

"What do you mean?"

"This is home for unicorns. They began to go missing. That is not normal. Unicorn is no worldwalker. For him to come back like this..." She shook her head, face full of concern. "It isn't possible, not with the veil."

I struggled to keep up with her words, wondering if I was understanding them right. "What is the veil?"

"It is protection between our world and yours."

"So, you're saying I'm in another world right now?" A calm knowing settled over me, followed by the awe of realization. "The Ancient Realm. You're Faeran."

A smile tugged her lips. "You know."

"I was raised by the Forest People," I said in a rush, trying to keep my voice calm despite my terrified excitement. "They are said to be your descendants, living in my world. I was told all about you and your ways."

The smile melted from Illian's face. "Many of us were left behind the veil. It was long ago."

"What happened?"

"A human. Like you."

I opened my mouth but found too many questions to choose from.

"Come. We must get you home. It is not safe for you here." She moved past us and beckoned us to follow. "Unicorn, where did you enter?"

Valorre looked at me. *I don't know. Wasn't trying to come here. Confused.*

I followed after Illian. "He doesn't know. Will you be able to help us get back through the veil?"

A male voice rang out.

I jumped and spun toward the sound, finding a man with milky-white skin, silvery-blonde hair, and piercing blue eyes standing beside one of the willows. He wore an elegant, periwinkle robe lined with white at the collar and sleeves. Two other men stood behind him in similar dress and with the same sharp, striking features. However, one man had black hair and the other had bronze. I had no doubt in my mind that these men were Elvan.

Illian grumbled and stepped in front of me. "She's done no harm."

The Elvan man replied in Illian's language. I extended my power to catch his words. "No harm, *yet.*"

"The veil may have torn. If so, this is a danger that she may be able to help us find—"

"And then what? There is no one to fix it."

Illian crossed her arms. "I found her first. She came to me. I will see that she leaves us."

The man strode toward us on long legs, the grass swirling around the hem of his robe as if it were water. His shadow reached us before he did, and I found him to be the tallest man I'd ever seen by at least a head. I swallowed hard and looked up at his stern face. He refused to meet my eyes. "As Steward of El'Ara, I am in charge of seeing how she leaves."

Illian glared at him, then relented and took a step back. She turned to me. "I'm sorry. You must go with Steward Fanon."

"Come." Fanon faced me but kept his gaze over my head. When I didn't move, he raised a hand, prompting the two men to come forward.

I felt the fire run to my fingertips as I prepared to fight. However, the men stopped behind the steward.

"Etrix, offer her your arm." The man with black hair did as told. His expression was less severe than Fanon's, but I wouldn't have called it warm.

I looked from Etrix to Fanon, making no move to accept. "Why should I go with you?"

Fanon grimaced. "I don't speak your language, human."

I gritted my teeth and felt my power surround me.

He finally looked me in the face, eyes growing wide. "She has human magic. She's just as dangerous as I thought."

"She is an empath," Illian said from behind me. "Raised by Faeran outside the veil."

Fanon wrinkled his nose with disgust. "Human magic, just the same. Every power they have is meant to invade, infiltrate, or conquer. Right now, she invades my mind to know my words."

Valorre, what do I do? I don't know what powers the Elvan have. Are they dangerous?

I could sense Valorre's panic. *I don't remember. It is like a dream.*

I took a deep breath. "What will happen if I go with you?"

Fanon averted his gaze, as if my words offended him. Etrix leaned closer, then said in his language, "You will show us where you came from and we will assess the best way to get you out of El'Ara."

Again, he extended his arm to me. My mouth felt dry as I accepted.

"Come then." Fanon turned on his heel while Etrix and the bronze-haired Elvan followed. Even though my grasp on Etrix's arm was light, I was unable to release him and found myself being pulled along. He was using his own magic on me.

Fanon paused and spun around. "Unicorn, why are you following?"

I looked over my shoulder at Valorre. "He's my friend."

Fanon sneered. "He's been tainted by the human. Very well. You'll need to come along too." He faced forward once again, and the retinue proceeded.

It may have been safer if you'd tried to hide until I found us a way out of here, I said silently to Valorre.

I stay with you.

I smiled. *I know, Valorre. I know.*

PLOTTING

Mareleau

I stared at Cora's hurried script on the piece of paper. No matter how many times I looked at the list of herbs, I couldn't stop the bile that rose in my throat.

"What are you reading?" Sera barged into my room, making me jump.

"Nothing."

"Oh, is it that recipe Princess Cora left you? What is it for?"

I folded the piece of paper and tucked it under the sash of my dress. "It's an advanced recipe for child-bearing sickness."

"Would you like me to take it to the kitchens?"

I narrowed my eyes. "Did I ask you to? No. I asked you to fetch Cora's cloak for me."

Sera frowned and looked down at the bundle in her arms. "Here you are, Your Majesty." She shook out the deep-blue cloak and held it up.

I went to her, crossing my arms as I examined the thick wool. "It's likely too short in length, but at least it's new."

"Such a pity you gave her your old one. However, I do think the blue suits you better than the gray did."

"And new suits me better than old." I wrapped the cloak around my shoulders, testing its warmth, then tossed it back to Sera. "Have the mountain clasp replaced with a rose—no, an eagle."

She nodded and folded the cloak in her arms. "You really should trade rooms now that Cora is gone. The master chamber is far better fit for a queen."

I scowled. "I'm not switching rooms, you fool. I'm getting out of here."

Moments later I was heading toward the great hall, neck long and head held high. *Today is the day I return home.*

I heard the rumble of quiet voices as I approached the great hall and found my uncles seated at the head table. "We can't allow him to be king. His claim is weak," Kevan said.

Ulrich opened his mouth to reply but halted as he saw me enter. "Your Majesty."

"Lord Ulrich, Lord Kevan, I would like to arrange my return to Dermaine."

Kevan spat a laugh. "Why in Lela do you presume to do such a thing?"

"I was sent here to aid Princess Coralaine. As she is no longer here, my services are no longer needed."

"Your Majesty, no one knows about the princess' disappearance yet," Ulrich said, "and we are determined to keep it that way."

I stomped my foot. "Why?"

Kevan scowled. "Kero's king has abdicated, the future queen has gone missing, and the future king is only heir through his marriage to her. Without Princess Coralaine to secure the throne, Kero could be on the brink of chaos."

"But Teryn and Cora have been married," I said. "Teryn can be King of Kero with or without her." My uncles chuckled, making my teeth clench. "What's so funny?"

"You know nothing about royal matters, Your Majesty," Kevan said. "Leave that to us. You will leave when we tell you to leave."

My cheeks flushed with heat. "At least let me send word to my husband."

Kevan's eyes flashed dangerously. "Until we have matters under control, not a single word about this leaves the castle."

I stared blankly at my uncles, at a loss for words.

Footsteps sounded behind me, and I saw Teryn enter. "Surely, you can't keep a woman in love from writing to her husband," he said. "In fact, word should be sent to Sele and Mena at once. As members of the Pact, King Verdian and King Larylis can council us in our time of need."

Kevan's face nearly turned purple, and Ulrich pursed his lips.

I regained my composure. "Thank you, Prince Teryn."

He bowed. "Anything for you, dear sister. Now, fret not, I will send a personal request for my brother's hasty arrival."

I eyed the two angry men, one side of my mouth

curled into a smirk. "You have been ever so helpful." I left the great hall, ignoring the curses my uncles hurled in my wake.

"You dropped something." I turned and found Teryn hurrying after me, unfolding a piece of paper in his hand. He paused as he read the list.

I felt the blood leave my face as my eyes bulged. "Do you dare read the private property of the queen?"

Teryn's eyes locked with mine as he handed me the paper. No apology was exchanged, and instead a sly smile crept across his face. "Your secret is safe with me, Your Majesty. However, if you would like that recipe made, leave it up to me. I can have it made with no suspicion on you."

My heart raced with fury. "You know nothing!"

"Cora taught me much about brews and tinctures. We even spoke last night about what she would do if she were to be with child from our first night together."

I crossed my arms. "Is that why she ran away?"

Teryn's expression grew hard as he looked away. "I'll never know why she chose to break my heart and leave me." His jaw shifted side to side as his eyes slipped back to mine. "I'm sure she'll be back."

"If that's all, I'll take my leave, Prince Teryn," I said, my voice sharp.

He stepped toward me and put a hand on my arm. "Dear sister, I'm on your side. Don't forget that. I'm the one bringing Larylis to you, am I not?"

My anger began to cool. "Again, I thank you."

He patted the hand I curled around the paper, then brought his lips close to my ear. "I won't say anything about our secret. If you want the recipe, just say the word." As he pulled away, his lips brushed my cheek. With that, he returned to the great hall.

My limbs trembled, and my gut roiled as I returned to my room. I was relieved to find my ladies nowhere to be seen. Tears pricked my eyes as I raced to my lounge, cringing at the thought of Teryn touching my hand, my arm, the disgusting warmth of his breath against my ear. *Our secret.*

I gathered the paper in a wad and threw it at the wall. My eyes slid out of focus and my stomach churned as an avalanche of feeling poured out in a rush of sobs. Everything that had been weighing heavy on my heart pressed down upon me further—fear of being a mother, guilt over my mountain of lies, shame that Teryn saw my list, worry over what Larylis would say if he knew what was on it.

At the thought of Larylis, my mind went still. Calm loosened my shoulders while memories of his smile dried my tears. Soon he would be at my side. Soon he would keep Teryn at bay. Soon I could tell him about the baby. His baby. *Our* baby. My palms went to my womb, circling over the folds of my dress, and I felt a smile touch my lips.

With a deep breath, I stood and retrieved the paper from the floor, smoothing it as I walked to my table. I took the cover from my lantern and placed a tip of the parchment over the flame. A hollow calm fell over me as I made my choice, sealing my fate as the words turned to ash.

~

Teryn

I breathed deep and focused on the racing of my blood through my veins as I watched Morkai return to the great hall. My heart pounded as I tried to shake the image of Morkai whispering to Mareleau from my mind.

"You don't have to watch." Emylia's voice shook me from my stupor. "You said so yourself; following Morkai hasn't helped."

I glowered at the back of Morkai's head as he approached the table. "I need to make sure he isn't going after Cora."

Emylia sighed, then nodded. We watched as Ulrich and Kevan greeted Morkai with venomous stares.

Morkai ignored their disdain. "I was thinking we should arrange my coronation ceremony."

Kevan's mouth fell open. "You have no right to expect such a thing. You aren't king without the Princess of Kero as your wife, and she has gone missing."

"Kero needs a king," Morkai said. "Dimetreus and Cora are clearly unstable. We must secure the kingdom at once."

"Without Cora's word, we have no proof your wedding was consummated, or that she's even alive."

Morkai threw his hands in the air. "You're the council, you have the power to say our wedding was consummated and crown me for the good of the kingdom. You don't trust Cora anyway. Why are you waiting on *her* word?"

The two brothers remained silent.

"I see. You don't trust me either." He put a hand to his

chin and paced along the length of the table. "Actually, I understand completely."

"Is that so?" Ulrich said with a smirk.

Morkai nodded. "You think Verdian made a mistake allowing Dimetreus to regain the throne. You think he made an additional mistake when he named me Dimetreus' heir. Worst of all, he made his own daughter heir to Sele when it should have been his eldest brother."

Kevan held his chin high but said not a word.

Morkai continued. "Sele should have gone to Kevan. Kero should have gone to Ulrich. That's what you believe, am I right?"

"If we'd been on the council, we would have fought for that," Kevan said.

Morkai nodded. "But instead of speaking to his council, he dismissed you and reassigned you here, where you'd have no say in his decisions. He placed my brother as King of Mena and made his daughter heir to his throne, so that she will inherit not only Sele, but Mena as well. Do you see what he's done?"

The brothers exchanged a glance. Ulrich shifted anxiously in his seat. "What are you implying?"

Morkai grinned. "It was obvious from the start. He wanted his daughter to have everything, and anyone who would fight that, he sent here."

Kevan's jaw moved side to side as he crossed his arms and leaned back in his chair. "Prince Teryn, you came here of your own accord. It was said you chose to abdicate your crown so you could marry Princess Coralaine."

Morkai let out a bitter laugh. "Do you believe those stories? Think about it. You yourselves have woven stories to serve the happiness of the people, but are they always true? I'll tell you what's true. Verdian knew I wouldn't be as easy to control as my brother. It's also true I wanted to marry Cora. I love her dearly. But Verdian refused to let his daughter be scorned by a crown prince. He threatened to ruin me if I didn't take his daughter as my wife. So I abdicated, making him think he'd won."

"He has, hasn't he?" Ulrich said.

Morkai shook his head. "His mistake was sending us —the three men he wanted to discard—away to the same place. Here we can unite as one, with one vision."

Kevan lowered his brows. "What vision would that be?"

"We will make Verdian and Larylis pay for the traitors they are."

Ulrich leaned forward in his seat. "You are speaking out against two kings of Lela. Two kings you are sworn allies with."

"Dimetreus signed the Pact, not I. Stand behind me as king, and I will stand behind the two of you and return you to your rightful places as Sele's heirs."

"How do you propose we do that?" Kevan asked, rubbing his hand along his jaw.

Morkai placed his hands on the table and leaned toward him. "When I told Mareleau I would summon Verdian and Larylis to Ridine, I did not mean as guests. We will hold them here as traitors while the two of you return Sele's original council to its former greatness. The other councilmen can't possibly agree with Verdian's decisions. There is no doubt you are the true heir." He turned to Ulrich. "And since Kevan has no male heirs, you shall be *his* heir."

Ulrich took a deep breath and rubbed his temples. "You are proposing treason."

Morkai shook his head. "Verdian was the first traitor. Unseating him is simply following your duty given by birth."

"Kero's Royal Force is still growing from nothing," Kevan said. "We can't face Sele's army like this."

"Gather men from your own houses. Send letters to those you know will support your cause. With Verdian held here, we won't need a large army. The word of the council is all it will take."

My mouth went dry as I saw the look in Kevan's eye. There was hunger for power and a thirst for vengeance clear on his face as he tasted Morkai's words. Ulrich opened his mouth, but hesitated, looking from Kevan to Morkai. "What about your wife? She will need to be found."

Morkai waved a hand. "No need to worry about her. She couldn't have gone far."

"We should send a search party," Ulrich said.

Morkai's lips curled into a grin, showing teeth. "It's already been taken care of. If she's alive, my men will find her."

I pulled away from the vision, and the great hall swept away until Emylia and I were surrounded by the temple room. My heart raced as I imagined Cora being pursued. "I can't let him find her."

"He won't hurt her." Emylia's voice was gentle.

I rounded on her. "How do you know? He's proved over and over that he's more than capable of hurting her."

She closed her eyes and turned her face to the floor. "Let me correct myself. He won't *kill* her."

"How can you be so sure?"

"No matter how angry he gets with her, I know he wants her alive."

"Why?"

Emylia lifted her head. "Remember when you asked why I'm still here? I told you Morkai has plans for me. Those plans involve her too."

Her words sent a shock of terror through me. What could she possibly mean? And why would she have kept something of such importance from me until now? I tried to keep my breathing steady as I met her eyes. "Tell me."

26

THE VEIL

Cora

We walked past the willow grove and entered a forest filled with dazzling shades of emerald, gold, ruby, and indigo. Everything I laid my eyes on—leaves, vines, trees, streams—looked both familiar and strange to me at once. A leaf looked like any leaf, yet the longer I stared, the more I realized the color was too vibrant or too iridescent to be any old leaf. The streams were filled with rich color and made sounds more like music than rushing water. Birds and animals flitted by with jeweled feathers or flowing fur, and eyes too big and round to be from my world.

Caught in the wonders around me, it was easy to forget I was a captive. Yet, aside from Fanon, my companions didn't seem too bothered by me. Etrix spoke to me now and again, and the bronze-haired Elvan, who I'd learned was named Garot, even offered me a smile.

"Where are you taking me?" I asked Etrix.

He looked down at me, his expression neutral. "To the veil."

"How is it you can understand me when Fanon cannot?"

Etrix laughed, a light trilling sound, although his expression barely faltered. "Anyone with the Mora can understand you if they tried."

It took me a moment to realize *Mora* meant something like the Arts or magic. "So, Fanon simply doesn't want to understand me."

"Fanon is Steward of El'Ara, a great burden to bear. He's no Morkara, and there hasn't been one in a very long time. Not since your kind destroyed the last. None of us are fond of humans, and Fanon is likely less fond than anyone else."

The word *Morkara* sent a chill down my spine, sounding much too close to *Morkai* for my comfort. "What is a Morkara?"

"Morkara is much like a steward, but the burden is given by blood, birth, and Mora. The Mora flowed from all around our world toward the capital city of Le'Lana. The palace in the center of Le'Lana was the seat of the Morkara. From there, the Morkara would decide how to evenly distribute the Mora back to El'Ara and our people. Satsara was the last Morkara we've had."

"What happened?"

I saw a flicker of emotion pass over Etrix's face before it returned to its usual, steady mask. "Your kind found its way to El'Ara. A human. A worldwalker."

Garot slowed his pace until he was walking alongside us. "Telling stories, are we?"

"She asked. No harm telling her."

Garot smiled, making his entire face glow beneath his bright, bronze hair and opalescent, sun-gold skin. "But you never tell stories right. Let me tell this part."

"Why would you relish telling such a dark tale?"

Fanon looked behind him and scowled at us. "Why are you talking with the human at all?"

"I thought she should know the deeds her kind is responsible for," Etrix said.

Fanon narrowed his eyes but returned his focus ahead. My mind spun from the effort it took to interpret three voices in such quick succession.

"Fine," Etrix said to Garot, "you tell the rest."

Garot puffed his chest and stood tall. "Morkara Satsara, most beautiful of the Elvan." His voice was rich and bellowing where Etrix's was soft and flat. "She was young when she discovered a human prince—a world-walker—lost in El'Ara. She went to banish him, but instead fell in love."

"Presumably," Etrix said.

Garot ignored him. "They began an affair, and Satsara grew with child. Her Elvan consort knew it was not his own, but he did not know it would be half-human. Upon the child's birth, Satsara confessed of her human lover and was forced to banish him once and for all. The child, however, was permitted to remain."

"A mistake," Etrix added.

"A very grave mistake indeed. Darius grew up alongside his Elvan sister, Ailan, while Satsara struggled to choose her heir."

"The eldest child of the Morkara is always made heir by right and blood," Etrix explained, "but as Darius was half-human, Satsara doubted he should be steward over the Mora."

Garot nodded. "As Darius grew, it was clear he was tainted with human darkness. Ailan was named heir instead. In a fit of fury, Darius wounded his sister, and Satsara was forced to banish him. She used the very same weaving she'd used on his father years before."

"Weaving?" The word seemed out of place, yet I could find no other to match the meaning I felt.

Etrix gave a sharp nod. "Many of us are weavers in different shades of talent. Satsara was the most powerful weaver of her kind. Only her daughter came close."

As I glanced down at my hand, I wondered what weaving he was using on me to keep me attached to his arm. I looked to Garot to continue the story.

"As she attempted a weaving around her son, making it so he'd never be able to return to El'Ara, Darius realized what was happening. With the power of the worldwalker, he disappeared into the human world before the weaving could take its hold."

"Only to return many years later to kill his mother and destroy the balance of El'Ara." Etrix's words came out in a rush.

Garot frowned at him. "That's a terrible way to end the story."

Etrix squinted his onyx eyes as he looked ahead. "We're close."

My attention had been so fixated on the story, I'd stopped watching my surroundings. I looked around and found the forest had gone quiet. No animals scampered through the undergrowth, and the plants themselves had taken on a dull tone. "Where are we?"

"Close to the veil," Etrix said.

As we walked along, the colors became more and more muted until I found myself stepping on dead roots and crumbling leaves.

"This is the way you came in, is it not?" Fanon asked from ahead.

I turned and looked at Valorre. *Did we travel through this?*

I don't remember. I was following home. Didn't realize my mistake until the willow grove.

"Possibly," I answered.

We continued, and I noticed a dense fog up ahead, swallowing the dead forest. The nearer we came, the more unsettled I felt. Fanon held up his hand, and we stopped. I looked from side to side, seeing nothing but the thick, colorless mist extending as far as I could see.

"Here we are," Fanon said with disgust. "The veil to your world."

My eyes shot to him. "This is the veil?"

Fanon refused to look my way. Etrix spoke instead. "If there is a tear in the veil, this is where it would be."

Fanon turned to us. "Find where you came in."

Come, Valorre. Try to remember. He went toward the veil, and I attempted to pull away from Etrix. I looked back at him, frowning.

He tapped the hand still linked around his arm. "I must accompany you."

I bristled. "If you let me go, I can try to find my way out."

"With your power?" Etrix raised a feathery eyebrow. "If the unicorn was the one who brought you, he should be able to find the way out. He's left once before."

"But he doesn't remember leaving or returning."

"If there's a tear, you should be able to leave without using your human magic. If it is your power that allows you to move through the veil, then you are a danger to us."

My eyes widened. I knew I'd had nothing to do with us entering El'Ara, but if Valorre could find no way out, what then? With a deep breath, I calmed my pounding heart and allowed Etrix to lead me along the veil, following Valorre.

Is anything familiar? I asked him.

Yes and no. Confused.

We walked along in silence until I decided to pry further into the history of El'Ara. "Why is the forest dying around the veil?"

Etrix looked toward the crumbled soil and the dead roots and vines, and I saw another flicker of emotion pass over his face. "The veil was never properly completed. When Darius returned to invade El'Ara and claim what he believed was his rightful place as Morkara—*Morkaius*, as he insisted—Satsara decided to weave a veil all around El'Ara. It would serve the same purpose as her original weaving had intended, but she'd be able to weave it around our world instead of only her son. Once complete, neither he nor any other from your world would be able to enter El'Ara again."

The blood left my face when I heard the word Morkaius, and I compared its meaning to that of Morkara. *High King of Magic. Steward of Magic.* I remembered what Morkai had said about being from the blood of the Ancient Ones. Could this Darius be his Ancient ancestor? "Why wasn't the veil finished?"

Etrix opened his mouth to speak, but squeezed his eyes shut. "Garot, I can hear you following, and I know you're going to interrupt me."

Garot stepped alongside him. "May I?"

Etrix pursed his lips, showing the closest thing to irritation I'd seen. "Fine."

Again, Garot puffed his chest as he prepared to tell his story. "From her seat at the palace in Le'Lana, Satsara began weaving her veil from the farthest reaches of our world toward the capital. She was nearly finished when Darius stormed the palace and killed her. But in her dying breath, she secured the edges of the veil and completed it where it had stopped—around the heart of the capital. What remained outside the veil was pushed into the human world, locking Darius outside with it, along with many other unfortunate beings. However, Satsara's heir, the beautiful Ailan, was stuck there as well. Without the heir of El'Ara, we have no true Morkara."

"Which is why I'm steward." Fanon's voice held deep bitterness.

"But why is everything dying?" I asked.

"El'Ara lost its heart," Garot said. "The capital city was where the Mora flowed, which is now in your world. The Mora still flows to it, yet no one can direct its return to us."

The capital city of Le'Lana, the heart of El'Ara, Lela. An Ancient land trapped outside the veil. Centerpointe Rock, the ruins of an Ancient palace. My mind raced to merge what I'd already known with what I was learning now.

"Satsara did all she could to keep Darius from controlling El'Ara," Garot said. "Yet in doing so, she unknowingly doomed our world. Not only has the land around the veil been dying, but the balance of our people has come undone. The dragons are restless, the unicorns are disappearing, and the cycle of give and take has been broken. The Faeran no longer direct the Mora of the soil to us. Since we can no longer direct its return, they now prefer to conserve it for their own kind. We may live indefinitely, but our powers aren't as strong as they were before. Some of us even choose Last Breath. El'Ara is nothing like it was before."

His sorrow crept into my heart. "Isn't there anything you can do about it?"

Garot shrugged. "Some believe El'Ara can only thrive when our world is whole again. However, Satsara and Ailan were the last weavers with their shade of talent. There's no one left to either complete the veil or tear it down."

"What if I can help?" Silence answered and Garot and Etrix froze. I could see the suspicion in their suddenly tense postures. "What if I can find a way to direct the Mora flowing into my world back to your world?"

Etrix's lips pressed into a tight line. "If you had the power to do that, you'd have the power to take it all from us."

My mouth hung open as I searched for the right words. How could I get them to believe I meant no harm? How could I convince them I only wanted to help? Then again, wasn't he right? It would take an immense amount of power to harness the magic seeping from an Ancient land. *That kind of power would belong to someone like...*

I shuddered. *A Morkaius.*

He was right; I didn't have that power, nor did I want

it. I turned my attention to Valorre, who slowly walked along the veil. *Anything?*

He swung his head toward me. *Nothing.*

Fanon folded his hands before him and tapped his foot. "Can the unicorn find where you entered or not?"

"We could have entered from anywhere," I said. "It could take hours to find it."

Fanon fixed me with his crystal-blue stare. "Then we have only one choice. Garot, weave us the fastest way back to the palace. She'll have to face the tribunal."

27

DESMOND

Teryn

Emylia raised her hand, and a fog rolled in, covering the floor, walls, and ceiling of the tower room. When the fog dispersed, it left behind the muted tones of Desmond's dark room at the inn. Emylia and I stood at the far end of the room while we watched the two figures of memory sit at opposite sides of the desk.

"Are you ready?" the Emylia of memory asked, an edge of excitement in her voice. "We're getting so close, Des. I can feel it."

Desmond nodded, but his expression held a hint of apprehension. "This is our last session before I return home to Syrus to report to my father. I hope what we've learned is enough for him."

"How could it not be? We've done so much work on his behalf, more than he's ever been able to do on his own. He'll have to appreciate it."

"I hope you're right." He folded his hands in his lap, eyes unfocused.

Emylia smiled, eyes sparkling with adoration. "Whether he appreciates it or not, I think you're amazing."

Desmond blushed, making him look younger than before.

"Let's hurry," she said. "I don't want to spend our last night together working."

He nodded and sat up straighter while Emylia closed her eyes. Desmond kept his voice low and steady. "Where is the Mother of Prophecy now?"

Emylia, crystal in hand, remained still while her eyelids fluttered. "Unborn."

"When will she be born?"

"The year of the Great Bear."

Desmond scratched his chin. "That could be three years from now, fifteen, twenty-seven, or more. How many years from now is it until she is born?"

Emylia remained silent.

Desmond moaned. "Fine. What will she look like?"

Again, silence.

He cocked his head, squinting. "She is said to have the beauty of Satsara. What does Satsara look like?"

"Eyes and hair as black as a raven's wing. Skin like ivory. Lips the color of raspberries."

A corner of his lips pulled into a crooked grin. "Beautiful."

Emylia grumbled. "Des."

His face melted as he watched her. "She can't be any more beautiful than you."

Her shoulders relaxed. "What else, Des?"

The image ended and shifted to the cot. Desmond and Emylia curled up together beneath a thin blanket. "I wish you didn't have to go," Emylia said, her head on his chest.

Desmond pulled her closer and kissed her forehead. "I have to tell Father what I've found. He was expecting me much sooner."

"How far is Syrus from here? I know nothing about the Northern Islands."

He pressed his lips together. "You know I don't like to talk about home."

She lifted her head to meet his eyes. "I just want to know how long you might be gone. I'll lose my mind thinking about you if I can't anticipate your return."

That seemed to please him. "It's only a few weeks' travel north. I should be gone no more than two months."

"Will your task be complete after this?"

"I hope so. Either way, I'm coming back to you."

Emylia smiled and brought her lips to his. When they pulled away, Desmond reached behind his pillow and brought out a gold chain.

"What is that?" Emylia asked.

"It's a gift for you." He lifted the chain over her head to hang from her neck. At the end was a coil of gold wire.

She moved her fingers over the wire. "What is it for?"

"Your crystal. Now you can wear it."

Her eyes widened, and a smile broke over her face.

The image shifted again. This time, Emylia was sprinting down the cobblestone street, hair flying wild in a mass of bouncing curls. Outside the door of the inn stood Desmond, who gathered her in his arms as she collided into him. They merged into tangled arms and breathless kisses.

"I missed you so much," Emylia sobbed. She took a step back and stared into Desmond's eyes. Her brows knit together, seeing the sadness there. "What's wrong?"

The image moved from the cobblestone street to the dark room in the inn. Desmond sat on the cot, eyes unfocused, while Emylia knelt at his side. "Father lied to me," he said.

"About what?"

"He can't bring my mother back, even if he becomes Morkaius. He doesn't have her ethera."

Emylia tilted her head. "Her ethera? Why would he have her ethera in the first place?"

"I've been reading about what it would take to bring my mother back. While there is no clear formula, I do know he would need her ethera. When I asked him about it, he tried to brush me off. But I wouldn't stop asking until he told me the truth." His eyes lifted and met hers. "He doesn't want to become Morkaius to bring her back. He wants power for himself."

She put a hand on his leg. "Des, I'm so sorry. What did he say about the information you've gathered for him?"

"He says it's not enough." His voice caught on a sob. "He told me I have to keep looking until I find the heart of El'Ara."

"Are you still going to help him, even though you know his motive?"

Desmond shrugged. "I don't know what else to do. He's my father. He's convinced it's his blood-right to become Morkaius."

"I don't understand why he needs *you*."

"Father is a powerful man, but he is physically weak. He gets disoriented every time he tries to talk about his past. I swear he's under a curse. How can I leave him like that?"

"Whatever you do, you know I'm here for you."

Desmond's face was blank. "Is that a promise? Will you do anything for me?"

"Anything."

The image shifted, and they were again sitting at the desk. Emylia held her crystal, now secured beneath the gold wire on the chain. "What would you like to ask this time, Des?"

He bit his lip. "Find my mother."

Her eyes flew open. "What?"

"I need you to channel my mother."

She shook her head. "I'm not a medium, Des. I don't commune with the dead."

"What's the difference?"

She narrowed her eyes. "There's more of a difference than I have time to explain."

His face fell. "You promised you'd do anything for me. I just want to speak to her."

Emylia pursed her lips as she glared at him. Finally, she relented. "I'll try." She closed her eyes. Silent moments passed.

Desmond remained patient, hands resting over his knees from his seat on the floor.

"I found her." Her voice came out in a whisper.

"Mother?"

Emylia trembled from head to toe. "Desmond? Why are you seeking me?" Her voice, while low in volume, reverberated through the room.

"I wanted to hear your voice again. I miss you."

She hesitated. "I missed you too. But this isn't right. You should leave me at peace."

"Mother, I want you to come back."

"That isn't possible."

"What if it is?" With slow, deliberate movements, Desmond came to his feet and crept toward Emylia. His hands framed hers, hovering above her fingers.

"What are you doing, Desmond?"

"I want you back. Aside from Emylia, you're the only one who ever loved me." He clamped his hands around Emylia's, securing the crystal between both their hands.

A wind cycled through the room, blowing Emylia's hair back and sending papers soaring. "I don't want to come back!" The booming voice that came through Emylia pounded my ears, even as I watched from the distance of memory. "Leave me at peace!"

"No, Mother. I need you." The wind increased, and the fire of the lanterns flared, sending the room beneath an orange glow. "Trust me, Mother."

Emylia's eyes shot open, burning orange like embers. "Let. Me. Go."

With that, the wind stilled, the lantern extinguished, and the room fell under darkness. I blinked but could see nothing. All I could hear was a quiet whimpering. "Why, Mother?" came Desmond's voice. A moment later, a flicker of light sparked over a candle. Desmond stood at the desk, watching the light fall upon the destruction of the room until he saw the toppled chair and a motionless body. "Emylia!"

He sprang to her side, cradling her head in his trembling hands. "Say something. Please!"

She mumbled incoherently as blood trickled beneath her nose.

"No, please no. I'm so sorry."

Her eyes fluttered open. "Des." She lifted a hand toward his face but dropped it. Desmond froze as he stared down at her, watching her breathing grow shallow. Then, with a chilling calm, he grabbed the crystal that still hung from her neck and grasped it in both hands.

"I'll make this right."

Emylia's lips moved but no sound came.

"Forget my father. He's never done anything to help me. Let him stay cursed. He never cared about me or my mother." He brought his lips close to her ear. "I'll find the heart of El'Ara. I'll find the Mother of Prophecy. And when I am Morkaius, I'll bring you back and we will rule together."

The image froze. I turned to Emylia. "Desmond isn't Morkai's son, is he?"

She shook her head. "The man I loved became Morkai, while I became prisoner in my own crystal. Desmond took over his father's mission as his own, adopting the name Morkai as he hunted down the black mountain and the Mother of Prophecy. Once he discovered the mountain represented a sigil, he became increasingly obsessed. I watched his every move, hoping to find a way to stop him, or at least a way to free myself."

"I still don't see what this has to do with him keeping Cora alive."

Emylia raised her hand, and the fog swept the inn away, replacing it with image after image of Desmond—*Morkai*—growing older, traveling, moving from kingdom to kingdom beneath banners similar to Kero's. I watched as fragments of images flashed by—the spilling of blood on stone, the dripping of liquid into a goblet of wine. I saw women lying lifeless while Morkai held the crystal above their bodies.

My eyes shot to Emylia.

"He knew it was no use without the power of the Morkaius," she said, "but he kept trying to find a body for me. Over and over he tried, knowing he wouldn't succeed. It didn't matter, so long as he tried. That is, until he found a body worth being patient for."

I looked back at the memory and watched Morkai enter a younger-looking Ridine Castle. He stood before Cora's parents, who looked exactly as I remembered them from my youth. Morkai himself looked as he had last I saw him living.

"Your healing talents have been spoken highly of," Queen Tiliane said as they led him through the castle. "Can you help our daughter? She suffers from pain she shouldn't feel, constant headaches, and wild emotional outbursts."

King Jeru leaned toward Morkai. "She says she hears voices."

Morkai kept his head held high. "I'll see what I can do."

They stopped outside a familiar door. King Jeru pushed it open, revealing a child's bedroom within. On the bed lay a child of four or five years. Her dark hair spread out over her pillow while long, black lashes rested on her round cheeks flushed pink. My heart stopped. *Little Cora.*

Queen Tiliane twisted her hands before her, eyes

glazed with tears. "We give her a sleeping draught when it's at its worst. We don't know what else to do for her."

Morkai sat at the edge of the bed and looked at Cora. He lifted a hand, extending it slowly until his fingers hovered over her forehead. With a sigh, he stroked the side of her tiny face and ran his hand along a strand of hair. "Beauty of Satsara, indeed," he whispered.

King Jeru cleared his throat. "So, can you help her?"

Morkai turned and smiled. "I have just the thing."

28

TRAPPED

Cora

Colors sped by in flashes of green, blue, brown, and gold, as if we were racing through a tunnel made of trees. Yet we walked at as leisurely a pace as we had before. The tone, however, had much changed since we began our travels to the palace. Etrix kept his eyes set ahead and Garot no longer shone his smile upon me.

"What are you going to do with me?" I asked for the hundredth time. "What is the tribunal, and why didn't you let me try to leave on my own?"

Again, no answer. I gritted my teeth and turned to look at Valorre, following behind with his head hanging low. *I'm sorry,* he said.

This is not your fault. His guilt was so strong, it made my heart sink. I faced forward, keeping my eyes on Fanon's back instead of on our dizzying surroundings.

"We're here," Garot said. The tunnel of color ceased,

spreading out into a green lawn dotted with flowers in shades of violet and lavender. A path of shimmering gold ran beneath our feet and over a bridge. A gentle stream danced beneath the bridge, and at the other side stood a towering palace of opalescent white topped with slender towers and shining, gold turrets. My mouth fell open; not even Verlot could compare to the beauty of the palace before me.

Fanon turned to Garot. "No one can see her." Garot nodded, and the tunnel of color again surrounded us, this time in shades of white and gold. Not a moment passed before the colors stilled and formed a bright room. I looked above me at a ceiling extending higher than any I'd ever seen, painted in a swirl of colors that seemed to move before my eyes. My gaze traveled to the walls where finely woven tapestries hung, along with intricately carved tables bearing painted vases.

"Etrix, Garot." Fanon eyed each in turn. They nodded, and my hand slipped from Etrix's elbow.

I shook out my limp arm, scowling as I felt the prickling of feeling returning to it. "It's about time."

"I'll speak to the tribunal," Fanon said. "Etrix, you stay with them."

Fanon and Garot left the room, and Etrix moved to guard the door. I took a step toward Valorre, glancing at the Elvan to see if he would stop me. He made no move. I closed the distance between me and my friend and placed a hand on his side. *Ever been in a palace before?*

His legs trembled, and his ears twitched back and forth. *I've never been inside anywhere before.*

You still don't remember this place? El'Ara?

No...a little.

I looked at Etrix and spoke out loud. "What will the tribunal do with me?"

Etrix met my eyes but didn't say a word.

I took a step toward him. "Please. I mean you and El'Ara no harm. I never meant to come here, and I would leave right now if I could. At least tell me what you think is going to happen."

"Your kind is not allowed here."

"I get that. What will the tribunal do with me?"

He took a few steps forward. "The tribunal has always supported the Morkara. Or, in this case, the steward. Fanon cannot make any final decision without them. They will help decide what is to be done with you."

"What are the options?"

"They will likely ask you to take Last Breath."

"What is Last Breath?"

"It is how we end our lives," Etrix said. "We live as long as we wish, so long as we are of service to El'Ara. Once we feel we have served our people and our children with our wisdom and talents, we take our final breath, and join the timeless ones."

My mouth felt dry. "You die by choice."

"We live and die for the beauty and greatest good of El'Ara. If we lived forever, there would be no room for us to multiply."

"And you think the tribunal will sentence me to this?"

He placed his hands behind his back and took another step toward me. "You will be asked to choose Last Breath for yourself. If you refuse, Last Breath will be chosen for you."

My hands clenched into fists. "No matter what, I'm expected to die."

"It would be for the safety of El'Ara."

"But I'm not a harm to anyone here! If it were up to me, I'd leave." I felt the fire course through my veins and tingle my fingers. My chest swelled, knowing I could use my power against him in that instant. But what then? Where would I go? How would I find my way out before getting caught? I inhaled deeply, letting the fire cool. "Is there any other way for me to leave?"

Etrix's brows gave the slightest flutter of concern. "No, I do not believe there is."

"So, I'm dead." I turned my back to him, my lip trembling as I looked at Valorre. "And him? What will happen to Valorre?"

"He's more human than unicorn now," Etrix said. "He'll be asked to take Last Breath too."

I narrowed my eyes and clenched my jaw. *Not if I have anything to say about it.*

~

Mareleau

Sweat prickled behind my neck as I watched out my bedroom window, looking for any sign of travelers moving on the road.

Breah joined me. "They say your father should arrive any time now. Are you excited to see him again, Your Majesty?"

"I'll be excited when he gets me out of here." Truth be told, I wasn't sure how I felt about seeing my father. I was still burning with fury from him forcing me to come to Ridine in the first place, and more so now that I was truly pregnant. What had he been thinking? When I'd first learned of my sentence, I'd been too full of guilt to understand the absurdity of his demand. But now, just thinking about what he'd forced me to do made my hands ball into fists.

But what if he's changed? What if he's sorry for banishing me here? What if he can get me out of here?

At that thought, my shoulders began to relax, and my hands folded across my waist.

My door opened, and in walked Sera and Ann. I spun toward them. "Any word of my father? Or my husband?"

Sera grinned. "King Verdian's scout just arrived. He will be here in moments."

"And King Larylis?" My heart raced, hoping word had finally been sent of his travels.

Sera's face fell, and she shook her head.

I cursed under my breath. "He should be here by now. He should have arrived days before my father."

Ann maintained a hopeful expression. "They may be traveling together. You never know."

"I *should* know. I'm his wife." My voice cracked on the last word, and I fought the tears that threatened to spill. I turned back to the window, hands on my belly in attempt to soothe the anxiety that boiled within.

It had been nearly a week since Cora had left, and in that time the entire castle seemed to go silent. Teryn, my uncles, and the councilmen had been constantly locked up in the great hall having hushed conversations. Guards were placed outside my door, and I was forbidden from walking the grounds or eating in the hall with the men. All was said to be done for my own protection, yet I couldn't help but feel like a prisoner. It even made me sentimental for the days when I'd first arrived at Ridine.

Breah gasped and tapped the window, shaking me from my thoughts. "Is that him?"

My heart raced as I leaned toward the window, squinting at the movement between the trees in the distance. I kept my eyes trained on the migration until it cleared the last line of trees to reveal a modest retinue on horseback beneath the gold banner of Sele. An assortment of guards flanked the front and back of the line, with my father at the center surrounded by what I assumed to be his councilmen. Nowhere in the crowd did I see a familiar head of sandy-brown hair.

My shoulders slumped, yet my heart increased its racing as my breathing became shallow. Horns blew announcing my father's arrival, and I began to pace in front of the window, shaking out my trembling arms.

Breah put a hand on my shoulder. "What's wrong, Your Majesty?"

"Is it the baby?" Sera asked. "Are you nervous to tell him?"

"I'm sure he'll be so proud," Ann said.

"Nothing is wrong," I snapped. "I'm simply preparing to greet him." I took a deep breath but could find no will to move to the door as moments stretched on. "Perhaps I'll wait until I'm called upon."

A sudden shout startled me. I whirled back to the window, but the procession had already passed out of view. The shouting escalated, followed by a clash of metal. I ran to the door and flung it open. Two guards faced me. "You must remain inside, Your Majesty."

I looked over their shoulders, hearing the raging

conflict coming from within the castle. "What's happening? Let me through."

"It's for your own safety," said one of the guards.

I crossed my arms. "Do you know who I am? I am Queen of Mena. I demand you let me through."

"King Teryn—"

"Oh, so *now* they're calling him king?"

"—has demanded you remain in your room for your safety."

"Where is my father?"

The guards gave no answer.

I lifted my chin, threw my shoulders back, and stepped forward. The guards stood shoulder to shoulder, blocking my way. "I am leaving this room."

"You cannot, Your Majesty."

"What are you going to do to prevent me? Push me, a pregnant queen? Pull your swords on me?" One man flinched and eyed the other guard. I raced at him and pushed at his chest. Stunned, he stumbled back, giving me room to slip between them. They called after me as I raced down the hall, and I heard the pursuit of feet as they pounded after me down the stairs. When I finally made it to the main hall, I froze.

My father's face was bruised and bloodied, his arms bound behind him by a pair of guards who pushed him through the hall. The other men from his retinue were equally bound and forced to follow. Teryn and my uncles stood by, faces smug as they watched.

"Father!" I raced toward him, but found strong hands grasping my arms, pulling me back. My father's eyes met mine. With the blood seeping from the cut on his forehead, it was hard to tell his expression.

"Yes, look at your daughter," Kevan taunted. "Was she worth your act of treason?"

"What are you talking about?" I strained to free myself from the grasp of the guards. "Father, what's happening?"

"Take them to the dungeon," Ulrich demanded.

"Father!" I shouted as he was pushed onward.

Teryn raced to my side. "Your Majesty, you shouldn't be here."

"What are you doing to him?"

Teryn looked over his shoulder, then brought his face close to mine. "I'm so sorry, sister. I didn't know what to do. Your uncles are furious about your father naming you heir instead of Lord Kevan. They consider it an act of treason."

I pulled my head as far away from him as I could. "That's absurd."

Teryn gave me a sad smile. "I know, but they are my councilmen. Without Cora to secure me as king, I owe my position to them. I must do what they think is right."

My lips pulled away from my teeth. "You're just as big of a monster as they are."

"Why would you say that? I'm the one who summoned your husband. He should be here any day now."

My eyes went wide, and I felt the blood drain from my face. "Will the same happen to him?"

Teryn's mouth fell open. "Of course not, Your Majesty. Larylis is my dear brother. Besides, your uncles only have issue with Verdian. I promise Larylis will be safe."

"Your promise means nothing to me."

Teryn sighed. "Oh, dear sister. I know this is hard for you. I'm here for you when you come around." His eyes left my face and his expression went cold. "Take her back to her room."

The guards pulled me back up the stairs while I struggled against their hold every step. "Larylis!" I called his name over and over, even though I knew he couldn't hear me. *Larylis, please don't come here. It's a trap.*

29

DISAPPEAR

Cora

I tried to close my eyes on the blazing night sky, but sleep would not come. Despite the deep, dark indigo outside the windows, the sliver of a crescent moon, and stars that looked like ordinary stars, the light burned my eyelids as if it were midday.

I rolled over on the plush cot I'd been provided and looked beyond the double doors to the balcony where Valorre slept. My heart ached to see him in such obvious discomfort, lying on a bed of hay as if he were a common horse.

I turned to my other side, where the silhouette of a shoulder showed between the doorframe and the door left slightly ajar. With a scowl, I wondered if it was Etrix or Garot. Despite their somewhat friendly attitudes toward me during our travels, neither had been much help to me once I'd been confined.

I rolled onto my back, hands clasped over my stomach, and closed my eyes. *How do I get back home?*

The word *home* brought another layer of conflict. *Where is home in the first place? With the Forest People? At Ridine? With Teryn?*

Thoughts of Teryn pierced my heart with guilt and terror. I thought of our last night together, his strange behavior, his voice when he told me to run. I shook the thoughts away, replacing them with more pleasant memories—the night of our first kiss, our dinner in the garden at Verlot, my delighted surprise when he showed up at Ridine.

A tear slid down my cheek as his smile filled my thoughts. *How could I have left him?* Yet, as soon as I asked, my mind was again filled with our most recent encounters, making my gut feel hollow. *How could he have changed so much?*

A more important question came to mind. *What did I neglect to see?* The calm of truth settled over me, and I realized I'd become so wrapped up in reacting to my experiences, I hadn't taken time to *question* them.

When did I stop trusting myself? The answer came to me quickly; it was the moment I'd found Morkai's poison and remembered what he'd done to me. After that, I'd become fixated on nothing but my pain and heartache, worried over what would come of my future. That obsession had made me lose touch with my present. *What happened while I was stuck in my pain?*

Memories flashed by. I remained detached from the painful emotions that accompanied them—Teryn's hurt expression when I shut him out of the secret room, my

shock at seeing him for the first time after he'd disappeared, his sudden aloofness, his strange behavior.

There. Something changed there. But what?

Grumbling with frustration, I rolled onto my side
again. *I need Salinda now more than ever.* I reflected on my
strange visit with her, still unsure whether it had been a
dream. Her wise words had given me so much hope, only
to have that hope come crashing down on my wedding
night. *Why did Teryn act so strange? Why did he tell me
to run?*

My eyes went wide as an idea crossed my mind. *Will it
work?*

Valorre lifted his head and eyed me through the glass
of the balcony doors. *Where are you going?*

Nowhere, Valorre, I said. *I'm just going to try something...*

I closed my eyes and breathed in deeply, filling my
consciousness with thoughts of Teryn. His terrible
laughter pursuing me as I ran from my wedding bed
came to mind, and I could feel my power draining. I
shook the thought away and focused on things that
flooded me with warmth—the moment we met, when I
shot an arrow over his head to keep him away from
Valorre, the pain of leaving him behind in the dungeon
when I made my escape from Morkai, the relief of finding
him alive at Centerpointe Rock, the moment I realized I
liked him when I was faced with marrying his brother
instead. I suppressed a bittersweet laugh and let the
memories build and build, until finally his face was clear
in my mind.

His hazel eyes looked back at me, the color of rich soil
speckled with summer leaves. His hair, the color of sand
and equally as fine, stood out at odd angles as if he'd just

woken. His lips parted in a smile, then pulled into a frown. "Cora?"

I jumped and found myself surrounded by blinding white light with Teryn at its center. My lips mirrored his, quivering between joy and fear. I took a step toward him. "Teryn?"

He remained still. "Is it really you?"

I nodded.

His shoulders fell, and his face crumbled. "No, it can't be. I told you to run, Cora! You should have stayed away."

I blinked away from his face to take in my surroundings, heart racing. "What is this place?" As soon as the words were out of my mouth, I knew the answer.

Teryn raced to my side and put his hands on my shoulders, eyes rimmed with red. "You need to get back before he finds you here. Where are you? Where did you touch the crystal?"

"She didn't." We whirled toward the voice, and I saw the same woman I'd seen before.

"What do you mean, Emylia?" Teryn asked, his tone sharp. "How could she be here if she didn't touch the crystal?" His wide eyes locked on mine. "No. Please tell me she isn't..."

The woman named Emylia approached me, lips stretching into a smile with every step she took. "No, Teryn. Look at her. This isn't her ethera."

Teryn's eyes moved from my head to my feet, and relief crossed his face. "How?"

Emylia shrugged, then put a hand on my arm. "How did you get here, Cora?"

I eyed her but offered no word of reply.

"You can trust her," Teryn said. "She's been helping me."

"Trying to." Emylia's smile faltered.

"I don't understand what's going on," I said. "I thought of you and found myself here. I was trying to see if I could find you. To talk..."

"It's not safe for you to be here," Teryn said.

I looked again at the white light. "Here...in the crystal?"

He nodded, eyes filling with tears. "I've been stuck here for weeks. The man you've been...the man you married..."

I felt the blood leave my face. "What are you saying?"

"It hasn't been me at all. It's been Morkai."

The name rang through my head, sending a stab of pain to my heart. "Dimetreus..."

"He was right. No one else knows the truth. He's using my body to take control of Ridine."

I tossed my head side to side. "No. This must be a dream."

Teryn put his hands on my face. "Pretend it is. Get out of here, go back to wherever you are, and don't come back to Ridine."

"I can't let him do this!"

"I need you to stay safe."

My eyes held his in all their warmth, soaking in the love and concern I'd missed from him. Calm flooded me. "I'm no safer where I am now than I would be at Ridine. Kero is my responsibility. I will not let Morkai take it from me."

"What can we possibly do?" he asked. "I've been trying to fight him, to regain control, but nothing seems to help."

My mind raced as I struggled to put the pieces of my past few weeks together. "I'll think of something. I'm not letting him take you or my kingdom."

Emylia's head swung to the side. She froze. Teryn and I followed her gaze, but before we could see anything, she grabbed me by the shoulders and forced me to face her. "You need to go back. Now!"

I looked at Teryn, wanting nothing more than to feel his touch one more time. "You must go," he said. "Whatever you do, stay away from Ridine. Don't even come near there. Morkai has men searching for you. Promise me you'll stay away."

I lifted my chin and smiled at him. "I'm sorry, Teryn. I can't."

"Cora—"

"I love you." Before he could respond, I closed my eyes and searched for the feeling of the cot beneath my back. The brightness of the white light faded, and I felt the night of El'Ara touch my eyelids.

I opened my eyes to a flurry of commotion, shouts filling my ears as hands wrapped around my wrists.

"She's here," Etrix said as he pulled me up to stand.

I struggled in his grasp, seeking Valorre. I sighed with relief when I saw he was still on the balcony. Garot had been leaning over the rail and now turned toward us, throwing his hands in the air. "I knew she didn't jump," he mumbled.

Fanon stormed over to me and brought his face close to mine. "Where were you?" His eyes burned like embers, and his lips pulled into a snarl. His Elvan beauty had been stripped away, his features distorted with monstrous fury.

"What do you mean? I've been here the entire time."

"I came in to check on you," Etrix said, his voice neutral as ever, "and you were nowhere to be found. I told you not to try and run."

"But I..." Words were lost as I contemplated the meaning of their surprise. *I'd really left, body and all. How is that possible?* I looked at Valorre. *Is it true? Was I really gone?*

Just as before.

You mean with Salinda?

Yes.

"She must be using human magic," Fanon said. "The tribunal can wait no longer. Take her. The unicorn too." He pushed me forward, and Etrix hooked my hand in the crook of his arm.

I looked behind me as Valorre began to follow.

"I told you not to run," Etrix said with the closest thing to regret I could have heard in his voice. "They will force Last Breath upon you. It will hurt."

With eyes unfocused, I made my way toward my death.

30

WARNING

Mareleau

My heart beat high in my chest as my eyes darted around the courtyard, investigating every corner and shadow for signs of hidden movement. A hand gripped my wrist, and I scowled at Teryn.

"I told you not to worry, dear sister," he said. "My brother will not be harmed like your father was."

I turned my attention back to the courtyard, focusing on the sound of hooves approaching. The sun was setting, sending an eerie light over the walls of Ridine to fall on those who awaited my husband's arrival. Every caw of a bird made me flinch. Every gust of wind sent me searching for hidden soldiers.

"You have nothing to worry about, now that your uncles are gone."

I clenched my jaw to refrain from spewing arguments and insults, and kept my eyes locked on the gate ahead.

My limbs trembled the louder the hooves became, and the blood left my face entirely at the first sight of a rider. I was nearly sobbing by the time Larylis appeared in the courtyard.

His eyes locked on mine, and he sprang from his mount to gather me in his arms. Our lips met in hungry kisses, making me forget my fear for one moment.

As we pulled away, his face swam before my tear-glazed eyes. I blinked to clear them, wanting nothing more than to study the expanse of his skin, eyes, and mouth in detail. "I've missed you so much." My voice came out with a rasp.

Larylis' eyes shimmered as much as mine. "I've missed you more than words can say."

A shadow fell beside us, and I tensed. Larylis turned his head toward Teryn and forced a smile. "Hello, Brother."

Teryn's face was full of false solemnity as they hugged. "I wish we were visiting on better circumstances, but I fear things have gone from bad to worse here at Ridine."

"I cannot believe Cora went missing." Larylis kept his eyes on Teryn and reached for my hand, as if to remind me I was still at the fore of his attention. "You must be devastated. Do you know where she has gone?"

Teryn lowered his head. "I don't know. I've sent scouts to search the woods, but she's nowhere to be found."

"Why would she have left?"

Teryn lifted his head and shrugged. "I think she was too upset by all that has happened. She had to witness her brother go mad and then was forced to marry unexpectedly. I tried to make her happy."

I burned Teryn with a glare that he refused to meet.

Larylis didn't seem to notice the tension between me and his brother as he scanned the courtyard, watching his men dismount. "Where is the council? Lord Ulrich and Lord Kevan?"

Teryn sighed. "That's where things went far worse, dear brother."

"What happened?"

"I fear they've been plotting against us all since they first arrived. Neither were happy about being sent here, much less about Kevan being passed over as heir in favor of the two of you. Seeing me become King of Kero was the breaking point."

"Where are they now?"

Teryn's eyes fell on mine, and he gave me a tender frown. I returned it with a deepening glare. "They have left for Verlot," Teryn said. "They have gone to reunite the original council and unseat Verdian. Kevan will claim himself the rightful heir."

Larylis' eyes went wide. "They can't do such a thing."

"They have more support than one would think. Not everyone was pleased with Verdian's choice of heir."

Larylis shook his head. "I don't understand. Where is Verdian? I was told he was on his way here before me."

My blood boiled as I awaited Teryn's explanation. "All I can say is thank goodness you didn't arrive with him," he said. "They formed a plot to arrest him and the councilmen most loyal to him."

"He's in the dungeon right now," I said through my teeth, eyes boring into Teryn.

Larylis looked from me to his brother. "Why is he still

in there? Shouldn't you free him and send men after Kevan and Ulrich?"

Teryn's face fell. "I wish I could, but I am king only in name. Ulrich and Kevan left loyal men here to watch over Ridine. They are guarding the prisoners in the dungeon, and no man is allowed anywhere near it."

Larylis' cheeks and neck became flushed with color. "We can't let this happen. My wife's father is prisoner. We must do something."

Teryn put a finger to his lips and looked around the courtyard. "Be careful what you say here. You never know where Lord Kevan's spies are."

Larylis took a step away from his brother. "Am I in danger too?"

"Of course not. No order has been made against you, and while Mareleau's uncles are away, we will be left at peace."

"At peace while the rightful king of Verlot is imprisoned beneath our feet."

Teryn's jaw shifted back and forth. "Give it time, brother. I'm sure we will think of something. Ah, Master Arther." Teryn extended his arm as Arther approached. "Please show Larylis his rooms." He turned back to me and my husband. "Would you like to stay in the master chamber together?"

Larylis opened his mouth, but I spoke before he could utter a word. "No, thank you. Master Arther, allow my ladies to share the master chamber. My husband and I will sleep in the room I am used to."

Larylis brought his lips to my ear. "In your last letter, you said you'd give anything for a bigger room."

"Much has changed since then. I feel safest where I am most comfortable."

He furrowed his brow as he looked at me, and I tried to convey the weight of my words through my stony expression. With light lips, he brushed my forehead and turned his attention back to Master Arther. "Her room then. It is getting late. We should retire now."

"Surely you must at least join me for dinner in the great hall," Teryn said.

I lifted my chin and faced him. "I haven't seen my husband in a long time. You must understand our need to be alone."

He nodded. "I'll have dinner brought to you then. And wine." He winked at me, then looked at Larylis. "For my brother."

~

Teryn

"I don't know how many more lies I can watch that man pour out of my mouth," I muttered as I paced within the crystal. "This cannot go on."

Emylia watched me, folding and unfolding her hands before her. "Teryn, I'm so sorry I haven't been able to do more for you."

"It's not your fault." I looked at my fingers, trying to remember what it was like to be more than my ethera. "If I had power like you or Cora, I could do this."

"You've been doing your best. You've remained connected to your vitale, and you've even managed to touch your cereba."

At her words, I felt the rise and fall of my lungs, the beating of my heart, the rush of my blood. "I wish it were enough. I must get my body back."

"You're so close, Teryn. I know you are. You just need more practice."

I stopped pacing and recalled the look in Morkai's eyes as he watched Mareleau and my brother ascend the stairs to their room. There was danger dancing within them. "He's going to kill my brother."

Emylia made no word to argue.

I rubbed my hands over my face. "And Cora. When Cora returns he'll have her where he wants her. For the love of Lela, why couldn't she promise to stay away?"

Emylia stood at my side. "You love her so much."

I nodded, feeling a lump rise in my throat.

She sighed. "I still remember what it felt like to be loved like that."

My eyes met hers. "Even after what he's become, how can you still think of him with sentimentality?"

"Who he is now is not the man I loved. Love doesn't die that easily."

I frowned and turned my head away from her. It was hard to stomach any word said in Morkai's defense.

"I do believe there is good in him, somewhere beneath the layers of darkness he's wrapped himself in. His darkness came from pain and loss. Loss of his mother, loss of his father's love, loss of me—"

"I don't want to hear it." I felt a twinge of guilt for the sharpness of my tone.

Emylia opened her mouth, then snapped it shut.

"I have to stop him, not save him."

Her eyes fell to the floor. She nodded. "I know. And you're right, he needs to be stopped. What will you do?"

"Everything I can. This ends tonight."

Larylis

"Sing me our song," Mareleau said with a smile as she brushed out her long, golden hair.

I sat next to her on the bed, my eyes straying from her face, to her nightdress, to the rosy hue in her cheeks. "Why would you have me ruin our first night together by making you suffer my singing voice?"

She swatted me playfully and rolled her eyes. "I've done nothing but read it over and over, imagining the sound of your voice." She set the brush on a table next to the bed and gathered my hands in hers. "It's been the only thing that has gotten me through being here."

My heart sank at the emptiness in her eyes. I'd anticipated her usual scorn over her situation, but I never expected to find her as I had in the courtyard that evening—shoulders low, voice weak and trembling. Even the looks she gave my brother sent a chill through me. "You really aren't doing well here, are you?"

"Everything was terrible to begin with, but then your brother arrived." Her voice was full of disgust. "I was starting to get along with him, I swear. And then...it was like he changed."

"What do you mean?"

A shudder ran through her. "I don't want to talk about

it. Let's just say he's been much worse since Cora ran away from him."

Her words made me pause. "Ran away *from him?* Why do you say it like that?"

"Do you really believe she ran away from her responsibilities because life was too hard? I don't know her well, but I do know she's stronger than that. She ran away on her wedding night and wouldn't even return to her room to fetch her cloak, for fear of seeing him again."

"You...saw her? Before she left?"

She nodded. "I gave her my cloak. I thought my duties to her would be over once she was gone, but I was stupid to believe that would be the case."

I chewed my lip as I pondered her words.

She continued, "I was terrified you were going to be arrested and locked up like my father. Teryn acts like he's sorry for what happened, and that keeping me in my room night and day is for my own good, but I don't believe him."

"He said your uncles are responsible for what happened."

She let out a short laugh. "Is that why he stood by and watched it happen without lifting a finger? Is that why he has no plan to free him?"

I shook my head. "Teryn wouldn't be like that."

Mareleau glared and crossed her arms over her chest.

"I'm not saying I don't believe you. I'm just surprised by your account of things."

She raised an eyebrow. "Sounds exactly like you don't believe me, plain and simple."

"Let's not fight, my love. This is our first night back together." I forced a smile and turned toward the table where a bottle of wine sat—a gift from my brother, brought up with our dinner. "Let's celebrate instead."

Mareleau opened her mouth to speak, but no words came as I moved to the table and began to fill our two goblets with wine. "I know how much you love your wine." I returned to the bed and handed her a cup.

She accepted but made no move to drink as she stared at its ruby-red contents. Her eyes lifted to meet mine, and she set her cup on the table. "There's something I need to tell you."

My heart quickened, and I set my cup next to hers. "What is it?"

Her eyes glazed with tears, and her hand slid over her belly. "I'm pregnant. *Really* pregnant."

Her words sent a rush of blood to my face and robbed me of all speech. My eyes darted from her face to her belly as I struggled to form a coherent word.

"Please say something."

Laughter was all I could produce, followed by a joyous shout. "You're serious? Please tell me you're serious."

Mareleau's face broke into a smile as tears ran down her cheeks. "I am."

I pulled her into my arms and covered her face in kisses. It felt as if my heart would explode with joy. "This is the best news. You can't imagine how happy you have made me."

She sighed. "I'm so glad, Larylis. I was terrified to tell you."

"Why?"

She shrugged. "No reason, I suppose. It just makes it so much more real."

I pulled back so I could take in the full beauty before me—my wife bearing my child. My eyes fell on the goblets, still full beside the bed, and laughed. "I suppose I will have to celebrate for the two of us."

Mareleau handed me both cups. "You mean for the three of us?"

I nodded. "The three of us." I raised the goblets, clinked them together, and brought one to my lips. But before I could take a drink, a knock pounded at the door.

∼

Teryn

It felt like an eternity as we waited for the sound of shuffling steps to enter the crystal. We stared into the bright, white light until we spotted the telltale waft of inky blackness creeping forth. Morkai's shadowy form floated in and away, as if coming in from one door and out another.

I looked at Emylia, and she nodded. Not a moment later, my bedroom in Ridine formed around us. On the bed was my empty body, face slack, chest rising and falling with breaths that echoed within me. I took my place on the bed, feeling the buzzing resistance surround me as I aligned myself within my body.

The racing of my blood and the beating of my heart felt more harmonious than ever as I poured my focus into my vitale. Next, I turned my attention to the resistance of the blankets surrounding me, of the mattress supporting my form, of my hair tickling my face where it rested. I felt the lightness of the air touch my skin, felt the coolness of it fill my lungs.

"Try to open your hand," Emylia said in a soft voice.

I focused on one of my hands curled at my side, feeling the muscles within, and the warmth of the blankets beneath it. One finger flinched. Then another. With a deep breath, I felt my entire hand uncurl.

"Now the other." Emylia led me from hand to hand, foot to foot, until I managed to control all four corners of my body. "Now open your eyes."

I resisted the anxiety that clawed at my mind as I imagined such a feat. Instead, I refocused on my vitale, on the sweat beading at my brow and within every fold and crevice of my skin, on the buzzing of my limbs as they responded to my command. I felt the muscles twitch in my face, felt the flutter of my eyelids. I opened my eyes.

Emylia's face stared back at me, a wide smile stretched over her lips. "You did it." Her voice was still soft, which allowed me to keep from getting too excited. I refocused on my body, on the suddenly heavy burden of my ethera, vitale, and cereba working under my command. With slow, jerky movements, I sat up in the bed. My head spun as if I'd drank too much wine, and my body felt as if it were made of mush.

"Take it slow," Emylia warned as I swung my legs over the bed and began to stand. "Slow. Step by step."

Sweat drenched my shirt as I moved from the bed to the door, every step feeling as if I were balancing a stack of uneven plates on toothpicks. I was nowhere near having full control over my body, but perhaps I had enough. *Enough is all I need.*

Time seemed to slow as I made my way through the empty corridor to Mareleau's room. Emylia kept her voice soothing as she encouraged me and reminded me what to focus on. Finally, we were outside the door. Sweat dripped into my eyes as I lifted my fist, heavy and unwieldy as if it were not a hand but a shield, and slammed it against the wood. I cringed at the sound it made.

I heard movement from within the room, followed by the opening of the door. I blinked into the pale light of the lantern-lit chamber and lifted my face to meet the wide-eyed stare of my brother.

"Teryn?" In one hand he held a goblet. Over his shoulder, Mareleau glared. "Is something wrong?"

My mouth twitched, and I felt a reverberating in my chest as I shaped words with air, mind, and muscle. They came out slurred and heavy, sounding completely unlike my own. "Don't drink anything I give you."

"Are you drunk?" A corner of Larylis' mouth lifted, as if he wanted to smile, but I saw blood leave his face.

"Do not trust anything I've said or anything I say beyond this moment. I am not...who you think...I am." I felt my energy fade as my breathing grew shallow and my knees began to buckle. "Morkai...has me. He's using...my...body."

"What are you talking about?" Larylis bent to lift me as I slid the ground. "What do I do?"

My words came out in a gasp before I lost control completely. "Kill me."

31

JUDGMENT

Larylis

I stared down at my brother's body, limp and lifeless aside from the sparse, shallow breaths he took as he laid upon his bed. Sweat dripped down my back from the effort it had taken to carry him back to his room.

Mareleau squeezed my hand from her place beside me. "What do we do?" Her voice was thick with fear.

My mouth gaped open before I could find my words. "I don't know. I hardly understand what we just witnessed."

"He told us not to drink anything. Do you think the wine..."

She didn't need to finish her sentence for me to grasp her meaning. Luckily, none had touched my lips. But why would the wine be poisoned in the first place? What did Teryn mean when he said Morkai was controlling his body? Nothing made sense. The words of his final request rang through my mind. *Kill me. Kill me.*

Mareleau squeezed my hand again, reminding me of the dagger I held in my other. My eyes filled with tears as I looked over my brother's body and imagined my dagger plunging into skin, tissue, and bone. "I can't do it," I gasped.

"Why did he even ask such a thing of you?"

I swallowed the lump in my throat. "If Morkai is truly controlling his body, Teryn's death might be the only way to stop him."

"But what about Morkai?" Her shoulder brushed mine as she shuddered. "How is it even possible he's controlling him? You saw the sorcerer die."

"I did. What he says is impossible." I turned to face my wife. "But you saw Teryn. You saw the look in his eyes, the strangeness of his movements. You told me yourself you witnessed a drastic change in him since he came here."

One shoulder lifted in a shrug. "I figured he'd been a jerk all along and had only been hiding it before. I never suspected a *sorcerer* was controlling him."

I lowered my head and squeezed my eyes shut. "I don't know what to do. I can't kill my own brother. I wish he'd been able to tell us more." I looked back at Teryn's body. "Damn you, brother. Come back."

Mareleau and I stood in silence as my mind raced over every option. Finally, Mareleau spoke, her voice almost a whisper. "We could run."

"Run." I rolled the word over my tongue as if it were new. "What good would that do?"

"It would keep us safe. And our baby."

"If Morkai is still alive, no one is safe no matter where we go."

"What would we do if we stay? What if the man who wakes up isn't Teryn?"

My knees trembled as her words filled me with a sense of urgency. "Your father is here, Mare. *Morkai* has your father. He's used Teryn's body to become King of Kero, right under everyone's nose. He will kill your father next, if he hasn't already."

"And what about you, Lare?" Her voice came out with a sob. "Don't you see? He now has the three kings of Lela under the same roof. If he's using Teryn, then all that stands between him ruling over all of Lela are the lives of you and my father. If I can't save my father, at least I can save you."

"And do what? Try to convince the others before it's too late? Gather an army to fight him? Start another war?"

Her jaw was set as her eyes locked on mine. "What other choice do you have?"

Again, I became aware of the dagger I held. My stomach twisted as I stepped toward Teryn. Still and sleeping as he was, he looked like nothing more than my childhood friend, the boy I'd grown up with. Despair shook me from head to toe as I suppressed a shout. *I can't do this. I can't do this!*

Teryn's hand flinched. I jumped, holding my breath as I watched his breathing begin to deepen. The muscles in his face twitched, followed by the fluttering of his eyelids. His head turned toward me, eyes open and locked on mine. His gaze slid from my face to the dagger in my hand. "Hello, brother," he said with a smile. "How good to see you."

~

Cora

The dark room began to fill as a dozen or so slender Elvan bodies filed through the door. At the head of the retinue was Fanon, while Etrix stood just inside the door. Garot stood on the opposite end of the room, a few paces from my left. Valorre and I stood on the floor at the center of the room, facing two tiers of raised platforms where elegant chairs had been placed.

I tried to keep my mouth from hanging open as I examined the beautiful faces, some male, some female, and some appearing somewhere in between. Each Elvan was unique in the color of their skin and hair, with every shade from ivory to onyx, yet their features were similar. Each had long, flowing locks, almond-shaped eyes in gemstones hues, and sweeping robes in shimmering, patterned fabrics.

Even though they weren't all pale-skinned and silver-haired like my childhood stories had claimed, they bore an opalescent sheen from head to toe. Another contrast between the tales and the evidence before me was their countenance. The Ancient Ones were said to be the epitome of kindness, fairness, wisdom, and generosity, but the faces before me showed nothing but fear and scorn.

I looked to Etrix and Garot, the two Elvan who'd shown me the least disdain, and wondered if they simply knew how to hide their hatred better than the others. Were they equally eager to see me die?

Once the tribunal was seated with Fanon front and center, I began to tremble. What would they do? Would my death come quickly? Or would I be given time to think?

Fanon cleared his throat, and his eyes darted to mine. I shifted under his gaze; it was the longest he'd ever looked at me. "The tribunal has gathered. Human, you are guilty of infiltrating El'Ara and using human magic. What do you have to say about that?"

I suppressed a smirk, finding it ironic that he was now acknowledging his ability to understand me. "I came to El'Ara completely against my will. Valorre can attest to that."

A round of gasps followed as I pointed to my unicorn companion. Whispers spread throughout the room, and I heard the word *named* uttered several times.

I ground my teeth, cursing myself for mentioning his name. "The unicorn," I corrected, "brought me here by accident, following memories of home. He didn't intend to come here either, and once we arrived, we wanted nothing more than to leave."

Fanon narrowed his blue eyes. "Yet when we brought you to the veil, you claimed the unicorn couldn't find where you'd come in. How are we to believe you didn't use human magic to get here?"

I threw my hands in the air. "Why would any human choose to come here, magic or no, considering the welcome you offer?"

"I have offered you fair treatment, considering your crimes. You have been unharmed during your stay." Fanon looked from Etrix to Garot. "You've been treated—by some —far better than your kind deserves. And how did you repay our trust? By using human magic to try and escape."

"Trust? I've seen no trust from you whatsoever. My disappearance from the room was another accident. Yet, if I *were* able to use human magic to leave, shouldn't you let me? Isn't it in all our best interests that I leave, regardless of how?"

A wave of angry grumbles rolled amongst the tribunal. Some of the Elvan shook their heads in disbelief. Fanon pursed his lips and curled his hand into a fist. He spoke through his teeth. "If it turns out you *are* able to use human magic to leave, then what is to stop you from returning? What is to stop you from bringing more of your kind to destroy us?"

The tribunal spoke their agreement.

"I promise you, I have no intention to return."

"Your promise means nothing to us. You are a danger." Fanon turned toward his comrades, meeting nods of agreement. He returned his gaze to me. "You will take Last Breath."

Fire flooded my veins as I opened my mouth to argue. I barely noticed when Etrix came to my side. Fanon's eyes went wide as Etrix stepped toward him and bowed.

"Steward," Etrix said, "it is our way to allow the ones under tribunal to choose Last Breath for themselves before forcing it upon them."

Fanon's face turned an odd shade of green as his eyes slanted dangerously. "You speak as if you know better than the tribunal."

"I speak only to keep our ways one with the Morkara. It is the human way to sentence a criminal to death, not ours."

Fanon curled and uncurled his fists, and I could see his temples pulsing. My heart raced as I worried over

Etrix's fate. Finally, Fanon let out a grumbling sigh. "The human will never choose Last Breath for herself. I chose a human sentence to suit the criminal."

Etrix nodded. "You very well may be right, steward. But will you allow me to try? If she will see the truth and accept Last Breath, we will remain pure in our ways. Her existence will leave us without the taint of her kind."

The tribunal nodded their assent, and Fanon was forced to nod his. "Fine."

Etrix bowed, then faced me. "Human. I have shared with you the stories of El'Ara. You have seen the pain and destruction brought into this world from your kind."

"But I had nothing to do with that. I've been taught to respect the Ancient Realm since I was a child. I would never bring harm here, and I never would have come if I'd been able to avoid it."

"I understand, and I sense goodness in you." The tribunal whispered amongst themselves at his declaration. "But you must understand the risk. You know what has happened to us, to El'Ara when mercy was offered your kind. We paid for it dearly."

"I am not the one who hurt you."

"You *are*. The human taint is within you. You carry the dark deeds of your ancestors and their potential for betrayal. We cannot let you go, nor can we allow you to stay. You must take Last Breath."

I looked into his eyes, my heart filling with guilt as I felt how hard he was trying to fight for me in his own strange way.

He continued, "Choosing Last Breath is an honor that the wisest of our kind have chosen. We are allowing you to leave your wisdom behind and ascend to the otherlife without force."

I calmed my racing heart and slowly nodded.

"You understand you must die?"

I kept my voice steady. "Yes."

"You are accepting Last Breath?"

I looked from Etrix to Garot, then to the tribunal. Awe-filled faces stared back at me, no longer scowling. I turned back to Etrix. "I accept."

No, Valorre said, tapping his hooves with agitation.

A flicker of relief passed over Etrix's face.

"And the unicorn?" Fanon asked.

No, Valorre repeated.

I ignored my friend. "He accepts too."

"Good. Do you know how to take Last Breath?"

I kept my face still, my mind empty. "I do, but I have one last request."

Fanon scowled. "We do not offer final requests."

I folded my hands before me as my lips turned down, eyes filled with tears. "I just want to say goodbye to Valorre." A sob escaped my throat. "He's my best friend."

Fanon's eyes shot from me to Valorre. "Very well. Make it fast."

I ran to Valorre and wrapped my arms around his neck, feeling his muscles twitching beneath my hands.

Why are you doing this? Valorre asked.

Calm, Valorre. It's going to be all right. I pressed my face into his coat and pulled my arms tighter around him. I thought of Etrix, of how he'd tried to help me, and guilt tugged at my mind. I pushed it away and instead thought of Teryn, my brother, Salinda, and Maiya. My heart swelled with tenderness as I thought of Lela, of Kero, of

Ridine. I thought of the cliff overlooking the valley, where Teryn had told me he loved me. Smells of grass, leaves, and flowers filled my nostrils. Cool wind touched my skin and pulled my hair into the breeze. Shouts surged toward me, but they sounded as if they came from behind a closed door. Then they were no more. I heard nothing but the rustling of grass, branches swaying with the wind, and birds singing as they swooped overhead.

I unwrapped my arms from around Valorre and opened my eyes to the morning light. The valley spanned out below the edge of the cliff toward the mountains that danced behind a misty, morning haze. I fell to my knees, dizzy from the power I'd used, but a smile melted over my face. We were home.

32

RETURN

Cora

Once my head stopped spinning, I gathered in deep breaths of air, letting it fill my lungs and return the energy to my body. I stood and lifted my face to the sun shining upon the cliff. Valorre quivered beside me; he was still recovering from our tense getaway.

"I'm so sorry, Valorre," I said as I stroked the side of his neck. "I'm sorry I didn't warn you about what I did."

I was so scared. Didn't understand.

"I know, but I needed to make sure no one could sense my motive. That's why I didn't tell you. Besides, I wasn't even sure it would work."

Dangerous.

"I didn't know what else to do. We're safe now."

Safe?

I understood his meaning. "You're right. Safe isn't the right word. We are no longer stuck in El'Ara, at least."

It gets more dangerous now.

My heart was heavy with the weight of truth. "Yes, it does."

I'll know the plan this time?

I smiled. "This time, we're in this together. I have an idea."

AFTER PARTING WITH VALORRE, I LEFT THE CLIFF AND made my way to Ridine. Once the castle came into view between the trees, I heard a rustling behind me. I paused. Footsteps neared, and I extended my power to seek who followed.

I spun around as four armed men dressed in Ridine's colors approached me with swords drawn.

"Princess Coralaine?" one of the men asked.

I raised my arms in surrender. "That would be me. Are you here to take me to my dear husband?"

"We are," the man answered.

"Well, then. Best get on with it." The men hesitated, as if they weren't sure how to proceed. My gaze touched each man in turn, taking in their hollow cheeks and pale complexions. Each man flinched beneath my scrutiny and refused to meet my eyes. "I haven't seen any of you as guards before. Are you new?"

The men exchanged a glance, and the one who'd spoken before cleared his throat. "We were hired as a special force to find you."

"It looks like you've found me." I narrowed my eyes at him, and his face lowered to his feet. Whoever these men were, they weren't trained hunters. While they each held their swords with ease and familiarity, they didn't seem comfortable with their task.

They led me to Ridine, swords trained on me despite the reluctance in their faces. Once we entered the courtyard, we paused, and one of the men ran into the castle. The rest surrounded me. My eyes wandered around the courtyard, finding it suspiciously empty for a castle that was in the middle of being rebuilt and re-staffed.

The sound of feet approaching brought my attention to the main door. I held my breath as they neared, forcing my face from falling into a scowl as the body of Teryn appeared. *Morkai.*

He froze when his eyes met mine, putting a hand over his heart as he let out a heavy breath. "My dear, I'm so glad they found you." With long strides he reached me, shouldering the men out of his way with a scowl. "Sheath those swords, you fools. I told you to find her, bring her home safe. *Not* hold her prisoner."

He's good. I allowed my face to soften as if I believed his words and looked down at my feet. "I'm sorry I left you. I...I needed some time."

His arms wrapped around me, and I suppressed the nausea that rippled through my stomach. "Don't apologize, my dear. It is I who should be sorry. I never should have rushed you." He pulled away and smiled at me in a way that was a near-perfect impersonation of Teryn. Yet his eyes remained narrowed where Teryn's would have turned down at the corners, brows lifted and knitted together.

How did I not see it before?

He rubbed his hand along my arm, far slower and heavier than Teryn would have. "You're home now, that's what matters. So much has happened. I've been worried sick for weeks."

Weeks. I recalled my time in El'Ara and could count no more than one day that I'd been there. I'd been sent to the tribunal at the end of my first night. Yet, when I really thought about it, it seemed impossible to measure the duration of my stay. Time in El'Ara was not as it was in my world.

Morkai cocked his head. "What's wrong?"

I shook my thoughts away and brought my attention back to him. "Nothing. I just feel terrible for worrying you so long."

"Like I said, you're home now, and that's what matters." His gaze swept over the men who'd brought me. "I have you to thank for this happy reunion. You have done well and will be greatly rewarded."

"It was nothing," said one of the men. "She was nearly here when we found her." The man next to him clenched his jaw and elbowed him in the side.

Morkai laughed. "You will be rewarded just the same. No one else has managed to report even a glimpse of her." He turned back to me and offered his arm. I accepted it with a false smile. "Where did you go, anyway? I've sent men all over Kero looking for you."

I kept my voice neutral and selected the most innocent of truths. "I wanted to find the Forest People."

"And did you?"

I shook my head. "I decided to come home before I found them."

He led me inside the castle. "Ah. Very good."

"And what of you? You said much has happened since I've been gone." I added some warmth to my voice and expression. "I've been as worried about you as you've been about me."

He met my eyes as we strolled down the main hall. "Terrible things have happened, my dear." I stared back at him, suddenly aware of the dark circles beneath his bloodshot eyes.

"What's wrong?" The words were meant more for Teryn than Morkai, but their effect was the same.

His face fell. "Lord Kevan and Lord Ulrich have done awful things here. They've all but taken over entirely. King Verdian is being held prisoner in the dungeon, guarded by their own loyal men. I'm not even allowed near there. Meanwhile, they've gone to Verlot to put Kevan on the throne."

"Why would they do this?" I asked with mock surprise. It took no power of mine to know he'd constructed the plan himself.

He shrugged. "They've been angry with Verdian for sending them here from the start, for making Mareleau his heir instead of Kevan. They believe their actions right Verdian's wrongs."

"That's terrible."

"What's worse, I fear Ulrich will turn on Kevan before they even make it to Verlot."

His words filled me with the calm of truth, and I began to see the tapestry of his scheme weave together in vibrant color in my mind's eye. "Why would you think that?"

Morkai turned away from me, hand under his chin. "Since Verdian has no sons, Kevan should have been next in line for the throne. However, Kevan has only daughters himself. Ulrich, on the other hand, has three young sons."

He lifted his face and looked my way. While his expression was soft and full of sympathy, I could see darkness in his eyes. "Ulrich said so himself. He's going to claim that *he* is the rightful heir to Sele."

Fire flooded my body as his pattern was made complete. I was filled with both terror and awe as I understood the intricacies of his weavings. He'd found a way to make himself King of Kero while manipulating others into destroying his next obstacles. Verdian was now his prisoner, and the two men who would oppose his rule were killing each other. Once Verdian was dead, his rule would pass to Mareleau and Larylis, who would rule Sele and Mena together.

Leaving nothing but Larylis' life between Morkai and rule over Lela.

Morkai studied my face. "I can see you are as upset over this news as I've been."

I nodded. My mouth felt dry as I tried to keep my voice and expression even. "How has Mareleau taken the news? And what of your brother? If Kevan or Ulrich win, they will certainly show no mercy to Mareleau and Larylis."

"Oh yes, they fear greatly for their throne. In fact, Larylis came to retrieve Mareleau very recently. They have returned to Dermaine to defend Mena from possible attack by the uncles."

"You mean, they were both here? Larylis too?"

He nodded. "Just long enough for him to take Mareleau home."

"But they left her father here?"

"They had no choice. I told you, the guards are loyal

to Kevan and Ulrich. They will kill before allowing anyone to enter."

My eyes went unfocused as I measured his lies.

Morkai put his hands on my shoulders. "I'm sorry to have you arrive to such a cold welcome. I wish I had better tidings for you."

I forced a smile. "I'm sure we'll get through this."

"We will. In the meantime, I have much work to do. I may have been left without much control, but I promise you I'm doing everything I possibly can."

"As your queen, shouldn't I help you?"

"No, my dear. You rest."

"Will I see you tonight?" My heart began to race, and my stomach churned.

He brought his forehead to mine and closed his eyes. "I remember how things last ended between us. I'd rather give you all the space you need. Come to me when you're ready."

I let out a heavy sigh of relief and pulled my lips into a tight smile. "I appreciate that."

He leaned in closer and brushed his lips over mine before turning away without a word. As he made his way toward the great hall, I let my face twist with the malice that burned in my veins.

As I walked down the hall of the great keep toward my bedroom, my eyes darted toward every corner and shadow, every flicker of movement. Aside from the occasional maid, it was empty. I paused outside the closed door to Mareleau's room. With hesitant steps, I reached for the handle and pushed it open. Daylight streamed through the windows, showing a perfectly clean room. Nothing seemed amiss; no signs of struggle, no clothing strewn about. It looked as if Morkai had been telling the truth—that Larylis had taken her and her belongings back to Dermaine.

I left her room as I'd found it and made my way toward my own, shuddering as flashes of my last night there ran through my mind. My hands clenched into fists as I cursed myself for not realizing then that Teryn had clearly not been himself.

As I approached my room, a trill of feminine voices came from within, quieting as soon as I pushed on the door. Locked. I pounded on the heavy wood.

Whispers responded, followed by the sound of soft footsteps. The door slid open, revealing a sliver of Sera. With a gasp she flung the door open completely. "It's just you, Your Highness...I mean, Your Majesty. You are queen now, aren't you? I can't believe you're back."

I ignored her words and entered the room. My eyes widened at the contrast between Mareleau's spotless room and the chaos within mine. It appeared Mareleau's ladies had made my room their home.

Sera followed my line of vision. "Mareleau sent us to stay here when King Larylis arrived."

Breah and Ann seemed to sink into the cushions of the couch, where they sat amongst what appeared to be my dresses.

Sera gasped and ran to the couch. The other girls followed her cue and sprang to their feet, rushing to hang my wrinkled dresses and straighten the bed. "We're sorry,

Your Majesty," Sera said with a tremor. "We honestly didn't think you'd be back."

"We...tried on your dresses," mumbled Ann behind my blue gown.

Breah's eyes were wide as she turned to face me with a deep curtsy. "Forgive us, Your Majesty. We were all alone. We didn't know..."

If matters weren't so grave, I would have laughed. While their actions were silly and would likely have gotten them a heavy scolding from Mareleau, I couldn't have cared less whether they played dress-up with my things. However, much more critical issues needed to be discussed.

"I don't care about any of that." I waved my hand at the girls to stop their anxious fluttering. "You can help me clean this room later. I need to know about Mareleau and Larylis. Why did they leave you behind?"

The three girls came forward, eyes downcast. Ann spoke. "We don't know. She never said a word."

"She must have been angry at us," Breah said.

"When did you last see her?" I asked.

Ann twirled a red curl around her finger. "The night King Larylis arrived. They went to bed in Mareleau's room, while we were sent to sleep here. In the morning they were both gone."

"Were you given a reason?"

"King Teryn said they left before dawn," Breah said, wringing her hands. "He said King Larylis insisted Mareleau return home to Dermaine with him."

Ann shrugged. "Something about the baby, perhaps?"

"Or the fact that her father is a prisoner," Sera muttered.

"But why did she leave you three behind?" I asked.

Sera shuffled her feet. "King Teryn said Mareleau left us to take her place and wait for your return."

"Which makes no sense," Ann said with a scowl. "She wouldn't have left without the three of us. She could have just left Sera."

Sera's mouth fell open as she rounded on Ann. "Me? Why would she leave me? Perhaps she would have left *you*."

"She'd already given you away as Princess Coralaine's chambermaid."

"*Queen* Coralaine now, you cow."

Breah put her arm between the two girls. "Stop bickering. She left *all* of us."

Ann and Sera exchanged a glare, then faced me with red cheeks. "I can't even imagine how she could travel without at least one of us," Ann muttered.

Their words confirmed my deepest suspicions. Mareleau and Larylis had not left by choice. Perhaps they hadn't left at all.

Teryn

The sound of my name came to me as if through water, echoing relentlessly until I opened my eyes. I blinked at the figure above me. Cora's face came into view, surrounded by Emylia's temple bedroom.

"Cora?" the words felt heavy, as if my tongue had to lift them straight from my heart.

She smiled, but the concern in her eyes could not be mistaken. "What's happening to him?"

Emylia appeared at her side and knelt next to me. "It's my fault. I shouldn't have encouraged him."

"To do what?"

"He...took control of his cereba. I thought the fact that he could do it meant he was ready. I didn't realize..."

"What is a cereba?"

Emylia's jaw moved as if she were considering her words. "Teryn needs certain connections to have full control over his body. Before recently, he'd had excellent control over his life force. But after he tried to integrate it with control over his mind, he lost control over everything. His life force connection has grown weak."

"What does that mean?"

Emylia opened her mouth, but I managed to summon my words before she could. "Cora, what are you doing here?"

Her eyes met mine, and her face fell. "Teryn, what happened?"

"You shouldn't be here. It's dangerous. He could find you."

"Tell me what I need to know, and I'll leave." Her words were stern while her face remained gentle.

A sudden thought occurred to me, and I attempted to bolt upright. However, movement refused to respond the way I wanted. I managed to lift myself a hand-span from the floor before my vision swam.

"You must rest," Emylia said. "Don't try to move until you reconnect with your vitale."

I felt a distant sensation of shallow breathing in my

chest. My eyes locked back on Cora's. "Where are you now? Please tell me you didn't return to Ridine."

"I'm not going to let you be taken over by Morkai."

I ground my teeth, knowing the truth behind her answer. "You came back, didn't you? You need to leave. He will...use you. There are things you don't know."

"Then tell me. Give me anything I can use against him. Do you have any idea what he has been doing with your body?"

"I used to."

Emylia added, "Before Teryn lost connection with his vitale, we'd spent much of our time watching Morkai."

"You can do that from within the crystal?" Cora asked.

"Yes," Emylia said, "but since the...incident...I've stayed at his side. I don't know what Morkai has been doing since."

"When was the last time you saw Mareleau? And did you see Larylis?"

Emylia's eyes turned to me.

I gathered my strength and my words. "I saw them. That's why I did what I did. I feared for my brother's life and gave him a warning."

Emylia raised an eyebrow, which was not missed by Cora. "What?" Cora asked, eyes darting from me to Emylia.

Emylia turned to Cora. "He told his brother to kill him."

Cora's face flashed between terror and anger. Her eyes were fierce when they turned on me. "How could you tell him to do such a thing?"

I held Cora's eyes with all the tenderness and truth I

could muster. "It's the only way to stop him. Without my body he is nothing."

Her eyes glazed with tears, and her lower lip trembled.

"You know it's true."

Her eyes left me. "You shouldn't have tried to sacrifice yourself."

"It didn't work, anyway. Either he didn't try to kill me, or..."

She swallowed hard. "Larylis and Mareleau are both missing." As much as her words pained me, I couldn't pretend I was shocked. She continued, "Morkai says they returned to Dermaine, but Mareleau left her ladies behind. Do you think they could have run like I did?"

I felt neither hope nor fear. "Perhaps."

Cora pursed her lips. "I'm going to end this."

I fought to stand, but it did no good. "Don't do anything. I said the same thing, and look where I am now."

"I have to do something."

I reached for her hand. "There's only one thing to do, and you know it. If you can do that, then I support you. Anything else will only get you killed or stuck in here with me."

She opened her mouth, then snapped it shut. A trickle of tears moved down her cheeks. "You can't ask me to do that."

"I gladly give my life to save yours, and to protect Lela."

"Teryn, I can't."

I lifted her hand in mine, feeling the buzzing resistance as I brought it to my lips. I tried to recall the feeling of flesh on flesh, but the memory was fleeting. "I love you. That's all I want to remember. Promise me you will do what needs to be done."

Cora did nothing but stare back at me, eyes swimming with tears, cheeks glistening as if they were covered in starlight. Finally, she nodded. "I will."

My strength drained from me, and my hand fell limp from hers. I tried to connect with my shallow breathing, with the faraway hum of blood rushing through my veins. I closed my eyes but could still tell Cora was near.

"Are you really going to do what he asks?" I heard Emylia say.

"I'll do whatever it takes. First, tell me everything you know."

33

THE PLAN

Cora

I sat at the edge of my bed as the first light of dawn crept into my room. Ann, Breah, and Sera were still asleep, sprawled over my bed. I'd decided to allow them to stay with me, seeing no reason to dismiss them, aside from their mindless chatter. Besides, if they stayed with me, perhaps Morkai would keep his word not to visit my room.

My eyes felt red and raw from a near-sleepless night. After everything I'd learned from Emylia about who Morkai really was, about his search for El'Ara, the prophecy she'd channeled, and his plans for using my body, I'd found it impossible to fall into deep sleep. My mind wanted to do nothing more than piece her words together with what I'd learned in El'Ara and link them to what I'd discovered before.

The result was a complicated puzzle spanning ages, with me at its center. The image chilled me to the bone.

I was supposed to be the Mother of Prophecy.

My hands slid over my womb, but tears would not fall. I'd done enough crying throughout the night, hidden beneath the snores of Mareleau's ladies. After everything I'd learned, pain threatened to tear me apart all over again, to send me agonizing over my past and what had been taken from me. Yet I made a promise to myself never to let my past cloud my present again. I was determined to keep that promise.

Besides, I have a plan to enact.

I dressed quietly in my simplest gown and pulled the cloak I'd borrowed from Mareleau over my shoulders. Around my waist I wore a leather belt. I checked in the mirror to make sure it fit with the look of my dress and cloak. Once satisfied, I tucked my knife in the back of the belt.

Once the sun fully rose into morning, the three girls began to wake. They admonished me for dressing without their help and insisted on fetching me breakfast. I ate in silence while their chatter filled the room, all the while going over the plan in my head.

After breakfast, the ladies moved their gossip to the couch. They barely heard me when I told them I was going to go visit my husband.

I extended my power as I walked down the hall, sensing Morkai stirring within his room. Outside his bedroom, I settled beneath a mask of grace and tapped on the door. "Teryn?"

After a few moments, the door opened and Morkai greeted me with a smile. "My dear wife. What a beautiful vision." His eyes moved from my face to the hem of my dress. I tried to keep my expression neutral as his eyes passed over the belt around my waist. "You appear to be ready for some kind of excursion."

"I was hoping we could take a walk this morning."

"A walk?" His eyes examined my cloak. "I take it you don't mean a stroll through the castle."

"I wanted to walk through the woods together. Maybe visit the place where you first told me you loved me."

"Ah. That does sound lovely."

"So? Would you like to?"

Morkai let out a sigh, and his shoulders fell. "I wish I could, my dear. Unfortunately, I have much work to do. Urgent news has come from Sele."

"What is it?"

"It's just as I'd feared. Ulrich has turned on Kevan. They hadn't even reached Verlot."

I worked my face into a look of surprise. "That's terrible. What will you do?"

"I must get word to my brother in case Ulrich decides to strike a blow upon Dermaine before he arrives home."

I resisted my urge to scowl at the lies woven through his words. "I see. When can I see you?"

Morkai's lips curled into a mischievous smirk so unlike Teryn's it made my blood boil. "Am I to understand you right in thinking you are eager to be alone with me?" He reached for my waist. I nearly played along, before I remembered the knife behind me.

I stepped away. "I am eager, but I still need time before...we can be intimate. That's why I wanted to start with a walk together."

Morkai narrowed his eyes while his smile remained as it was. "I understand, my dear. Like I said, I will allow you to take all the time you need. I'm happy to take a walk with you this evening."

"This evening?"

"Yes. A moonlit walk will surely be more romantic than one now, while I'm in distress over the state of Lela."

The look on his face said anything but distress. However, my plan didn't require any special time of day. "That sounds perfect."

"Meet me in the courtyard at sunset."

"I'll eagerly await."

THE LIGHT OF THE SETTING SUN THREW THE COURTYARD under a blanket of glowing shadow. I kept my mind clear and my breathing steady as I listened for the sound of footfall. When I heard Morkai approach, I turned with a smile planted over my lips. He came toward me, and I tried not to focus on how thin his hair looked and how much darker the circles beneath his eyes had become. Perhaps it was suspicious that I *hadn't* remarked upon his ragged appearance, but I knew I wouldn't be able to mention it without trembling.

Morkai offered me his arm. "Where are we off to?" he asked, eying the lantern in my hand.

"I told you. The place where you first told me you loved me." When he gave no response, I held back my desire to force him to admit he had no idea where that was. Instead, I led us past the charred field and into the shadows of the darkening forest. I held the lantern before us as we made our way through the trees. I closed my eyes and sought Valorre. He was close.

"Where's Valorre?" I jumped at his words and tried to keep heat from rising to my cheeks, grateful for the cover of shadows.

"He's probably wandered off somewhere. I'm sure he'd love to see you."

"And I'd like to see him as well."

I tried not to consider any hidden implications of his words and kept my focus on the path ahead. Once we neared the cliff over the valley, my heart began to race.

"You're trembling."

I let out a small laugh. "Am I? I must be cold."

He put his arm around me and pulled me close as we stepped out onto the cliff. We stared over the moonlit valley and the dark silhouettes of the mountains beyond. "What a beautiful place."

I turned to face him. "Thank you for coming here with me." Keeping my eyes locked on his and a smile on my lips, I reached my mind to Valorre. He wasn't far.

Danger.

My eyes flashed over Morkai's shoulder. I could see no sign of Valorre. *What do you mean?*

Morkai followed my gaze. "What has gotten you so spooked, my dear?"

I relaxed my expression when he returned to face me. "I thought I heard something."

He pulled me to his chest, arms around my waist. He brought his lips to my ear. "You seem terrified."

This time I *knew* his words held double meaning. *Valorre, where are you?*

Danger. There are others. All around. Swords.

Sweat beaded behind my neck. *Run, Valorre. Now.* I

took a step to pull out of Morkai's grasp, but he wouldn't release me. "Teryn, you're hurting me."

Morkai threw his head back and laughed. When his eyes returned to mine, they were burning with malice. "You can't fool me."

I calmed my mind and reached for my power, letting the fire flood me until it poured from my chest. It struck the space between us, sending him reeling back as I reached behind my belt. My hands grasped at nothing. I looked back at Morkai and saw him flourishing my knife with a grin.

"Looking for this?"

I ran forward. His empty hand shot toward me, as if he meant to wrap it around my neck from where he stood. I paused, hands flinging to my throat, expecting pain to constrict my breathing. Nothing happened.

Morkai grimaced at his hand and lowered it to his side. "As you can see, my powers are not what they were when I had my own body." He walked toward me, and I stepped back, keeping my hands in front of me. We slowly circled each other, his eyes locked on my face while I watched the blade.

His eyes flicked to the knife in his hand. "Is this what you want?" He pressed the blade to his throat, and I froze. "Were you hoping to do this? To plunge this blade into the body of your beloved just to free him of me?" A trickle of blood poured down his neck while he grinned.

My hands shook as I considered my next move.

"I see." He lowered the blade, leaving the wound open and bleeding, then walked toward me once again. "You are undecided. You made a promise you aren't sure you can keep."

I let out an unsteady breath. "I'd rather be the one to do it, that's all."

"You are a terrible liar, Coralaine. I, however, have made a promise I fully intend to keep. I will rule Lela and become Morkaius. Thanks to your beloved, that process has become easier than ever."

A rustling in the trees stole my attention. *Valorre?* Yet as soon as I looked, I knew it couldn't be him. A dozen men moved out of the trees and surrounded me. When I looked back at Morkai, he was directly before me.

Hands pulled my arms behind my back as Morkai brought his face next to mine. "While I may not have my full magic, I still have many assets at my disposal. I've always had a way with words. And poison."

Before I knew what was happening, he pressed a damp cloth over my mouth and nose. I tried to keep from inhaling, but already the bitter aroma went to my head. My eyelids fluttered, and the face of my beloved, features distorted with Morkai's terrible smile, swam before me.

34

ROIZAN

Mareleau

I woke with the feeling of cool air touching my skin and grass tickling my face. With a jolt, I realized I was no longer in the dungeon. I tried to lift my hands but found myself bound at my wrists and ankles. A whimper escaped my throat, but no sound came through the gag between my teeth. My neck ached as I lifted my head to take in my dark surroundings—a field expanded as far as I could see, bathed under moonlight. Flickers of fires or torches danced at the edges of my vision. I rolled to my other side and found myself face to face with a sleeping Cora, who appeared to be in the same predicament as I.

"Wake up," I tried to squeal through the cloth in my mouth. I lifted my bound ankles and sent them into her calves. She stirred but her eyes remained closed. I turned away and struggled into a seated position.

"I see you are awake." Teryn—or Morkai—stepped out of the shadows and stood over me.

I glared back at him and tried to hurl words through my gag.

"I can't hear you, Your Majesty." Morkai bent down and roughly pulled the cloth from my mouth.

"Where is my husband?" My lips felt raw at the corners.

"You will see him shortly. He has quite the show for you. First, there is someone else I want you to see. However, I think we should wait for Cora, don't you? She wouldn't want to miss this."

I looked over my shoulder at her unconscious form, wondering if it would be best if she stayed asleep.

Morkai, on the other hand, didn't seem to share my sentiment. He leaned over her and slapped her on the cheek. She mumbled and curled in on herself as her head rolled side to side. "Wake up. I have something to show you." He pulled the gag from her mouth and slapped her cheek again.

Her eyes fluttered open, widening as they moved from him to me. "Where are we?" She spoke as if her tongue was coated in syrup.

"We're in your favorite place, can't you tell? The place Teryn told you he loved you."

Her head moved from one edge of the field to the other, eyes heavy. "The wildflower meadow? Why?"

"You know how easily I will become ruler of Lela. But what's the one thing I'm missing?"

Cora's eyes went unfocused for a moment before her gaze snapped back to Morkai. "A Roizan."

"Exactly. However, it took me years to make my Roizan as strong as it was. I don't have years to start over."

Cora wriggled until she was sitting upright and narrowed her eyes at the man who wore Teryn's face.

"Ah, I see you are more awake now. Guards." A dozen men sprang forward, swords drawn. "Keep her surrounded. If she suddenly becomes invisible, stab the place where you last saw her, then kill the other girl."

Cora flinched as the blades paused mere breaths away from her skin. She eyed the guards, careful not to move too much. "Who are they? If you don't have your magic, how did you find men stupid enough to be loyal to you?"

"You'd be surprised what men are willing to do for freedom."

Cora pursed her lips. "They're men from the dungeon, aren't they? But most of those men had been your slaves. They never would have returned to do your bidding without your mind control."

I struggled to understand what she was talking about and regretted I hadn't paid more attention to what I'd heard about the Battle at Centerpointe Rock.

Morkai seemed entertained by her words. "I agree, many of the men held for questioning were more loyal to you than they ever would have been to me. But you forget something. As far as they know, I am Teryn. By serving me, they are serving *you*. They do what they are told in honor of King Teryn and Cora, the unicorn princess. Or shall I say unicorn queen?"

Again, she eyed the armed men. "I still don't understand. These men clearly hear you speak and see what you are doing to me. If they are loyal to me, why aren't their swords trained on you instead?"

Morkai shook his head. "Not all the men in the dungeon were loyal to you. Those I've kept closest to me understand my mission and the security they are building for themselves and their families by allying with me. They couldn't care less about you."

"And the others? What did you do with them?"

"I sent some of them to find you. The rest I sent to follow Kevan and Ulrich, to make sure they never reached Verlot."

Heat flooded my cheeks at the mention of my uncles. "What?"

He turned to me. "Haven't you heard? Ulrich turned on Kevan, and a bloody battle ensued. However, my men showed up in time to stop it, loyal as they are. I warned them of Ulrich and Kevan's dreadful plot to take over Sele and Mena, only to return to rip the throne from their beloved Queen Coralaine. Unfortunately, both your uncles are now dead."

I couldn't say I felt sorrow for my uncles, but I was far from joyful over their demise. Neither of them had ever thought highly of me, but that didn't mean I'd wanted them slaughtered. My eyes slid to the ground at Morkai's feet.

Cora brought his attention back to her. "Where are they now? The men loyal to me?"

"They are on their way back here, but none will make it in time to stop what I've already begun."

"What have you begun?" Cora asked.

Morkai clapped his hands, and a rumble responded on opposite sides of the valley. Shadows moved toward each other in the forms of two gigantic, hunched silhouettes. As they drew nearer, I saw several men had each hulking form in heavy chains as they led them to the center of the field.

"What are they?" Cora asked.

Morkai frowned at her as if she were a child. "You know what they are."

"You've created another Roizan—two new Roizan. But how? You said you didn't have time."

"I don't have time to create one in the way I had before, feeding it horns to grow its strength. It was a brilliant plan, but it was too time consuming. I've discovered a faster way to create a powerful Roizan."

"You said your powers aren't what they were before. How are you able to do this?"

"I don't need my full powers as a narcuss to create a Roizan. A Roizan comes from necromagic, needing precise conditions and incantations, much like a spell or a potion."

Cora's lips trembled as if she wasn't sure she wanted to ask any more questions. I too was torn between not wanting to hear another word and needing more of an explanation. Even the word *Roizan* escaped my understanding. I'd heard Larylis and my father speak of it, but it had never seemed like something I'd needed to concern myself with. *Looks like I was wrong.*

Morkai clasped his hands in front of his waist. "Would you like to meet them?"

"Who?" Cora asked. "The Roizan?"

He grinned. "I think you will be pleasantly surprised by how they were created."

Cora shook her head, and I tried to back away. Morkai

ignored us both and turned toward the mountainous silhouettes. "Bring them forward." The men kept the two Roizan a good distance away from each other as they brought them forth. The moonlight showed two hairless creatures with rough, raw skin, one in the shape of a bear, the other in the shape of a boar. Yet as they moved into the torchlight, I saw something far more terrifying than anything I could have imagined.

Each wore an unmistakably human face.

"Do you recognize them?" Morkai asked.

My eyes were glued to the two creatures, but I refused to seek recognition. *It's nothing. It's no one. None of this is real.*

Cora let out a strangled cry. "Dimetreus?"

Morkai's laugh reverberated throughout the field, sending a chill down my spine. My eyes rested on the Roizan that stood across from Cora. It swung its bear-like head from side to side as it panted with its human mouth. Its fleshy face was wide and merged seamlessly into the body of the naked bear, but its eyes, nose, and lips were those of a man. *Is that truly the face of her brother?*

With a shudder, my eyes moved to the creature before me. Air puffed out from its human nostrils as its boar-like hooves tore impatiently at the dirt beneath it. My eyes lifted to meet its own—dull and gray and lined with creases. Creases that I'd likely caused with my years of defiance.

"Father." My body fell into a fit of convulsions as a sob tore from my throat, followed by a scream.

Morkai put his hands behind his back and looked down at me, smiling. "Let it out, dear girl. No one will hear you scream."

"Where is my husband?" I thrashed about as I craned my neck to look into every shadow. "What have you done with him?"

He crouched beside me and grabbed my chin, forcing me to meet his eyes. "Your father is dead. Your uncles are dead. The rule now passes to you and Larylis. Can you guess what happens next?"

I wanted to fight my way from his grasp, to bite, to spit, to kick. But all I had the strength to do was glare.

"Next, I become King of Lela."

35

SHADOWS

Larylis

Every part of me twitched with rage as I watched the Roizan standing mere steps away from my wife. I was unable to blink as I strained to hear Morkai's words from across the field. My mind spun as I tried to assess any possibility of defeating the four armed men who guarded me. The bindings around my wrists made any such plan difficult.

Keeping my eyes on Mareleau, I imagined every option. I considered grabbing the sword from the nearest guard, somehow cutting my bindings with the blade of the first man who fought me, then beating the rest in battle. Every step went through my mind. My blood raced with the clarity of it all.

One of the men took a step closer, and my eyes flashed to his sword. My fingers trembled as I prepared to lurch toward him...

A man on my other side nudged me in the shoulder,

startling me from my plan. "Move," he said. The four guards pushed from every side as they forced me onto the field. I'd lost my chance.

The two Roizan were led further away from each other, putting Mareleau in center view. He'd forced both her and Cora to standing as they watched me approach. Tears streamed down Mareleau's cheeks as she stared at me.

Morkai greeted me with a maniacal grin. It made my stomach churn to see him manipulating my brother's face in such an obscene way. "Are you ready to put on a show for your wife, dear brother?"

"Don't call me that," I hissed through my teeth.

Morkai threw his head back with laughter. "Touchy, are we?" He jerked his chin at the guards. "Cut his bindings."

The guard at my left exchanged his sword for a dagger and moved toward me with an uncertain expression. My muscles twitched as I forced my hands to remain still while he cut the rope around my wrists. As soon as my bindings fell away, I reached for the guard's sword, unsheathed it, and spun around to face the four surprised men.

"I like your spirit," Morkai said from behind me. "But your battle isn't with them."

I ignored him and surged toward the men. A scream made me pause before our blades could connect, followed by Morkai's order for his men to stand down. They did as told, but I refused to take my eyes off them.

"You should turn around, Larylis. The view is better over here. Your wife looks lovely in red."

My heart raced as I spun toward Mareleau. A gash

was open over her cheek, revealing rivulets of blood raining down with her tears. I took a step forward, but Morkai held his hand toward me. His other hand held a knife to his own throat.

"Don't come nearer, or I will end your brother's life and find a more suitable home for myself."

My eyes widened when I realized a purple crystal hung around Mareleau's neck.

Morkai's grin stretched from ear to ear. "You will do what I say. I grow tired of this body, and I will dispose of it if I find it should motivate you. Being Queen Mareleau will suit my needs just fine. However, I won't hesitate to spill her blood. Or the blood she carries within her."

"Don't touch her or our child!" I shouted. "I will do anything you say."

Mareleau shook her head as more blood poured down her neck, soaking the collar of her white nightdress.

I closed my eyes and steeled myself. *I will do anything for you.* "What do you want, Morkai? Let's get this over with."

He took the blade from his throat and held his hands at his sides. "Impatient, now? Very well. However, we are expecting one more guest. Guards." He tilted his head toward Cora, and the men urged her forward. Morkai looked beyond me, eyes boring into the trees at the edge of the field. "Valorre, come here, please."

"No!" Cora shouted. She nearly ran forward before she seemed to remember the swords surrounding her.

"Hold out her arm," Morkai ordered. One of the guards did as told while Morkai strode toward her with the knife. In one quick motion, he drew a line of red across her forearm. "Come now, Valorre. I know you're out there. Would you rather see her cut into pieces?"

"Valorre, stay back," Cora said, eyes looking anywhere but at the gash on her arm.

Morkai moved his blade below the first cut. "Come, Valorre. Or she will be covered in red stripes until she bleeds out."

Cora narrowed her eyes at him. "Do it. You won't kill me."

He drew another line of red across her arm.

Cora hissed but kept her eyes fixed on his. "You won't kill me. You need me."

"Don't be so full of yourself. I've never needed you."

"What about Emylia? You need me alive for her." Cora grinned, looking as smug as a cat with a mouse between its teeth. However, Morkai seemed far from surprised.

He took a step away from her and put his hands behind his back, empty hand clasped around the wrist that held the knife. "I admit, I do enjoy irony. There was a time I thought there could be no better vengeance than seeking the Mother of Prophecy, destroying the one thing about her that could stop me, and then using her body to house my lover. In fact, there was even a time when I imagined having you by my side would be pleasant, even if my plans for Emylia failed. But now," he leaned in until their noses were almost touching, "I rejoice the day when I never see your face again."

He straightened and turned away from her. "You've served your purpose. You would have made a lovely companion for me, if you'd agreed to serve me when I gave you the chance. As much as I love irony, you aren't worth it to me anymore. At this point, any woman will do.

I'm sure I could find one even prettier than you." His gaze moved to Mareleau.

I clenched my hand around the sword and contemplated sending it through his heart. Yet I hesitated, remembering the body before me was my brother's, and putting a sword through it would mean his death. Sweat dripped down my face as I forced my feet to remain planted.

Morkai put a hand to his chin. "Now, where were we? Ah, yes. Valorre, show yourself or your friend dies. You must be able to feel her fear now. She knows her life is no longer protected. If you want her to live, then—"

"No!" Cora shouted. "Valorre, go back!"

I turned and saw a white form step from the shadows of the trees. After a few moments, he was at my side, muscles quivering and ears twitching. It was hard for me to do anything but stare at him. Even though I'd seen him once before and had even been surrounded by unicorns on the battlefield, nothing could dull the awe of seeing a unicorn at my side.

"So good of you to join the party," Morkai said. "I would like you and Larylis to put on a show for the two queens. You each know what is at stake. Teryn's life, Cora's life, and Mareleau's free will."

"What do you want us to do?" My voice sounded empty.

Morkai's gaze alternated between the two Roizan flanking me and Valorre on the field. "A Roizan is created by death," he explained. "Two creatures fight in a carefully conducted battle until their lives end at precisely the same time. After this, they merge into one and become a Roizan. My first Roizan I made stronger by feeding it darkness—specifically the dark horn of the unicorn. For my new Roizan, I will make it stronger in a new way. I will pit Roizan against Roizan and allow it to strengthen in leaps and bounds."

I looked at the fleshy faces of the two Roizan and then at Valorre, realization dawning on me. "You want us to become your next Roizan."

Morkai nodded. "There's my new sense of irony. I will have three Roizan made from the men who stood between me and my throne. Then my three Roizan will battle and merge into a new Roizan. He will be unstoppable."

I shook my head, wishing I could wake from my nightmare.

"I know I needn't remind you what will happen if you disobey."

My eyes flashed to Mareleau and the crystal she wore around her neck. If I didn't do what he wanted, he would kill Teryn and jump into Mareleau's body. I couldn't let that happen. But what could I do? There had to be another way.

"Fight!" Morkai shouted. The guards released the chains of the two Roizan, and the beasts closed in on us. "Face each other, you fools." It took me a moment to realize Morkai's order was meant for me and Valorre. "One attack at a time."

The Roizan with Verdian's face bared its teeth and snorted, swinging its bore-like tusks into my ribs, forcing me to turn toward Valorre. I cried out as the tusk tore through my flesh. The other Roizan swung its heavy, razor-sharp claws over Valorre's neck, revealing streaks of red in his white coat as he faced me.

I crouched into a fighting stance, pointing my sword at Valorre. Valorre lowered his head and aimed his horn at me. We faced each other, motionless, until I felt the tusks gore me in the thigh. I raced toward Valorre as the other Roizan clawed the unicorn's rear, sending him to meet my blade with his horn. Our weapons clashed, and I was surprised at the strength of his horn. We faced each other again, and I now stood in front of the Roizan wearing Dimetreus' face.

We danced toward each other again and again, trying to move before we met the wrath of the two Roizan that constantly prodded us toward each other. Yet we continued to meet blade with horn, never grazing each other's flesh. I panted, my arm heavy as I prepared for another attack.

"This is getting boring," Morkai called out from his place next to Mareleau. "If I don't see the two of you draw blood from each other, I'll have the Roizan begin to remove one limb at a time."

For a moment, I considered the peace of simply letting the Roizan end me, tear me limb from limb into nothingness. But where would that leave Mareleau? What would he do to her? *What will he do to her if I become his Roizan? The same thing. I'm not helping her by doing this. There must be another way.*

I saw the bear-Roizan reach a heavy paw toward Valorre's flank and took my cue to race forward. My sword grazed Valorre's chest as his horn pricked my shoulder. I watched the blood run down Valorre's leg and felt a lump rise in my throat. *I hate this. I hope you know that, Valorre.*

We raced toward each other again. This time, my

sword met nothing as Valorre knocked me to the ground with a blow to my already wounded ribs. I struggled to stand as sweat and tears poured over my face. My eyes moved from the blood-covered unicorn to the two hovering Roizan. I imagined Dimetreus and Verdian in similar battles, facing a boar and a bear. I almost envied them. It must have been easier to kill an animal like that, one full of rage, confusion, and an instinct for survival, rather than a gentle unicorn.

We circled each other as we prepared for the next attack. My eyes flickered to the Roizan behind Valorre, heart racing. I looked back at the unicorn, trying to fill my eyes with everything I wanted to convey. *I know you can't hear me like you can hear Cora, but I hope you can understand.* My eyes widened and then darted between the two Roizan.

The boar-Roizan swung its tusks toward Valorre, giving us the cue to attack. We raced forward and passed alongside each other. My sword plunged into the neck of the boar-Roizan while Valorre attacked the bear. Madness erupted in a flurry of tusks, claws, blades, and blood.

36

LIGHT

Cora

Morkai shouted, but his words couldn't be heard over the snarls, snorts, and growls on the field. The faces of the guards turned toward the chaos while I closed my eyes and focused on my power. The bindings fell from my wrists. With my hands free, I sank to the ground, beneath the circle of blades. I let the fire flood me, surging through my blood until it burst from all around me. The force sent the men flying, landing on their backs. I crawled to the nearest guard, unsheathed his dagger, and cut through the bindings at my ankles.

Morkai was still watching the field while I ran to Mareleau. He turned around as I cut her last binding. He leapt forward, but before he could reach us, I held out my hands and sent him reeling back. I tore the crystal from around Mareleau's neck and threw it onto the field. Morkai stood, lips pulled into a snarl as he glared at me.

His eyes moved to Mareleau's chest, widening when he saw the crystal was no longer there.

He clenched his jaw and squeezed his eyes shut. When he opened them, he immediately turned toward the field where I'd thrown the crystal. He shot one more look of fiery malice my way, then stomped onto the field.

"Valorre, now!" I shouted.

Valorre was tangled with one of the Roizan, but at the sound of my voice, he darted away from the creature, circling Larylis and the other Roizan, and raced toward Morkai. Morkai bent toward his feet, eyes flashing forward as the unicorn surged toward him. He stood and held out a palm, but Valorre's horn went through his torso, lifting him off his feet. I could see the tip of the horn protruding from the middle of his back. Tears poured from my eyes as I watched blood rain down Teryn's body.

Valorre halted and tossed his mane, sending Morkai to the ground. Tendrils of what looked like black and gray smoke began to float from the grass where he laid motionless. "Valorre, the crystal!"

Valorre ran back to the field. Mareleau whimpered and clung to my arm, nails digging into my flesh. I followed her line of vision and saw the bear-Roizan approaching Larylis while he was still locked into battle with the boar. I looked back at Valorre; his horn hovered over the ground while the smoke-like mass, now bearing the form of a man, walked toward him. Valorre plunged his horn down, and a bright light erupted in streams of violet, sending the dark form back. Valorre plunged his horn again, and more streams of light spilled forth, growing brighter and brighter until the whole field was bathed in purple.

The two Roizan froze as if paralyzed by the light, and Larylis sent his sword into one and then the other. The Roizan let out screams both human and animal as they fell, writhing on the ground until they grew still.

The purple light extinguished faster than it had come, sending the field into darkness. I blinked as I tried to readjust to the light of the moon and torches. When my eyes fell on Teryn's limp form, I raced to his side. Blood spread out from the wound in the middle of his chest. I tapped his cheeks but got no response. I put my ear to his chest, listening for his slow, quiet heartbeat. "Come back to me."

"Teryn is dead." I sprang to my feet and looked at the dark form that was Morkai.

His face was a translucent gray yet looked as it had before he'd died at Centerpointe Rock. The rest of his figure undulated beneath a smoky shroud, in blurred lines of gray and black. "You don't scare me. You're nothing but a wraith now."

Morkai smiled, showing teeth. "Did no one ever teach you to fear a wraith? Let me fix that." He stood tall and spread out his arms, the waves of black trailing behind him like wings. His eyes burned red as his features twisted into a mask of fury, reminding me of Fanon. However, where Fanon's face had turned from beautiful to terrible, Morkai's turned from terrible to deadly.

"Morkai." A female voice rang through the field. He spun around. Emylia came forward, a translucent version of the woman I'd met in the crystal. She appeared to be a wraith like Morkai, but instead of being shrouded in black, she was a mixture of white, blue, and gray light, shimmering in the darkness.

Her expression was soft as she approached him. "Is this how you want to live the rest of your days?"

Morkai seemed to constrict, all the tendrils of black pulling in until his wraith-form bore a more human semblance. "I've wanted nothing more than to live out our days together," he hissed. "Don't you dare condemn me. Everything I've done has been for you."

Emylia shook her head. "You're wrong, you didn't do this for me. You did it all for you. Look around, does this look like something I'd want?" Her eyes moved to me standing next to Teryn's lifeless form, then slid to Mareleau and Larylis huddled together and covered in blood. Valorre approached my side, streams of deep red spilling from his many wounds. "I never wanted this. I never wanted you to become Morkaius."

"You were the one who helped me learn how to become Morkaius in the first place."

"I didn't know what I was doing. I regret what I channeled for you."

Morkai seemed to shrink further. "I promised we'd be together forever."

"But I didn't."

Morkai hissed and stepped back. "You told me you loved me. You said you always would."

"I don't love you. I love *him*." She put her palm on his chest, then pushed her hand inside his wavering form. When she pulled her hand back, she held something—a dark, pulsing object slightly larger than her fist. It was surrounded with layers of black and gray smoke. "Somewhere in here is the man I love."

"*He* had no power," Morkai said. "*He* got you killed."

"We both made mistakes. I never should have helped you learn what you learned. It has become the demise of so many." She put a hand on his cheek. "You know that's not me."

"And he is not me. Not anymore."

Emylia's arms fell to her sides. "Then I'm leaving. I'm ready to be at peace. You can have this back." She returned the pulsing object to his chest and turned away from him.

"You can't leave."

"I can and will." She looked over her shoulder at him. "You can either come with me to the otherlife where we can be together, where you can see your mother again, or you can remain here to torment people as a wraith."

"I can't. It's too late for the otherlife."

Emylia faced him and put her hands on his shoulders. "It's not. It's never too late. Let this darkness go."

"This darkness belongs to me."

"It doesn't. It simply envelops you. Shrug it away and let me see the man I love." Again, she reached inside his chest and pulled out his heart. This time, the face of a young man I'd never seen before emerged, as if Morkai were simply a cloak he wore. "See, Desmond, you're still there."

Desmond smiled, then made a choking sound. "It hurts. It's so heavy."

"Let it go. That darkness doesn't belong to you. It has accumulated from things you've done. Actions you've taken. Those things were never you."

Desmond took another step away from the dark mass of Morkai, revealing a wraith-like form similar to Emylia's with colors of white and blue, but primarily gray. He closed his eyes and stepped fully out of the dark shroud. Streams of it still clung to his back, like tiny threads of black. It roared around him like a storm, hissing and taunting as the threads grew thicker, trying to stitch the shroud back into him. "I can't do this. It hurts!"

"Stay with me, Des. Let it go."

"Everything I've done. It burns. It feels like fire."

"It isn't you." Emylia's eyes were frantic as she took his hands in hers. "Come with me. Just let it go." She pulled him forward, and again the shroud was torn away. But the threads would not be severed from his back, as if they were anchored deep within.

"What have I done? Emylia, it burns! It won't let me go." He pulled his hands from Emylia's and covered his face. The threads grew thicker, tearing into his back.

"Let it go, Des!"

With a shout, he threw his head back. White light spilled from his mouth, spiraling through the darkness, growing brighter and brighter. Holes pierced the shroud, burned by the light. Desmond's limbs flailed, arms fluttering as if made of paper while the light streamed from his hands and feet. It continued to burn until nothing remained, neither light, nor shadow.

He was gone.

Emylia stared at the empty space where Desmond had stood just moments before. She put her face in her hands and silently wept.

A lump rose in my throat as I tore my eyes away. While I was glad Morkai was gone in all his forms—Desmond included—watching someone weep for him scratched at my heart in an unsettling way. Valorre nudged me in the shoulder, and I pressed my face into his neck.

Teryn? Valorre asked.

"I don't know."

I'm sorry.

"Don't be sorry. You only followed our plan, even though it went nothing like I thought it would." I returned my attention to Teryn and sank to my knees at his side.

Footsteps approached. "Is he...dead?" Larylis asked.

I could find no words to reply as my eyes roamed over Teryn, searching for any sign of life.

Larylis crouched next to me, face devoid of color, and put a hand over his mouth. "You did the right thing, Cora. He knew it was the only way."

My hand hovered above Teryn's chest, then slowly lowered over his heart. Ignoring the blood still soaking his shirt, I closed my eyes and searched for the rhythmic beating below his cold flesh. It was there, but weak and growing slower with every beat.

A light gust of wind brushed my cheek, and when I opened my eyes, Emylia was kneeling on Teryn's other side. Her brow furrowed as she stared at his face.

Larylis gasped. "Who is she? A wraith?"

"Don't worry," I said. "She's a friend."

He made no word of reproach but didn't come nearer.

"Where is Teryn, Emylia? Why can't I see him like I can see you?"

"He isn't a wraith like I am." Her voice sounded muffled, like it was made with air. "His ethera is in there."

"How do we get him to wake up?"

"I don't know." Emylia leaned closer to Teryn. "Teryn,

if you can hear me, then you know what I'm going to tell you. Breathe. Feel your lungs fill with air, no matter how small an amount it is. Feel the blood still warm within you. Feel each beat your heart still makes." I felt a light pulsing beneath my palm, and she continued, "Feel each beat grow stronger. Your body is yours now. Nothing stands between you and your vitale." Her airy voice grew fiercer with every word. "Take it, Teryn. It is yours. Let your lungs be full. Feel them expand in your chest."

My eyes widened as I watched Teryn's chest rise. Tears streamed down my cheeks as I felt the beat of his heart grow stronger beneath my hand. Warmth flooded my body and flowed from my fingertips. *Come back to me, Teryn.*

Emylia wore a satisfied smile. "That's it. Breathe. Take your vitale back, feel the vibrancy of the blood rushing through your veins."

Larylis took a step forward. "He's breathing!"

"Now take hold of your cereba. Feel the grass tickling your neck, the cool breeze brushing your skin. The warmth of the hand pressed over your heart."

Unable to blink, I kept my eyes fixed on Teryn's face and watched as a hint of color began to fill his cheeks. I leaned down and brought my lips to his, ignoring the crushing disappointment that his lips gave no response to mine. "Come back to me. I love you."

A calmness settled over my heart, while a warm hand landed softly over mine. I sat upright, eyes widening when I saw the hand belonged to Teryn. His eyelids fluttered, and a moan escaped his lips.

"Teryn!" Larylis and I shouted at once.

"I'm...alive," Teryn struggled to say.

I wanted to press my body into his, to wrap my arms around him with all my might, just to experience the full truth of his return. Remembering the wound in his chest, I settled for a gentle squeeze of his hand. "I'm so happy to see you."

"I thought I'd lost you," Larylis said.

"So did I." Teryn pulled his hand from mine and propped his arms behind him as he tried to sit.

I put a hand on his shoulder, easing him back down. "Not yet, Teryn. You're wounded."

"Wounded?"

I bit my lip. "It was all I could think to do."

Teryn looked down at his chest, wincing as he lifted his blood-soaked shirt from his skin. "What happened?"

My eyes flashed to Valorre before resting back on Teryn. "I had Valorre stab you."

"Then why aren't I dead?"

"And shouldn't we dress the wound?" Larylis asked.

"I don't know if that's necessary." I took Teryn's collar between my hands and pulled until his shirt split in two. I wrinkled my nose at the sight of blood bathing his chest.

"Why wouldn't you think it necessary?" Larylis looked at me as if I'd gone mad.

I sighed with relief and nodded toward the wound. "The wound has already stopped bleeding. He's healing."

Teryn craned his neck to try and see for himself. "Healing? How?"

Now that I knew my plan had worked, I was able to find a smile. "Valorre's horn. I'd learned that some of the men from Centerpointe Rock had been healed by the unicorns that had stabbed them during battle. Kevan described them as *men brought back from the dead*. They woke up after being on the brink of death, confused but with their wounds healed. I wasn't positive how it had happened, but it was the only way I could think to free you from Morkai."

Teryn's eyes went wide as he tried to sit again. "Where is he? Where is Morkai and the crystal?"

"He's gone." I kept my voice gentle. "Being stabbed by Valorre forced Morkai from your body. Valorre crushed the crystal before Morkai could get to it."

"You finally found a way to destroy the crystal?"

I nodded.

Teryn turned his head toward Valorre. "Thank you."

Valorre tossed his mane, although I could tell the movement caused him pain. Teryn appeared to be the only one who'd managed to escape the need for bandaging.

Teryn's eyes returned to mine. "What about Morkai's ethera? If he didn't get to the crystal..."

"He's no more," I said. "Not even his wraith form survived. I saw him burned by light. And Emylia—" I turned my head from side to side and looked out at the field. There was no sign of her. My heart sank, realizing I'd never thanked her for her help. At least I knew she was finally where she wanted to be—at peace.

Thank you, Emylia.

37

WOLVES

Mareleau

The first light of dawn peeked over the mountains, illuminating the valley. I was sprawled on the grass watching Larylis and Cora huddled around Teryn, feeling no will to join them. My legs felt as if they'd been turned to liquid, my skin twitched, and my muscles quivered. The morning breeze blew through the thin cloth of my nightdress, but it felt like nothing compared to the sting of the gash in my cheek and the ache in my heart where my father resided.

Cora lifted her face, eyes meeting mine. She stood and came over to me, leaving Larylis crouched beside Teryn, and looked out at the field. I didn't follow her gaze, knowing exactly what horrors she beheld. Her voice sounded empty when she spoke. "We'll burn them and give your father and my brother a proper ceremony."

"How are you so calm?" My words came out broken

through my chattering teeth. "Why aren't you falling apart like I am?"

She looked down at me with a blank expression. "I am falling apart. I've just been in enough crises by now to know I have to keep it together, at least for a little while. I will mourn my brother for a very long time."

Her words burned me, reminding me of the privileged life I'd led compared to her, of my ignorance to war and suffering. Everything that had previously caused me distress—being forced by my father to marry a crown prince, being told I couldn't love Larylis, being separated from my husband and sent to Ridine—had felt like terrible injustices. Only now, as I turned my head to meet the disfigured animal that bore my father's face, did I know what injustice meant.

Bile rose in my throat. "How do we move on from this? My father died a monster. How do I tell my mother?"

"You don't. Your father and my brother died defending their kingdoms. That is a fact. They did what they could, and I *know* they fought with all their strength. Your father wouldn't have died willingly. Neither would my brother. That's all anyone needs to know."

"You don't think we should tell the truth?"

Cora shook her head, and her eyes flickered to where the guards last stood. "Morkai's men have fled. Even with witnesses, it would be hard for anyone to believe Morkai had returned from the dead to cause this chaos."

"Then what do we do?"

"Like I said, we will burn them. Give them the ceremony they deserve. We may not have bones to lie beneath their effigies, but there's no way I'd let the bones of a Roizan mingle with my brother's."

I shuddered at the thought. "Nor my father's."

"We will have to put the truth back together in a way everyone can accept." Cora grimaced at her own words. "As much as I disagreed with your uncles, they were right about some things. One of those things being this: there are truths our people will accept, and the rest needs to remain hidden from them for the safety of our kingdoms. The truth of what really happened would terrify our people and make our kingdoms appear vulnerable."

I crossed my arms over my chest. "I see you've suddenly learned how to be queen."

"I've had my kingdom taken from me and thrust into dangerous hands one too many times. I can't let that happen again."

"So, what do we tell our people?"

Cora looked lost in thought. When she spoke, her voice was firm. "Upon my marriage to Teryn, Dimetreus abdicated his throne to us. Meanwhile, Lord Kevan and Lord Ulrich rebelled against King Verdian and destroyed each other. "

I narrowed my eyes. "Who killed my father, then?"

"We will have to say your uncles killed him and Dimetreus before they left for Sele."

"They may not have been honorable men, but they weren't murderers," I said through my teeth.

Cora's expression softened. "I know, and I'm sorry. It may not be fair to them, but it is in line with the truth." She turned to Teryn and Larylis, who were watching us with keen expressions.

"I agree," Teryn said, his voice weak. He propped himself up little by little until he was sitting upright.

Larylis' hands hovered around him, as if he expected his brother to break. Teryn continued, "I witnessed much of what Morkai did while he was using my body. He may have been the one to encourage Kevan and Ulrich to do what they did, but the desire was already in their hearts. I don't know if they would have resorted to murder, but I do know they would have done whatever it took to reclaim what they believed was rightfully theirs."

I let out an exasperated sigh. As much as the story grated on my nerves, there was no better explanation I could think of. I'd have to add one more lie to the mountain I already carried.

Larylis looked down at his bloodstained clothing, torn nearly to shreds by his wounds. "What do we say happened to us?"

"Luckily, Morkai doesn't keep a tight household around him," Cora said. "Whomever remains currently at Ridine will know nothing more than we got swept up in the plot and managed to escape."

Teryn looked at Larylis. "Do you know what happened to your retinue, or any of the councilmen who were put in the dungeon with Verdian?"

Larylis shook his head. "Morkai had me and Mare seized by his men and taken to the dungeon, but it seemed empty the entire time."

"He must have already begun working on his Roizan," Cora said. "Hopefully some will have survived. We will need to form a strong council for each of our kingdoms."

"What about the men Morkai sent to fight against my uncles?" I asked. "What will you do with them?"

Cora's eyes went wide as she considered my words.

"They will be returning soon, but we can't punish them. They thought they were following orders from their king and may be the only loyal fighters Teryn and I have."

Teryn's eyes went unfocused. "I'll have to accept responsibility for everything Morkai did in my name."

Larylis stared at the ground. "Are we ever going to recover from this? Verdian's gone. Father's gone. Ridine's council has been destroyed. My councilmen may be dead, and Mareleau and I are supposed to rule two kingdoms. How do we do this ourselves? None of us are qualified for this."

"My father was right all along," I whispered. "We've sent our kingdoms to the wolves."

Cora turned to me. "That may be true, but wolves are survivors, and they protect their pack."

They protect their pack, I repeated to myself. My hands slid to my womb, reminding me of what I already had to protect. There was much to mourn and much to repair. Some wounds might never heal after this. But if there was one thing I was good at, it was surviving.

Teryn

Flames rose high into the sky over the two massive bodies, sending plumes of smoke into a dark cloud over the field. I wondered if it could be seen from Ridine. The four of us had said all we could to honor the two kings who died by Morkai's sorcery, and we now stood wordless.

Cora sniffled at my side as she gazed into the flames. I squeezed her hand, feeling her flesh against mine as if for the first time. After spending weeks as nothing more than my ethera, I knew I'd never take physical touch for granted again.

She returned the squeeze. "Why do I get the feeling our troubles are far from over?"

"They aren't," I said. "This is only the beginning. We have months of work ahead of us."

She nibbled her bottom lip. "It's not just that."

"You mean Morkai? He's gone."

"We've said that before."

I turned to her, brow furrowed as I studied her anxious face. "You said so yourself, you saw him destroyed."

"But what if there's a bigger threat than Morkai?"

That was not something I wanted to ponder, but her words stirred dark memories within. "You mean his father? The Blood of Darius?"

She nodded. "When I last visited you in the crystal, Emylia told me about Desmond, his search, and the prophecy. She said he'd begun his search for his father, who I think may have been Darius himself, the very man who'd tried to destroy El'Ara."

"Morkai's father wasn't looking for Lela like Morkai was," I argued. "He wanted El'Ara. It was Morkai who decided to claim Lela instead. Besides, Morkai seemed to think his father was under a curse, that he couldn't find El'Ara without help."

"I don't think it's a curse. I think it's because of the veil. An Elvan woman by the name of Satsara created a veil between our world and hers so that Darius could never return."

I cocked my head. "I remember the prophecy mentioning a veil and the name of Satsara, but I don't remember Emylia mentioning anything about how the veil was created."

"Emylia didn't know," Cora said. "I learned that on my own."

I was taken aback, prompting a thousand questions to rise to my mind. I shook my head to clear it. "That shouldn't matter to us. We're safe, and so is El'Ara. If there's a veil in place to protect them—"

"The veil keeps Darius out, but El'Ara is dying because of it."

This time, I couldn't resist my curiosity. "How do you know so much about El'Ara? Emylia told me everything she knew and everything she'd channeled."

Cora looked deep in thought, eyes unfocused. "I went to El'Ara when I ran away."

My jaw went slack as her words battled logic in my mind. "You actually went to the Ancient Realm? To El'Ara? How is that possible?"

"Valorre unknowingly brought us to his original home. I hardly escaped with my life." Her eyes met mine again, and clarity returned to them. "I can't imagine what they would have done to me if they'd known I was the mother of a broken prophecy meant to save them."

The pain was heavy in her voice. I put my hand on her shoulder. "You can't save everyone, Cora."

"No, I can't." She looked at the flames, eyes dancing with fire, and I immediately regretted my words.

With nothing left to say, we returned to our silent

mourning, hands locked together as we watched flames burn to embers, embers burn to ash, and ash burn to nothing. In its place a secret remained—a secret the four of us would carry, heavy as stone and sharp as thorns, in the deepest reaches of our hearts.

ABOUT THE AUTHOR

Tessonja Odette is fantasy author living in Seattle with her family, her pets, and ample amounts of chocolate. When she isn't writing, she's watching cat videos, petting dogs, having dance parties in the kitchen with her daughter, or pursuing her many creative hobbies. Read more about Tessonja at www.tessonjaodette.com